THE REMARKABLE STORY OF AN
ORPHANED BOY IN WWII JAVA.

EVEN WITHOUT BLOOD

a novel

Birgit Treipl

For my dear father, who permitted me to tell his life story. I love you and miss you.

Not flesh of my flesh,
nor bone of my bone,
but still miraculously my own.
Never forget for a single minute,
you didn't grow under my heart but in it.

— Fleur Conkling Heyliger

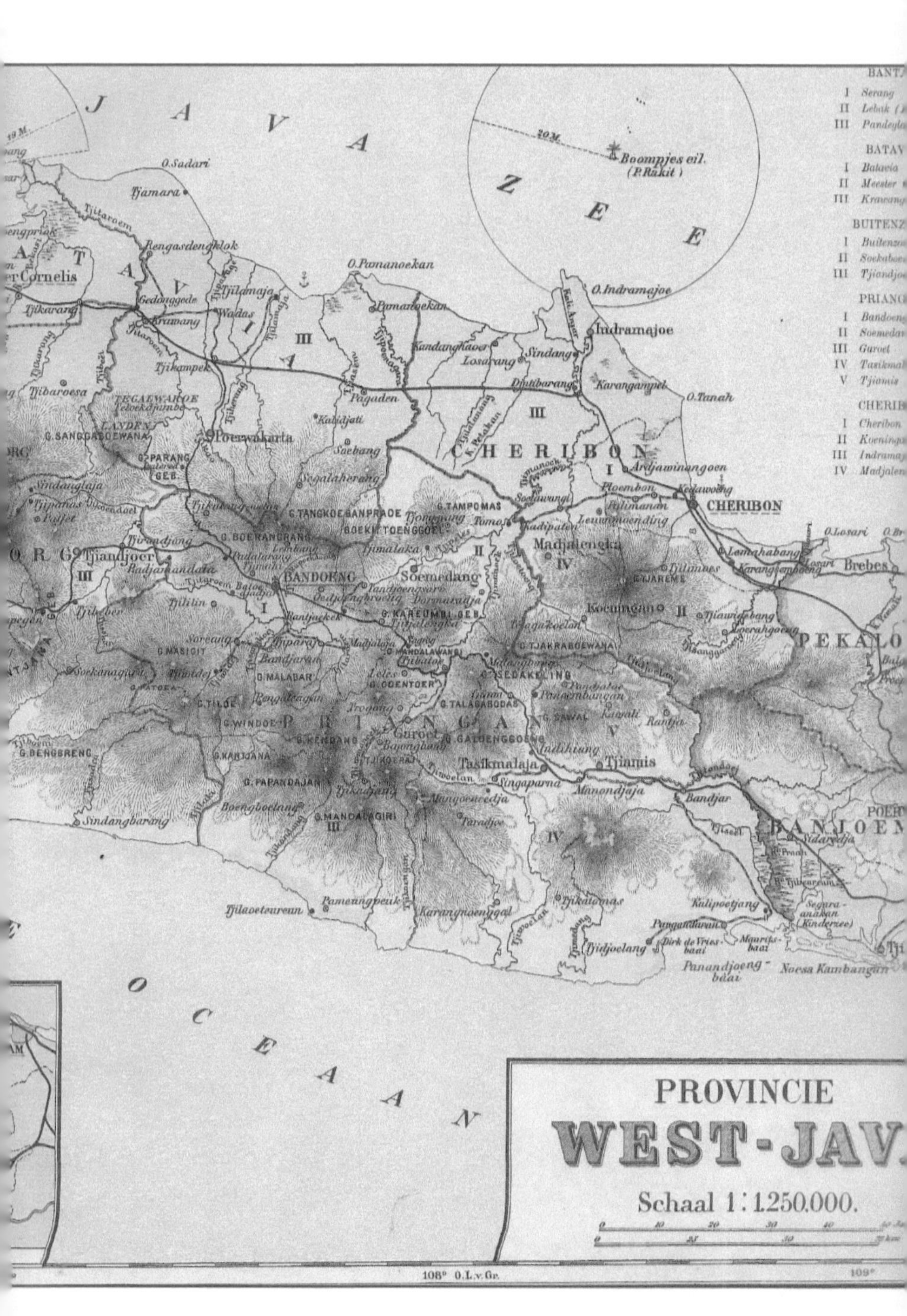
JAVA ZEE
BANTAM
I Serang
II Lebak
III Pandeglang
BATAVIA
I Batavia
II Meester Cornelis
III Krawang
BUITENZORG
I Buitenzorg
II Soekaboemi
III Tjiandjoer
PRIANGAN
I Bandoeng
II Soemedang
III Garoet
IV Tasikmalaja
V Tjiamis
CHERIBON
I Cheribon
II Koeningan
III Indramajoe
IV Madjalengka
Boompjes eil.
(P. Rakit)
O. Sadari
Tjamara
Tjitaroem
Rengasdengklok
O. Pamanoekan
O. Indramajoe
Koff Angor
Indramajoe
Priok
Cornelis
BATAVIA
Gedonggede
Tjilamaja
Wadas
Krawang
Pamanoekan
Kandanghaoer
Sindang
Losarang
Tjikarang
Tjikampek
Pagaden
Dintiborang
Karangampel
O. Tanah
Tjibaroesa
TEGALWAROE
Kalidjati
Tjikaoe
CHERIBON
Poerwakarta
Saebang
III
Ardjawinangoen
G. SANGGABOEWANA
Sindanglaja
G. PARANG
Soeklawangi
Ploembon
Kedawoeng
Tjiparnas
Segalaherang
G. TAMPOMAS
Tomos
Kadipaten
Leuwimoending
CHERIBON
O. Losari
G. TANGKOEBANPRAOE
Tjongrang
Madjalengka
Lemahabang
Losari
Brebes
Tjimalaka
II
IV
Karangsemboeng
Tjiandjoer
G. BOERANGRANG
Lembang
Tjilimus
Koeningan
PEKALONGAN
BANDOENG
Soemedang
G. KAREUMBI GEB.
Tjiareme
Tjiungberang
Loerahgoeng
Tjilitin
Ranjackek
G. KAREUMBI GEB.
Tjakraboewana
Soerang
G. MASIGIT
Tjiparay
Madjalaja
G. MANDALAWANGI
Ledes
Soekanagara
G. PATOEA
G. TILOE
G. MALABAR
G. GOENTOER
SEDAKELING
Malangbong
Tjibatoe
G. WINDOE
PRIANGAN
G. TALAGABODAS
G. KENDANG
Goeroe
Bajongbong
G. GALOENGGOENG
SAWAL
Karali
Ranja
V
G. BENGBRENG
G. KARLJANA
Tjikoeraj
Tasikmalaja
Indihiang
Tjiamis
G. PAPANDAJAN
Tjikadjang
Singaparna
Manondjaja
Bandjar
Sindangbarang
G. MANDALAGIRI
III
Mangoenredja
Paradje
IV
BANJOEMAS
Tjilaoeteureun
Pameungpeuk
Karangnoenggal
Tjikatomas
Kalipoetjang
Segara anakan (Kinderzee)
Pangandaran
Tjidjoelang
Dirk de Vries baai
Maurits baai
Panandjoeng baai
Noesa Kambangan
OCEAAN
108° O.L.v.Gr.
109°
PROVINCIE
WEST-JAVA
Schaal 1:1.250.000.

PROLOGUE

When I was a teenager, I told my best friend that one day I would write down my dad's life story: a moving family legend in which happiness and tragedy and the unbreakable bond between my dad and my grandmother are central. Theirs is a story that casts new light on the history of the Dutch East Indies as many people know it. That is because my father wasn't born in Java as a Dutchman but as an Austrian. The story gets quite complicated, so as a little girl, I asked Dad to repeat it again and again. Only after he turned eighty-six did I begin this project in earnest; I'd needed to live my own life before I was finally ready to turn my long-held wish into reality.

Just like my grandmother and my dad, I too have emigrated—the third generation of world travellers. I now live in British Columbia, Canada, in the small mountain town of Nelson, on the west arm of enormous Kootenay Lake. Vast forests, waterfalls, clear lakes, and snowy peaks surround us—a wilderness inhabited by bears, deer, and cougars. Being so close to nature inspires me and brings me peace of mind. Away from busyness, the crowds, and the noise, my heart opens up. I like to hike and ski. When I get home from walking the rails-to-trails or hiking to the rocky bluffs, streams, and gorgeous views of the lake and of the Kootenay Rockies, I'm ready to withdraw to my cozy little office. The old chandelier that I brought with me from the Netherlands spreads a pleasant, warm light. I take a seat behind my desk, on my pink yoga ball. My mind becomes quiet, my thoughts wander to times gone by, and I write.

I'm standing at her grave, a simple grey stone and some greenery around it, in the old municipal cemetery in Salzburg. The cemetery offers magnificent views over the Hohen Salzburg Fortress, and with an area of around twenty-five hectares and twenty thousand graves, it is the largest in the province of Salzburg. I needed a map to find her grave.

There she is, entirely by herself. I hope that up there, or wherever her spirit lives, she's together with my grandfather again, who is buried in Indonesia and whom I've never known. I can still picture her clearly, my strict petite Austrian grandmother, whom I loved dearly. She passed away at the age of ninety-three, in 1981. Where would Dad have been if she hadn't been by his side?

My grandmother had once been a rich woman and the owner of the Grand Hotel Lembang in Java. At only twenty-three years old, possessing an incredible amount of courage, strength, and discipline, she'd taken a boat from Austria to her alien destiny in Indonesia. I'd be remiss not to mention her softness, too, although it wasn't easy for her to show that openly. She poured her soul into that hotel before it all came crashing down. When she returned to Austria after WWII ended, she was sixty-five years of age, alone and penniless.

I remember Grandma staying with us in the Netherlands, where I grew up. She'd come for six weeks. Year after year, she'd take the night train from Austria, and we'd pick her up at the small station half an hour from our house. She'd be standing on the platform in her suit, her hat on and her little suitcase in hand. I remember her pulling my ear when I played false notes on my violin. She had studied piano at the Vienna Conservatory, so she could hear my mistakes.

She was religious. Catholic. But she didn't force her belief on anyone. She said grace before having her meal without asking us for silence. On Sunday—when it was dry outside—she'd walk to the church in the nearby town, her purse around her wrist and her lace handkerchief in hand. She wore a copper bracelet, believing that it protected her well-being. After all, it has been claimed since ancient times that copper has positive effects on health. Now I often wear her bracelet, and when I touch it, my thoughts go back to her.

To me, she was an example of great daring and entrepreneurial spirit. At only five-feet tall, she was my greatest role model. She encouraged me to deal with difficult situations promptly and directly, to get educated and work hard, to become an entrepreneur, to seek adventure, and last but not least to follow my heart.

Standing here at her grave, I realize again that she was born on January 18, exactly in-between my parents' birthdays, January 17 and 19, as though that fateful timing indicated the strong bond that existed between them. The irony in my dad choosing to marry my mum, who is of Dutch descent, is that her people had taken everything from my grandmother. And yet, my grandmother embraced my mother. My mother, in turn, along with my father, committed to pay for my grandmother's living expenses for the rest of her long life.

My grandmother loved my dad dearly, more or less since his birth. His existence thrust an almost impossible task upon her, but she was brave and magnamimous, and she set aside her internal barriers so that they could be together. They went through life together, through WWII. They lost everything. And they shared everything.

But only when dad was a young adult did she tell him the whole story about his origins. It shook his existence to its foundations.

Birgit Treipl, Nelson, BC, Canada, 2020

Chapter 1

THE AMBULANCE

It's the month of November, 1938. A long, black Chevrolet with a flashing light on the roof, a wide door at the back, and a white cross with the word AMBULANCE painted on the side is parked on the gravel road beside the hotel. Seeing that car at our door, I know something is terribly wrong.

I run to Mami's—my mummy's—bedroom. The ambulance drivers have just placed her on a stretcher. Her face is pale, almost grey, and her eyes are cloudy. Because she's so tall—much taller than Papi, my daddy—her feet protrude a little over the edge of the stretcher. Mami always dresses according to the latest fashion. Even though she's sick, she's wearing her fancy black satin pantsuit with the brightly coloured embroidery at the bottom of the legs, and she has fur-lined leather slippers on her feet. Mami has an elongated face and blue eyes. I find her face a bit dull and ordinary compared to Aunty Hilda's, who always has a twinkle in her eye, and a thin, pointed nose, but Mami has a stunning bunch of curly hair. I guess that's where I get my curls.

I'm walking alongside the stretcher to the back of the ambulance. The door is already wide open. Mami has a pile of pillows under her head and shoulders. Suddenly she starts coughing quite badly. She's holding a cloth over her mouth. The roaring sound with which she's trying to suck in air terrifies me and so does the murmur with which she's exhaling again. Her face is red and there's blood on the cloth. I'm used to Mami being ill, but this time she's extremely ill. My body is trembling and my hands are sweating. Tears are burning behind my eyelids, but I don't want to cry. I want to be strong. For Mami.

The coughing stops. Mami sighs deeply and leans back into the pillows. She closes her eyes while the paramedics tuck her in with a sheet.

My Mami has TB, tuberculosis. She has little bugs in her lungs, and that's why she has to cough so hard. Once when I asked her why she was sick so often, she told me the disease first touched her before I was born, when she was still living in the city of Vienna, in Austria. She used to live with her mother in a damp house, and that's where she inhaled those bugs. When she's sick like she is today, she can't do anything. She can't work or take care of me. She's in bed all day long. When Mami is sick, Aunty Hilda takes care of me. Aunty Hilda takes care of me very often.

The ambulance will transport Mami to Bandung, to the tuberculosis clinic of Dr. Boon von Ochssee, where she'll be examined and operated on by a lung doctor. I know that doctor because I'm also regularly sent to him for check-ups, but today I won't be going.

Before she is hoisted into the ambulance, I give Mami a hug and a kiss on her cheek. "Bye-bye, Mami. I love you!"

A soft smile appears on her face, and I feel warm inside. My Mami is the sweetest Mami in the whole world.

Aunty Hilda is standing next to me. She has put her arm

around my shoulder, and together, we're watching the ambulance drive down the gravel path. All of a sudden, the tears I wanted to hold back appear anyway, and my shoulders start to shake.

"Shhh…Shhh…," Aunty Hilda kneels down beside me and tries to comfort me. "Mami is in good hands, Bubi."

"What if she never comes home again?" I moan.

"Don't think that way, sweetie. The doctors will make her better again."

Sniffling and then sobbing, I watch the ambulance drive off until it disappears around the corner.

"Come, Bubi. It's time to go to school. That'll distract your thoughts," Aunty Hilda says. I wipe my eyes dry with my arms and blow my nose into Aunty Hilda's handkerchief.

I'm being schooled according to the Dutch Clerkx method for home-schooling European children of five years and older. My teacher, I call her Missy, is an Indo—someone of mixed European and Indonesian descent—and in addition to our Dutch language lessons, she also teaches us Malay words and expressions. I really like my teacher, and I like to learn. The two other students in the class, Helga and Jutta Waldstein, live in our hotel, in one of the apartments beside the main building of the hotel. They speak German at home, just like me, because they are from Bohemia in Austria. Helga, with braided blond hair and big blue eyes, is my age, and her sister Jutta is a year and a half younger. They live in our hotel with their mother because the air in Lembang is healthier than in the big city of Batavia, where their father works. He's an engineer and head of the Topographical Service at the Dutch Ministry of Water Management. He only comes home on weekends, which I don't mind because I don't like him that much. He's always grumpy and short with me, even though I'm only eight years old.

I'm the only boy in my class, though my blond curls are long like the sisters'. Every day I wear the same thing: shorts, a shirt, socks, and sandals. My beloved slingshot dangles halfway out of my pocket. I often make slingshots myself, out of sticks, but they are fragile; they break with one or two shots. This one is special. It's as smooth as a rounded river rock, which makes it comfortable to hold. Our head gardener carved it for me from the hardwood of the Djambu tree that grows in our hotel garden. I shoot at almost everything—trees and bushes and the water in the ditch, at snakes and spiders, too—but never at people or pets.

This morning in class, before checking our homework, Missy singles me out. I have noticed that the adults are being extra nice to me now that Mami got taken away.

"Bubi, how are you?" Missy asks me.

"Good."

"Your Mami is ill again, isn't she?"

I nod.

"I'm very sorry to hear that, darling," Missy says. "But let's talk about something more fun. Tell us something special about your Mami that we don't know yet."

I don't have to think about that one for too long. "There's a piano in our small living room. My Mami plays the piano very well. Much better than Aunty Hilda, who plays complicated music on her grand piano. Mami plays every night before she brings me to bed, and she sings with it too."

I look away for a second. Mami's playing her piano while I'm standing beside her in my pyjamas, her voice echoing in my chest.

"I love my Mami very much! She takes care of me and protects me. I find her pretty and sweet."

"Thank you, Bubi, that's an adorable story," says Missy. "And tell me," she continues, putting on a mysterious smile. "Is your father not there with you when Mami plays her piano?"

I chuckled. "Not at all. Papi lives on the other side of the hallway, just like Aunty Hilda," I respond.

"How does that work exactly, Bubi?" Missy asks.

"Well, just like I'm saying…They have their living room, where Aunty Hilda has her grand piano, and they also have a bedroom. Papi and Aunty Hilda are the owners of the hotel, and they often work in the evenings, when I've already gone to bed. Aunty Hilda checks all the orders that Papi gives to the staff. She checks everything and everyone, and makes sure that the work is being carried out properly. Even though Aunty Hilda is strict, I'm never afraid of her. But sometimes she gives the male servant a reprimand if the beds aren't made properly. Or if she thinks the bedding isn't clean enough. Then the servant runs to my Mami in the linen room to get new bedding. My Mami is the head of the linen room."

"Aah," Missy says. "Now I understand!"

There's a strange undertone in her voice, and I suddenly wonder why Missy is so interested in the way things are organized at my home.

After school, Papi, Aunty Hilda, and I are having a hot meal for lunch together, and then, as usual, it's siesta time. Papi and Aunty Hilda sleep for an hour, and I have to stay in my room and play without making a sound.

I miss Mami. Normally she would have lunch with us, then she'd take her siesta in the bedroom right next to mine, but her bed is empty now. She has to stay in the hospital all week. I'd never heard her cough so loudly. And now, remembering the blood on the cloth, my stomach cramps up. I put my hands on my belly and bend forward until the cramp goes away.

My thoughts are restless, and I can't concentrate on my toy cars. My eyes wander around the room. I have to get out of here! But what if Papi finds out? If he discovers I've gone out on my own, without an adult, there's no doubt I'll get a beating with his hippo whip, a braided length of hippo skin with some fringes on the front. The thought of its lashes makes me shiver, but I can't help myself—I climb out the window and clamber over the six-foot-high fence. I take a quick look behind me. I don't see anybody coming after me, so I start running up the hill to the Bosscha Observatory.

The white walls of the observatory contrast sharply with the fresh green of the forests. The striking metal dome shines in the bright sunlight. My Dutch friend Karel's dad is the director of the observatory and says it's the oldest observatory in the entire Dutch East Indies. I bang hard on the heavy wooden door. Its copper fittings glint in the high sun. Soon, the sound of running feet echoes in the hallway, then the door is thrown open and I'm looking into Karel's grinning face.

"Bubi! Come in quickly, my dad's gone to run some errands."

My real name is Victor, but everyone calls me Bubi, which means "little boy" in Austrian. We run up the stone stairs. I take a seat in the swivel chair under the giant stargazer and Karel makes it spin as fast as he can. The chair turns, and I turn, and we're laughing our heads off until I start to feel a little light-headed. I bring the chair to an abrupt halt, jump up, and promptly fall over. It takes a few seconds for the dizziness to go away. I look up and grin at Karel.

"You okay?" he asks.

"Yes! Let's open up the dome," I say. I feel fluttering in my belly. Opening the dome is the pinnacle of fun. The large metal roof opens up in the middle, exasperatingly slow, as the gap gets bigger and bigger, until finally we see the blue of the sky. We're lying down on our backs on the floor, squinting up as the sunlight pours in, while the enormous stargazer shines like a mirror. Only for a moment, the observatory is our private playground; then, out of fear of being caught by Karel's father, we quickly close the roof again. All of a sudden, Papi's whip comes to mind; more specifically, I recall its sting on my behind.

"I have to go home, I'll see you later," I shout while jumping up and running towards the stairs.

Once outside, I look up from the observatory to the Tangkuban Perahu, the mighty volcano. From a distance, the slopes look blue and the gorges almost black, but when you're standing on top of that mountain, what you see is a lush green tropical rainforest that blankets the hills and valleys. It's inhabited by wild animals—snakes, spiders, panthers, and monkeys. Winding paths run through the jungle, used by the charcoal burners and wood gatherers and sometimes by guides taking tourists to the top.

To the right of the mountain is the small lake. You can swim in it, but it's not very clean. And you can walk all the way around it, through the bamboo forests that grow along the lake's edge. I find it alluring but scary at the same time because weird things have happened out there. I think back to that foggy day when, as I so often do, I walked around the lake during one of my excursions alone. Several men were at work, digging large holes in the ground, so deep that half their bodies disappeared into them as plumes of dirt shot out.

Somehow, I knew—I felt, in my tummy—that these men wouldn't want curious bystanders hanging around, so I quickly crouched behind the thick stems of bamboo. *Why are they digging those holes*, I wondered, *especially on a foggy day like today?*

Nearby, I saw large, dark heaps lying around. I squinted to see better. They were cows. They lay in the grass without moving, swollen bodies with legs stiffly raised in the air. It looked quite spooky.

I tried hard not to move as I watched the men from behind the bamboo. My heart was beating in my throat. Sweat dripped from my forehead. All of a sudden, my right calf seized in a cramp. I grabbed my foot and pulled it up, trying to change position as quietly as possible. Instantly the digging stopped. The men looked around nervously. I held my breath and crouched down a little farther.

"Hey, you! Get out of there," a deep, masculine voice roared.

Though I was horrified, I jumped up and started running as fast as I could. I ran to the stables of the nearest farm and sheltered there for a while, reflecting on what I had seen. I suddenly understood. Those cows were dead and had to be buried in those holes. But why were they being buried on the sly? And who were those men?

Only when I was absolutely sure no one had come after me did I dare to emerge. Once home, I confessed the story to Mami, and she explained that the cows might have been ill and that they should have been burned or buried on the farm grounds. She forbade me from going to the lake again, but of course I've broken that rule on many occasions, and I break the rule again today.

I wander down the mountain and turn right towards the vast farmlands and the many cowsheds owned by our neighbours, the Ursone family. Their place is called Baru Adjak. I walk past the metres-high fields of elephant grass. I don't understand how the cows can eat this grass without cutting their tongues to pieces, because when I walk through it, the grass regularly opens my shins, slashing painful red stripes into me. The Ursone cows are the best in Java, I've heard. They give at least twelve gallons of milk a day.

Behind the meadows of the Ursone family lie their kina plantations. These medicinal plants are high as trees, so high that they block the view of the Grand Hotel Lembang behind them, on Lembang Street, number 272. That's where I live: the hotel.

I accelerate my pace and run to the slow-flowing canal on the side of the hotel garden. I pick some red sorrel and chew on it. It has a lemony flavor. The canal is full of catfish. They have barbs that look like a cat's whiskers. I like poking sticks or throwing stones into the canal because it makes the fish shoot away in the mud. The native people eat them, so our servants eat them as well, and when I'm with them, I eat them too. They taste like the mud they live in.

I jump over the canal into the garden. Our garden is enormous, over seven acres in size, and I know every little corner of it. It's a pity, though, that I'm always alone. That's why I often visit friends outside the garden. I have Indo and European friends. Sometimes

I go to the pasar, the native market, where I buy tasty Indonesian finger food for a cent. Of course, Papi doesn't want me to leave the yard by myself, but he has no time to check on me. He's always busy.

The siesta is almost over. I climb over the fence, through the window, and into my bedroom. I walk to Mami's bedroom. The door is open and her bed is empty. How might she be feeling? She'll be in the hospital for a week. I hope the lung doctor will make her feel better.

Chapter 2

SKYPE CONVERSATION

Birgit Treipl, Nelson, BC, Canada
Victor Treipl, Loupiac, France
January 2, 2017

"Do you still miss Java?"

I'm sitting on my pink yoga ball in my office in Canada and see my father live in the attic of his French home, behind his large Apple computer screen. The connection is as clear as if I were sitting opposite him at the desk. The technology still amazes me. I'm interviewing my dad and want to know everything about his life in the Dutch East Indies. I'm so grateful that he's still alive. His mind is still sound, I find, but his memory is fading.

"Do I miss Java…" Dad mumbles, and his mind seems to wander. In the background, someone is singing, her voice accompanied by an electric piano—my mum, who's practicing downstairs in the kitchen with her French choir friends.

"In a way, I do, yes," he continues. "It is wonderful out here, and life in the French countryside comes much closer to that in the Dutch East Indies than the narrow-minded behavior I encountered in the Netherlands during the years after the war. But nothing beats the Indonesian hospitality. The warmth of the people. The tastes and smells. The phenomenal finger food I used to buy at the pasar, the Indonesian market. And nature…It was a paradise, out of this world!"

His eyes wander off the screen. The collar of his checkered shirt frames his round face. His white hair departs in a wave from his broad forehead. He wears glasses. He used to have a head of big, bouncy curls, just like me. I look like him.

"I can still picture the gardens of our hotel, and I can almost smell the fragrant scent of the Hibiscus chalices…You know, Lembang is located in the Preanger, one of the most beautiful regions of West Java," he continues. "It is located four hundred and sixty-five miles south of the equator. The sun rose at six a.m. and set at six p.m. Within a few minutes of sunset, it would be pitch dark. As if someone had turned the lights off. Lembang lies on a plateau, four thousand feet high, on the slopes of the Tangkuban Perahu volcano, which towered high above our small mountain village. It was pleasantly warm during the day, and the mornings and evenings were cool. The fresh mountain air was good for your health, like a natural spa. That's why my dad and Aunt Hilda felt so attracted to that place."

Dad's face fills the screen while my thumbnail is visible in the upper right corner. The window behind me is dark. It's eight a.m. here in Nelson, whereas in France, the rays of the late afternoon sun illuminate the room, and it's almost time for happy hour.

"That all sounds nice, Dad, but a lot has happened there. You've been uprooted twice," I say with a serious face. "First as an eight-year-old boy when you lost both parents and the war started, and the second time when you left your homeland."

He nods. "Yes, you're right. I was born Austrian in a Dutch colony that ultimately turned against me. When I arrived in Europe, I felt like a stranger. For years, I was searching for my identity. I was born white, but it was as if Indonesian blood was also flowing through my veins. Even though I'm not an Indo, I felt just as displaced as that part of the population. Your mum understood that. The Dutch East Indies also played a significant role in her life. That was important to me."

He pauses for a second. "And Aunt Hilda didn't have an easy life either. One has to wonder whether emigrating to the Dutch East Indies was a good decision for her. It has left an immense mark on her life."

I lean forward. "Fortunately, she had you."

"Yes, I think that kept her going all those years," Dad replies.

"Your parents had a mission, they were driven and incredibly successful.... Yet something very essential was missing," I say. "They had a deep longing for children and they were childless."

"Indeed. Until I was born. My arrival caused quite a storm," Dad laughs. "But for the longest time, I didn't know anything about that. I grew up in luxury and freedom, amongst family members who loved me, and I was the Indonesian staff's little darling. The apple of everyone's eye. My early childhood was like a long, lazy summer, although I felt lonely quite often. I also wondered why my dad spent so little time with me. He was always terribly busy. Why did he have that urge for children? Strangely enough, I did the same thing myself."

"What do you mean?"

"Well, I was always busy too. With a sports store that went completely sideways, a bankruptcy and all the consequences that entailed, and I was busy with other unimportant business adventures as well. I did it all alongside my job as a German teacher. I've been a haggler, more or less all my life. I wasn't a real entrepreneur, but I tried to be one. And because of it I've spent too little time with your brother and you, and I left too much work for your mother to do. I shouldn't have done that. She also had a full-time job.

"When we eventually got into financial trouble due to me, Aunt Hilda told me: 'You're just as naive as your father.' That hit me tremendously, and I wasn't proud of it. She passed away not long after that. In her sleep. As if she didn't want to be a burden to me anymore. I blamed myself terribly. She could have lived longer."

"But Dad, she turned ninety-three. Isn't that a remarkable age? You've cared for her all her life. It's true that, at home, most of the work came down to Mum, and yet I don't feel like I missed you as a child. Mum organized all the ins and outs of our lives, and it was always she who stood on the sidelines of the hockey field, but you were there for me in completely different ways."

Dad's face turns red, and I can see he's fighting his emotions. His eyes are getting a little watery.

"You need to be gentle on yourself, Dad. You weren't a bad father at all. We were very active as a family. Every holiday we went somewhere, off to France, skiing, and windsurfing. And you taught me how to pour concrete," I say with a grin.

"Thank you, darling, you're already making me feel better." His voice sounds hoarse. He stands up for a moment, sits down again, and changes position on his seat.

"On December 12, 1939, everything changed," he says all of a sudden. "Fate struck. Three times in a row."

"I know. It's incredible what you had to endure already as a young boy. What kept you going?"

"From a very young age, I've learned to be invisible in this world, to shut up to protect myself and mine. I became a survivor. This quality came in handy several times in my life. But in the long run, it got in my way and even made me physically ill. Remember that time I fainted in front of the classroom while your brother and his classmates were writing an exam? It was the drop that made the bucket overflow. I had to start talking. Eventually, with the support of a psychologist, I got to the point where I could forgive myself for specific events that happened in my life. I was able to be at peace with the choices I made and the disappointment I created for others."

He turns his face away.

"What are you thinking about?"

"I'm thinking about my dad. About my mother. Aunt Hilda. I think of everything she had to endure. I think of that moment sitting on the bare white hallway at the police station in Madiun, Java, that turned my world upside down…Life is a road filled with potholes and bumps. It's a good thing we don't know in advance what it has in store for us."

There's a moment of silence.

"Perhaps we should leave it at that for now, Dad."

"That sounds good, dear. I'm a little tired. It's been a long time since I dug in my past like this. I hear our choir friends at the front door. They're leaving. I'm going to pour your mum and myself a nice glass of wine."

"Wonderful! Enjoy that," I smile. "Bye, Dad!"

"Have a great day, my little girl, I'll see you again next week."

We're waving at each other. He has tears in his eyes. He's so close, yet so far away.

Chapter 3
GRAND HOTEL LEMBANG

"Girlie! Girlie!"

The children of hotel guests are playing together in the swimming pool. I'm jealous that they have brothers and sisters. I've asked Mami several times now if she can make me a little sister, but my Mami is ill and a sister still hasn't come.

I distract myself from my envy by collecting empty bottles I find on the hotel grounds. When the drinks supplier comes by, he refunds me the deposit: one cent per bottle. For a cent, you can get a tasty snack at the market and for a gobang, two-and-a-half cents, you can buy a whole meal. Collecting empty bottles is a big hobby of mine.

Again there's shouting: "Girlie! Girlie!"

I turn around. They're ridiculing me. I turn my face away, and then they all start to laugh. I put down the bag of empty bottles and start running. I have tears in my eyes. I'm not a girl at all. Can't they see that? I'm wearing shorts and a shirt, not a dress or a skirt. My name is Victor, and I've had enough of this.

I run straight to Mami's bedroom and look in the mirror. My ringlets are long and blond. Far too long. Almost to my shoulders. Mami loves my curls, sure. But why do they have to be this long? I've always hated them, and now even more so. I don't want to be called a girl. I get an idea. In a quiet moment, when nobody's watching, I'm going to cut these curls off myself. I steal the scissors from Mami's drawer and hide them under my mattress.

I'm quite proud that Papi and Aunty Hilda built the largest and most exquisite hotel in the entire area. We have a hundred and twenty beds. It's always hectic, and we're usually jam-packed. Aunty Hilda says that there's not much work in Europe for the time being because of some economic crisis. That's why a number of family members from Austria have moved to Indonesia to work at our hotel.

Uncle Ferdi, Mami's brother, a career waiter, is the head of the dining room and manager of the male servants. Papi's sister Aunt Lintschi, who worked in a sewing shop in Austria, works in the linen room. Now that Mami is in the hospital, Aunt Lintschi has to do the work all by herself. Her husband, Uncle Pepi, is a plumber, and he does a lot of things that have to do with water. He's very handy and he knows a lot, and I find him interesting, but Aunty Hilda doesn't like Uncle Pepi much. "Er ist ein gemeiner Mann," she says. He's a rude and abusive man. He swears and rages and, to be honest, that makes me laugh. But when he hits Aunt Lintschi, and she shows up in the linen room with bruises, I don't like him either. I feel for her because she is such a kindhearted person. She never gets mad, not even at Uncle Pepi.

Uncle Pepi was already here when the swimming pool was being built. It's a crystal-clear, large pool at the back of the hotel grounds. Uncle Pepi makes sure that the water in the pool stays clean. He has also installed faucets and showers in all the hotel rooms, so that our guests can enjoy running water at their convenience. Uncle Pepi has the key to the lid of the deep well, which is always locked. There's a pump in the well that pumps the water into a high tower with an enormous water tank on it. The well produces enough water for the entire hotel.

And then there's Aunty Hilda's cousin Bruno. They call Bruno "the entertainer," but I don't know exactly what kind of work he does. Aunty Hilda once said that Bruno wanted to join Adolf Hitler's party, but his father was totally against it, and that's why he sent Bruno to us in Lembang. Bruno is good looking and athletic and is always well dressed. He can often be found at the tennis court or at the swimming pool, joking with the hotel guests. I'm always a little wary when Bruno is around. Back when I still couldn't swim, he grabbed me and threw me into the pool, clothes and all. The water swallowed me whole, and, for a few seconds, the world disappeared behind the fizzy wash of blue. I shut my eyes tight. I kept spinning and spinning. It felt endless. Then my feet finally touched the pool's tiled bottom, I pushed off as hard as I could, and I came up again, coughing, spewing, and gasping for air. I floundered like a fish on dry land and tried to get to the poolside as quickly as I could.

As I pulled myself up, tears streaming down my face, I screamed, "Why did you do that, Bruno? That was so mean. I couldn't breathe! It wasn't funny!"

Bruno was bending over laughing.

I stomped off to my bedroom, but after this episode, I started practicing, just in case he ever tried that stunt again, and I eventually learned to swim. At first, I swam like a splashing doggie, but now I swim like a water beetle, and I hold my breath underwater.

All of our family members live in the row of apartments linked to the hotel, except for my granddad. We call him Opapa. Opapa lives with us, in the main building. His bedroom is to the left of Papi and Aunty Hilda's living room. Opapa is old. He only came to live with us a year ago. He loves the sun and good food. I like him very much. We feed the rabbits together every day.

"Opapa, are you there?" I cheerfully shout from the dining room.

"Yes, Bubi, I'm coming," he shouts from his bedroom.

Opapa is little, and he's also slightly bent. When he comes out to see me, he's wearing his white tropical uniform: the button-up with the epaulets, shorts, socks pulled up over his calves, and brimmed helmet. Opapa likes uniforms a lot because he used to be in the navy. We walk along the garden paths to the rabbit cages. The gardeners are busy weeding.

"Selamat pagi tuan."

"The gardeners are saying 'Good morning, sir' to you, Opapa."

Opapa nods politely. He only speaks German and doesn't understand Malay. Opapa walks very slowly. It makes me a little impatient and I tend to run back and forth on our walks. He doesn't mind.

"Opapa, what did you do in your old life, before you came to Lembang?" I yell from a distance.

"I worked as a rear admiral with the Austrian Navy. I was in charge of various navy ships."

"Ah, yes.... What places did you visit then, Opapa?"

"I have sailed around the world, Bubi."

I look at Opapa admiringly and wonder how he did it all, because he's such a tiny man. I'm almost as tall as he is.

"Please, tell me again about the time you went to China?"

I've heard the story ten thousand times, but I still find it fascinating every time Opapa tells it.

"Well, you see, I once traveled to China to connect with the Chinese government. As a special tribute to the Austrian government, they took me to a Chinese prison. They did me the honour of letting me watch a series of beheadings of crooks who were sentenced to death. Just before their beheading, the crooks smoked one last cigarette, made jokes amongst each other, and then they said goodbye."

The story always ends here because Opapa doesn't want to share the horrors of those beheadings with me.

"And how did that go, Opapa?" I try.

"The rest of the story is not suitable for the ears of little boys like you, Bubi."

"Ahhh…come on," I beg him.

"No, Bubi."

"Oh well, I do have have an idea of how that went, you know," I say.

Opapa grabs some carrots and starts feeding the rabbits. My thoughts are stuck on his story. I have often staged those decapitations for myself and shiver while thinking about it. The men are standing in a row, a burlap bag over their heads, their hands tied behind their backs with a piece of hemp rope. Suddenly a giant Chinese man appears, dressed in black and wearing a large golok, a sword-like tool, on a belt around his waist. With a big stroke, he chops off the men's heads. The blood sprays everywhere and makes red spots on Opapa's immaculate white uniform. Imagining it all now, I scream.

Opapa looks up, startled. "What is it, boy?" he asks.

My gaze quickly glides over his uniform. Not one spot on it. I sigh with relief.

"Nothing."

The rabbits are rushing around in the cage. One rabbit jumps up high and twists in the air like an acrobat.

"Look! That rabbit is a circus rabbit," I shout.

Together we stick the carrots through the mesh. The rabbits are making a cozy, soft, gnashing sound with their teeth. But after a few minutes, I get bored.

"Opapa, I'm going to take a look a little farther down the garden path."

"That's okay, Bubi. Don't do anything stupid, okay?"

"No, Opapa…"

It's a Saturday, which means I'm off school today. I walk toward the hibiscus hedges at the far end of the hotel garden. They are over six-feet high and in full bloom. It's a sea of gigantic white- and salmon-coloured flowers. The largest have a diameter of six inches or more. I stick my nose in them. They have such a strong smell, it almost makes me dizzy. They are called kembang sepatu in Malay, which means "shoe flower." The servants use the fallen flower buds to polish their shoes until they shine. Behind the hibiscus hedges are the servants' outbuildings; whatever happens there, the hotel guests never get to see. It's where the servants eat, laugh, live, and sleep, and where the laundry gets washed, dried, and ironed.

I visit the wash man. He's a very strong native guy, with big muscular arms, and he works with a bare torso because of the heat. His work area smells of soap, and it's wet everywhere. He swings a sheet with great force against a washboard, which he holds slightly tilted. The white foam splashes in all directions. After many strokes, the sheet is clean, and the wash man throws it in a large bin full of clear water. He looks so strong and powerful, I find it exciting to watch him. I always have a lot of questions for him, so I like to stand there while I watch and talk to him. (My Mami calls this "constant chatter.") Now and then I get an answer.

"Mister, what are you doing?" I ask him.

"Washing," he answers.

"Why are you doing that?"

"It's my job."

"Oh." I wait a bit while he whips a sheet against the washboard. "How long have you been doing that?"

"As long as I can remember."

"Why does that board have ribs?"

No answer.

"Why do the sheets need to be so white?"

No answer.

I decide to go over to the man who irons everything. I'm jumping around, and my long blond curls are swinging up and down. The ironing man is a rather small, sturdy Indonesian and sweat is dripping off his forehead. He strokes the sun-dried sheets with a gigantic iron that is at least sixteen inches long. It is heated with charcoal. He irons for hours at a time in the sweltering, tropical heat.

"Mister, aren't you hot?" I ask him.

"Yes, I am," he says.

"How hot is the iron?" I ask.

"It's so hot, I'm almost burning the sheet."

"How do you know not to burn it?"

"I learned how."

"How long do you have to iron?"

No answer.

Papi doesn't let me hang out in the outbuildings. He has forbidden me from going there. "As the owner's son, you don't belong there," he always says. He wants me to grow up as a European boy and doesn't want me to become like a native child.

It's even more taboo to visit the servants during their lunch hour, but I like their Indonesian food much better than the European meals at home and there's always such a great ambiance in their kitchen. I love it there, so I secretly slip in when I can. They cook their dishes on anglos, portable heaters with glowing charcoal in them and a metal grill on top. Pans and woks go on the grills. The servants sometimes have seven anglos in a row going. It smells wonderfully sweet and spicy today. They're cooking rendang padang, spicy beef simmered in coconut milk, and steamed white rice. They're sitting on their butts on the floor, their legs slightly bent. The floor is cement, but there are mats lying on it. These are our regular employees, always the same group of people.

"Sinjo Bubi—Master Bubi—come over here, sit beside me and have a bite to eat," the cook says to me.

I don't need further encouragement. I squat in-between the servants and get a bowl pressed into my hands with rice, meat, and cooked vegetables. I inhale the delicious scents and start eating. I eat with my fingers, just like them. The mood is pleasant and cheerful. Occasionally someone will say something, then the others chuckle. I feast with all my senses, the fat dripping down my hands, and I lick my fingers one by one.

All of a sudden one of the servants whispers, "You'll have to get out of here now, your mother is coming."

I look up and see my Aunty Hilda appear in the distance.

"Thank you for the delicious food," I say and jump up. "That is not my Mami, by the way," I yell as I skedaddle.

A few weeks later, Opapa dies in his sleep. He is buried in the large European cemetery in Bandung and gets a tasteful stone. Only our family members are present at the funeral. Opapa was very old, ninety-five years old, to be exact, but still, I am sad.

I don't feel like feeding the rabbits anymore.

Chapter 4

GUNA-GUNA

I'm sitting on the steps outside of the hotel lobby, on the lookout for my Mami, who is coming home soon. The driver drove Papi to Bandung to pick her up from the hospital. I've been counting the days. I've been longing, too, for her piano-playing and for her kiss on my cheek before bed and her loving arms around me.

Suddenly the car shows up on the gravel path, and it comes to a crunching halt in front of me. I'm so excited I hop around. As soon as Mami gets out, I wrap my arms around her. I don't want to let go of her.

"Darling, I can hardly breathe," my mother laughs.

"I'm sorry!" I say, and I let her go.

"I'm glad to see you again," she says, as she gives me a wink. "You've become stronger overnight."

I'm blushing. We walk over to our small living room. She tells me she has had surgery on her lungs and that it hurt a lot, that the nurses gave her milk to drink, and pushed her out in the sun and fresh air every day with her bed and all. That has done her much good.

She doesn't tell me how they did the surgery, but I imagine the doctor has zipped open her chest so that he could suck out those little bugs with a little vacuum.

But now that Mami is back home and feeling better every day, Aunty Hilda has suddenly fallen ill.

I stand near the edge of her bed, watching her. The bedroom is dark. The European doctor and Papi are whispering. Aunty Hilda is not saying a word. She's lying in bed without any movement. Nobody understands what's going on with her. I bring my face close so that it's just above hers. Her eyes aren't blinking. They're wide open.

"She has a heartbeat of five," the doctor says. "That's impossible! I can hardly feel it."

"She's not drinking or eating either," Papi replies, worried.

I find it scary that Aunty Hilda doesn't move at all, and I sneak out of the room.

In search of distraction, I walk outside, towards the cages at the back of the hotel garden. One pen in particular is very large. Our birds live in it: small parrots and brightly coloured songbirds. Fieps lives in another cage. He's a big, tall, slim Javanese monkey, with a shiny black coat and a brown glow on his legs. His tail is three feet long. Fieps is agile; he jumps around with considerable force in the sturdy metal cage and shows me his long, dirty teeth. We have a bit of a rivalry, Fieps and me. He scares me.

One of the servants is his caretaker. He feeds Fieps and cleans his cage. He's good friends with him, and he's stern with me because I always try to tease Fieps. Sometimes I pretend I'm going to feed him, and then I withdraw the food. It isn't right to do that, but I don't care. I just like to see his reaction. Today I've found a long stick and I try to poke him with it. Fieps gets furious. I start to giggle. He shrieks and jumps into the iron fence with a mighty dive. I somehow lose my balance; I fall on my back, and the stick flies out of my hands. Fieps moves fast. Before I find the time to think, he sticks his long arm through the mesh and gets hold of my hair.

"Ouch! You, ugly bastard," I scream. I start screeching. The caretaker comes running at me at high speed and Fieps lets go of my hair.

"Tidak boleh!" the caretaker reprimands me while raising his finger. That is not allowed!

I give him my most innocent look.

"You shouldn't bully Fieps like that." He saw me do it.

I lift myself up and rub my aching head. It feels awfully sore where the monkey grabbed my hair. I raise my head and Fiep's gaze finds mine. He grins amicably, his thoughts transparent in the twinkle of his eyes: good for you, nasty bugger. I look sheepishly at the caretaker and wander off.

I stroll to the front garden and climb into one of the tall ironwood trees. There are many of them in the hotel garden. They produce a lot of sticky resin and I love its strong odor. Climbing trees is my favourite hobby. I enjoy watching everything and everyone from their leafy heights without people below being aware of me. I hoist myself onto a large branch and lean my back against the thick old trunk, my legs dangling on either side of the branch, like I always do.

I love it here in the garden. Playing outside always makes me in a good mood, and I feel as free as the breeze. I take my slingshot out of my pocket and mess around with the elastic. In my idleness, I scout the garden looking for entertainment while keeping an eye on the black caterpillars crawling around the tree. They're big and have long hair, and if they touch you, your skin will be itchy for hours. It has happened to me before. Now I'm always careful around them. I have almost forgotten the incident with Fieps until suddenly a huge commotion echoes through the garden. I look up. The noise is coming from the direction of the pool. Two seconds later Fieps runs through the hotel garden, various gardeners chasing him, some of them raising garden tools at him, and there's a lot of shouting from all sides. They can't catch Fieps, though. He's making triumphant monkey sounds, the kind you hear in the jungle all the time. He grasps the branch of an acacia tree with his long, muscular arm and swings around, clearly enjoying his escape. The caretaker is running after him, but Fieps is always too fast for him. I can read the distress on the man's face. The situation is getting out of hand. He probably didn't close the cage door properly after feeding Fieps. "I'm going to get help," he shouts to one of the gardeners and runs towards the main hotel building. They don't see me up here in the ironwood tree.

A little farther away, a group of boys are watching, standing in their bathing suits with wet hair, talking feverishly. They're the same boys who were bullying me before. There's movement in the corner of my right eye. It is Fieps. He bolts toward the boys and bites one of them, right in his thigh. The boy wails in terror and drops to the ground. The other boys scatter and scream for help, and Fieps dashes off. Almost as quickly, Papi hurries out of the hotel lobby, wearing his always flawless white tropical suit, Fieps's caretaker following. Papi has got his shotgun. I jump out of my tree and run towards the two men. I want to see this spectacle up close.

The bitten boy is still lying on the ground, crying miserably. His friends are standing around him, their eyes wide and their faces frozen. Two gardeners help the injured boy to his feet, wrap a large bath towel around him, and carefully place him in a wicker lounge chair.

Remarkably, Fieps's sense of submission kicks in upon seeing Papi and his shotgun. Focusing his gaze on the ground, he walks on all fours in the direction of his cage, occasionally looking back as his bare butt wiggles side to side. He calmly jumps into the cage, which the caretaker quickly closes behind him. The man gives a deep sigh of relief, takes a hanky from his pocket, and wipes the sweat from his head and neck.

I am standing next to Papi, who's now tending to the son of the hotel guest.

"Would you mind holding my gun, Bubi?" Papi asks me.

Sure! I like doing that, because now everyone can see that this man is my dad. He taught me how to hold the gun, with the barrel up. The boys' eyes are on me, in awe.

Papi turns around and beckons a servant to come disinfect and bandage the boy's wound. Then he gives them all an ice cream, and I get one too. I'm proud of Papi. Of us. Fieps looks serenely at the scene from his cage. He's had a lot of fun today.

The next morning the doctor comes to see Aunty Hilda again. Nothing has changed, though. Papi paces back and forth while talking to him.

"I think this is it," the doctor says.

I don't know what he means by that exactly, but Papi is emphatic, "No! No, I don't believe that. There must be something we can do."

The doctor leaves the room, carrying his large bag, and we are left sitting next to Aunty Hilda's bed. Papi moistens her lips with water and squeezes the doctor's drops into her eyes. He then walks out of the room. I run after him.

"What's wrong with Aunty Hilda, Papi? Why can't the doctor heal her?"

"I don't know. Come, let's ask Soma for advice," he replies.

Raden Somawidjaja, or Soma for short, is our chief bookkeeper, a wise Indonesian man. He's a good friend of Papi's. We find Soma working in the office, sitting behind his desk. Papi takes the seat in front of him. I remain standing next to Papi.

"Soma, my friend, you must have heard. Hilda is terribly sick. She isn't responding to anything. The European doctor has already visited a few times, but her condition has not changed. He thinks she's dying, but I don't believe it. Do you have any idea what to do?" Papi asks.

Soma sits in silence for a second. "Is there anyone who wants to do you harm, Boss Franz?" he asks. Papi's first name is Franz Viktor.

Papi looks surprised. "Not that I know of," he answers. "Why?"

"This may be a case of guna-guna," says Soma.

"I'm sorry?" Papi asks.

Soma leans forward across the desk and says in a muted tone: "Guna-guna is part of our traditional indigenous beliefs. It's a magic tool that can be used to generate love or to harm some-one—or both."

"But...how is that applied?" Papi asks.

"Everything and everyone has a soul. The soul possesses a supernatural power that can be manipulated."

Papi is startled. "Black magic?" he whispers.

"Yes. The guna-guna uses mantras, formulas, the force of thought, special ingredients, and the intervention of nature spirits," Soma explains.

I have no idea what to think of what Soma tells Papi, so I wisely shut up and listen.

Papi doesn't seem to understand either. "I can't imagine how that works exactly, but perhaps more importantly," he trailed off for a moment as if he was searching the room for a solution. "How do you get rid of the curse?"

"Boss Franz, I advise you to consult a dukun immediately," Soma says. "But not just anyone. One of the highest level. He must be able to break through the secret forces. I know a very good one for you."

A dukun is an Indonesian medicine man who works with native medicines and herbs, which they also sell at the pasar.

"Would you please ask the dukun to come by as soon as possible? I'll be forever grateful." Papi grasps Soma's hand firmly.

Soma nods and stands up. "The man lives on the outskirts of the Indonesian settlement."

As Soma leaves the hotel, Papi and I walk back to Aunty Hilda's room. He trickles the drops into her eyes again and moistens her lips. We sit there for a while without talking.

"I need to get back to work, Bubi," Papi whispers in my ear. "It's almost lunchtime for the hotel guests."

He walks out of the room.

While sitting on the edge of the bed, something weird is going on. My eyes have already adjusted to the dark, so I stand up and move my face above Aunty Hilda's to look into her eyes, which are still wide open. And even though she doesn't move or blink, I'm suddenly convinced that she can see me. I startle and jump back a little, but then move my face above hers again. Her eyes, the colour of the sky, are reflecting her energy back to me. It's as if I can look straight into her soul.

I hold my hand close to her nose and feel the warmth of her breath. It's very weak, but I can feel it.

"Aunty Hilda, Aunty Hilda, you must wake up again."

But Aunty Hilda doesn't answer.

All excited, I run out of the room, looking for Papi. I find him in the dining room, uncorking wine.

"Papi, Papi, I think Aunty Hilda can see me!"

"What do you mean, Bubi?"

"Well, I put my face over her face, and I'm one hundred percent sure. She recognized me."

Papi puts the bottle and opener down on the table. He lays his hand on my shoulder and stares at me with a serious face.

"Thank you, Bubi. I will discuss this with Soma when he gets back. We will have to wait for the medicine man to solve this problem."

After lunch, everyone is in bed for the siesta, as always. While I'm playing with my toy cars in my bedroom, I suddenly think of the scissors I took from Mami's drawer. They have been sitting under my mattress for over a week now. I tiptoe to the door of my mother's room, put my ear to it, and hold my breath. No sound, nothing, except the loud pounding of my own heart behind my rib cage.

I sneak back to my bed and take out the scissors from underneath the mattress. They're large and shiny. There's no mirror in my room. The only thing I have is the windowpane. I'm standing on my bed, looking at the outline of my head in the reflection. I stick out my tongue, which makes me grin from ear to ear. This look will be very different in a minute or so. I grab the scissors in my right hand, cut off a few curls, and catch them in my other hand, while I look contentedly at the head in the glass. I toss my curls out of the window and watch them as they slowly flutter down and land on the pavement. I keep going for a while. When I'm done cutting, I hide the scissors under the mattress again.

After some time, there's the shuffling of a body tossing amongst the sheets in the room next to me. Mami's awake and getting up. A tingling sensation runs down my spine, and a slight vibration quivers in my throat. Will she notice my hair? Of course whe will. Will she get mad?

When the door opens, I'm on the floor playing with my cars, trying to act normal and behave while feeling Mami's eyes, her piercing gaze, staring at me.

"What have you done," she exclaims.

I cringe while my mother's voice suddenly rises in pitch... "Your beautiful ringlets, completely ruined. Your hair is all higgledy-piggledy. Look at yourself!"

She grabs my arm and pulls me up, grabs me roughly by the chin, and turns my head to the window pane. Seeing my short hair, I have trouble suppressing a triumphant smile. Mami sighs deeply and stomps out of the room. Unfortunately, I know what's coming: she'll call in Papi. I'm not looking forward to that. He usually gets really angry when Mami's reached her breaking point because of something I've done.

And indeed, moments later, Papi rushes into my room with the hippo whip in his hand. His fearsome weapon.

"What have you been up to, Bubi?" Papi's anger lights up like a storm and his face turns red. "You cut your hair? How, for crying out loud, did you get that idea in your head?"

Before I can say anything, he folds me over his knee and strikes me with the whip several times on my backside.

I scream and start crying loudly.

But Papi doesn't stop and continues whipping my butt a number of times.

I scream again. "Papi, all the kids are making fun of me. They were calling me 'girlie,'" I whine, "but I'm not a girl at all!"

The whipping suddenly stops, and Papi stands me back up. My buttocks are glowing painfully.

"Bubi," he says in a stern tone, "I don't want you to cut any part of yourself with scissors. Ever! Woe to your bones if you do this again. You could have asked politely. We'll go to the barber in Bandung and have this mess turned into a normal boy's head."

Papi leaves the room. I stay behind and rub my butt with my hand. I'm sure there are red stripes on it, and I won't be able to sit comfortably for two days. Then I start to chuckle and the tension slips from my body. I drop down onto my bed and roll back and forth, giggling.

I won. We'll go to the Hungarian barber and my hair is going to be cut short.

Suddenly, from the corner of my eye, I see my father's whip lying on the table. He must have forgotten all about it. I conveniently throw the thing behind the wardrobe.

"There, I solved that in a hurry." I cross my arms and feel quite proud of myself.

That night the medicine man comes over. He's a small, slender indigenous man in traditional Javanese costume. His batik headscarf is neatly folded around his head. He's wearing a plain cotton shirt with long sleeves, two colourful sashes draped over his shoulders, and a batik sarong around his waist that reaches down to his feet.

He rolls out a wicker mat on the floor next to Aunty Hilda's bed. On it he places a bronze bowl in which he lights some incense. He walks over to Aunty Hilda and cuts her fingernails and snips off a swatch of her hair. He then sits down on his mat, cross-legged, behind the bowl. A lump of wax appears in his hands, which he rolls in his palms along with the bits of Aunty Hilda's hair and nails, and then he starts to mould the hand-warmed wax into a doll.

Papi and I are watching, silent, from a corner of the room. I feel so tense that it isn't until leaning against the wall I realize I'd forgotten the painful marks on my butt. I take Papi's hand. Soma is standing next to us and looking quite relaxed. I wonder whether he has watched such a scene before, and if so, whether that person survived. Aunty Hilda doesn't budge an inch.

The medicine man begins to make strange noises. He casts a spell, and it sounds like a prayer. He repeats it three times. After each prayer, he blows incense over the doll's head. Then he starts rubbing the doll's body and recites his prayer. Again, and again, and again. Even though I don't catch the wording, there's a clear start and finish to his prayer. I counted them all. Twenty-two times. He then stands up and opens Aunty Hilda's mouth with his fingers. He produces a tiny bottle, drips some of the contents onto her tongue, and closes her mouth again. He picks up his bronze bowl, places it on her nightstand and starts rolling up his wicker mat. He nods at Soma, who guides him out of the bedroom.

The ritual is complete. Papi and I stand motionless and stare at Aunty Hilda. She still doesn't budge. Soma comes back into the room and talks to Papi.

"Boss Franz, the dukun has driven away the evil spirit. We now have to take turns keeping a watch over boss lady Hilda."

For two days and two nights, Soma and Papi keep watch. Nothing happens. But then, at the end of the third morning, while the three of us are in the room, holding vigil, Aunty Hilda suddenly starts to move very carefully. She's blinking her eyes. It's a miracle!

She starts to cough loudly. I jump up from my chair. Papi and Soma rush to her and help her sit upright in the bed. They help her drink water and the coughing calms down. She sighs deeply and drops back onto the pillows.

I sit down on the bed next to Aunty Hilda. She starts to talk with a crunchy, raspy voice. "I could see you, Bubi," she says. "I just couldn't move and I couldn't say anything to you. I was trapped in my own body."

Papi shakes Soma for joy.

It takes a long time for Aunty Hilda to be back to her old self again. Every day she has to take all kinds of nasty herbal remedies. My teacher Missy never comes back. After extensive research, Soma's medicine man discovers that Aunty Hilda was poisoned by another medicine man of a lower rank hired by Missy. Soma says Missy wanted to get rid of Aunty Hilda so that she could seduce Papi and become a rich woman.

What a witch she was. I think of the questions she asked me during that one morning class. Did I tell her too much? Did Aunty Hilda fall ill due to me? Imagine if she never woke up again...

Chapter 5

THE PASAR BARU

Papi has a car. A beautiful red Chrysler convertible. That's very special because vehicles are scarce and expensive and most people travel on foot, by bike, or with a horse and buggy. We have three vehicles because the hotel needs them, but the red Chrysler convertible is definitely my favourite. The driver drives us to the Pasar Baru, the large Indonesian market in the city of Bandung, to buy fresh vegetables, fish, meat, and other food items for the hotel. I'm off school today, so I can come. I sit in the back with Aunty Hilda. Mami never goes to the market because she has to work in the linen room.

For me, going to the market is always a big party. I can already smell its stalls from a few hundred yards away. Above it, the sky fills with the intense aromas of meat and fish, all kinds of fruit, ready-made Indonesian food, incense, and other fragrances. It is one big jumble whose potency the heat of the tropical sun reinforces. The vendors all shout to promote their products and capture our attention. With hundreds of stalls, the sound is deafening, and as we get closer, my excitement grows. As the son of a good customer, I always get yummy snacks at the stalls of the regular suppliers.

The driver parks the car near the market. Papi, who was sitting in the front passenger seat, steps out, while the driver opens the back door for Aunty Hilda. I jump out on the other side and eagerly grab my father's hand. He smiles. I glow. I love to walk through the market with him. Here, Papi has plenty of time for me—not like at home.

"What are you going to buy, Papi?"

"I need fruit, vegetables, meat and fish, and Aunty Hilda wants to run a few more errands on Braga street. Let's go get some fruit first, Bubi."

I hop happily around Papi, my hand in his, while our driver carries the baskets. The stalls look so inviting. Hundreds of types of fruit, richly displayed in shades of green, brown, golden yellow, and red, smell wonderfully sweet and slightly overripe. I know all the different kinds because I eat them every day. I pick them from the trees on our property or get them at home in the kitchen from Aunty Hilda or the cook. Small, sugary bananas and mangoes. Guava, which also hang in the tree above our well. Jackfruit, Java apple, lychee, and soursop, whose flesh we spoon right out of the peel. Can't forget the big smelly durian, the fruit of the Durio tree—I love it! My mouth waters at the sight of all those goodies stacked together in barrels and on tables. One of the vendors knows me and gives me a wink. As we approach, he peels a mango and drops fresh, juicy pieces into my palm. I stuff them into my mouth one by one and lick the juice from my hands. We've been at the market for less than ten minutes and already my face and hands are covered in sticky liquid.

"Terima kasih banjak, pak," I thank him politely and run my tongue over my lips. A broad grin appears on the man's face, and Papi looks proud. I speak a hodgepodge of pasar-Malay and

Sundanese. I also speak Dutch fluently because I learn it in school, and at home we speak German because we're Austrians.

Aunty Hilda and Papi are on their way to the vegetables. I fall behind trying to take in all that I see. Hundreds of people are walking around the market, rich and poor, in all possible clothing, a mix of everything.

European ladies stroll through the crowd. Their long, flowing white dresses sway in the humid breeze. Clutching delicate fans, they gracefully use them to cool their faces. The European men wear Western-style clothing: white pants, shirts, jackets, and sometimes even a tie. Some of them have pens or pocket watches in their suit pockets. The Indonesian men wear traditional sarongs, shirts, and sandals, although a few prefer pants. Many of the Indonesian merchants don't wear shirts. The Indonesian women look elegant in their traditional sarong kebaja—an embroidered tunic over a sarong of long batik cloth wrapped around the waist, reaching the ankles. And many of them wear a conical hat made from handwoven bamboo, called a sawa paddy hat. Many of the Indonesian women are buyers. They carry baskets in slings on their hips. Some of the women chew constantly, even while they're talking. Suddenly one of them spits a massive squirt of black liquid into a drain pit in the road.

I make a face. "Yuk! What is that, Papi?"

"They're chewing the betel nut. It's made from fresh leaves and fruit of the sirih bush. They roll small pieces or finely ground sirih, chalk, and cloves into the leaves, and that's what they're chewing on," Papi explains.

It doesn't sound like anything I would like to taste.

"They have a crooked face, because that nut is always sitting in one cheek," I say.

A little farther down the street, Indonesian men balance their merchandise in baskets on either side of a bamboo bar on their shoulders. I admire them. The baskets are gigantic and incredibly full. The men themselves are no taller than my father.

"Could you carry those baskets too, Papi?"

"No, I wouldn't dare to try," my father grins. "Those men are very strong because they carry those baskets up and down the hill every single day. They have calluses on their shoulders because of it."

While we're on our way to the big hall to buy meat and fish, our driver and the market vendors carry our fruit and vegetable purchases to the car. All the walls in the market hall are tiled in white. The meat has been set out in baskets on the tables, behind which slaughtered chickens hang by their necks on hooks. Aunty Hilda hands one of the vendors her basket while pointing out different chickens and pieces of meat. The woman covers the bottom of the basket with banana leaves, then lays the pieces of meat and the chickens in the basket, one by one, with leaves in between.

I'm highly attracted by the fish stalls. A massive selection is spread out; many look alien, like fish from another world. Small ones, large ones, some even larger than me. The small fish are still alive, and now and then one jumps out of the aquarium. There are freshwater fish and saltwater fish. Their scales shine in the sunlight that reaches through the building's tall windows. You can buy the whole fish or just pieces, and you get to choose whichever fish you want.

On the way back to the car, we walk past the stalls with clothing, hats, knives, household items and knick-knacks, sandals, and incense, not to mention all sorts of different djamus, native medicines and herbs, like dried roots, flowers, leaves, tree bark, and bottles with oils and potions. I find those stalls intriguing and stare at the various bottles. "Could this one make my muscles stronger?" I wonder aloud. "Does that one make bald men's hair grow?" The djamus vendor is wearing a starched white coat over her dress. She isn't shouting like the other salespeople. She mainly hawks her merchandise using gestures. She waves to Aunty Hilda, then pours a drink in a coconut bowl, stretches her arm out, and makes a face. I look up at Aunty Hilda. She smiles and kindly shakes her head no.

"I will definitely stay away from those," she whispers to me. "I barely survived the guna-guna."

The Hungarian hairdresser cuts my hair even shorter than I did. After that, Aunty Hilda wants to visit Toko Tjijoda, which is a Japanese department store, and Maison Bogerijen, the pastry shop on Braga street. I'm starting to feel bored with the shopping now.

"Papi," I whine, "when are we finally going home?"

"We'll have a bite to eat here first."

My face brightens. "At the Chinese restaurant?"

My father nods, and I'm already on my way to the corner of the street.

The car is packed and bagged and then we head home, up the hill, back to the hotel. Tired and satisfied, I fall asleep in the back seat, unaware of the dark clouds gathering above my head.

Chapter 6

THE ANGEL
OF DEATH

Aunty Hilda enters my bedroom, interrupting my game, and squats down beside me. She strokes her hand through my hair, looks at me seriously, and takes my hand in both of her hands. I can see that she means to comfort me, but I sense trouble.

"Bubi, Mami will not be coming home anymore," she says. "The doctor at the clinic couldn't make her better, and she passed away quietly."

I can't bring out a word.

Mami fell ill again a few days ago and had to be taken by ambulance to the clinic in Bandung. But I expected her to come home again soon, like last time.

I look up at Aunty Hilda. "Passed away? What do you mean?"

Aunty Hilda doesn't answer and wraps her arm around my shoulder. "Come, let's go say good-bye to her."

She takes my hand and hesitantly I walk with her to the lobby, where Papi is already waiting for us.

"Mami is dead," he says gloomily.

That Mami would be dead is entirely impossible to me.

"Will I never see Mami again? No! It can't be true," I shout, bewildered.

It is quiet in the car while we're driving down the hill to Bandung. Bruno and Uncle Ferdi are with us. I look out the window and see the green farmlands and gracefully terraced rice fields glide by. Everyone is turned inward and stares ahead.

My Mami is laid out in a small room of the sanatorium. She lies in a strange bed with a wooden frame around it, like a box, amid pretty flowers. The place is sunny and warm. I find her extremely pretty—all those flowers!—and walk over to her.

"Mami?"

Of course, she doesn't answer. Mami is dead; the fact echoes through my mind. I look up and cast a questioning glance at my father. His face is sweaty and red, and he blows his nose in a handkerchief. I've never seen him cry. Fathers aren't supposed to cry. I bite my lower lip and quietly watch my gorgeous, captivating mother, who can no longer speak.

Suddenly, I feel the urge to touch her. My fingers brush against her cheek, and the feel of her cold skin startles me. I pull my hand back and start to cry. Aunty Hilda hugs me and tries to calm me down, but it doesn't work. After a while, Bruno grabs me by the arm and drags me outside, towards the car.

While driving back to the hotel, I have a massive cry. It is starting to dawn on me that Mami is no longer with me.

"Bubi, big boys don't cry," Bruno says in a reprimanding tone.

"It's my Mami who's dead, so I may surely cry," I shout back at him. I have earned the right to be rebellious. Something has been taken away from me.

Once we're back at the hotel, I run to our small living room. I stare at the piano. I'll never hear my Mami play again. Never hear her sing again. I run into her bedroom. Her nightgown is hanging from a hook on the back of the door. I stick my head into the fabric and try to absorb her scent. I start to cry, and soon the sobs rack me so hard, my whole body is shaking. I lower myself to the floor and curl up behind the door.

Aunty Hilda squeezes her way through. She helps me to my feet.

"Shhh…shhh…," she whispers, stroking my head.

She walks over to the bed, sits down, and gestures for me to join her.

But I'm upset and start yelling, "You see, I told you so! When I asked what if Mami never comes back? The doctors didn't do their best at all! Otherwise, she would be home again and take care of me and play the piano!"

I dissolve into tears. I'm tired. So, so tired. Aunty Hilda pulls me towards her, takes me into her lap, and wraps her arms around me. She wipes my tears dry and cleans my nose with her handkerchief and rocks me back and forth.

"You know, Bubi, Mami was very ill, and she was in a lot of pain. The pain had become unbearable for her. It's better that she went to heaven," Aunty Hilda says softly.

"I don't want her to go to heaven. I wish she were here," I shout. "I want to talk to her. I feel so miserable now that she's no longer here!"

"I know, darling. You're sad because you loved Mami so much. Grief hurts, but it's also very beautiful."

I can't see what's so beautiful about grief. I'm in pain. "Aunty Hilda. My heart hurts," I say while sobbing.

She rocks me back and forth on her lap.

"It feels like my heart has shriveled."

"When your heart has shriveled, you need a lot of hugs," Aunty Hilda answers while squeezing her arms firmly around me. She feels warm, and I love the smell of her perfume. I sob softly and my breath trembles. We sit there for a long time until my breathing calms down.

"Where's Papi, Aunty Hilda?"

"Papi's at work, dear."

"Isn't he sad then?"

"I think he is, Bubi."

I wonder why Papi is always and forever working. Even now that Mami has died. His work seems to be more important than anything else.

"Where's heaven, Aunty Hilda?"

"Heaven is everywhere above us. Mami's now a star in the sky. Every time you look up in the dark, you can see her shine," Aunty Hilda says.

That reassures me, that I will still get to see Mami. Aunty Hilda takes me to my bedroom and puts me to bed. I wrap my arms tightly around Mr. Bear, my favourite stuffed teddy bear. I fall asleep from exhaustion. When I finally wake up, she's there, nodding on the chair next to my bed. She has been keeping watch over me for hours.

As soon as she notices I'm awake, she sits up and says, "I will always be there for you, Bubi, and I will always take care of you."

It's true, because she has always done that.

It's December 12, 1939. Mami is dead, and nothing will ever be the same.

Chapter 7

PAPI

Aunty Hilda, Papi, and I are having lunch in the family dining room. If Mami were still alive, she would have been here with us, but now it's just the three of us. Everyone is being extra nice to me, gentle and understanding, but I can't help it, our home feels terribly empty. Aunty Hilda and Papi are talking to each other. Grown-up talk. I only half listen to what they say.

"Hilda, Christmas and New Year are just around the corner. It'll be hectic, and you'll need to be well rested and fit. There's one more week before things will start to gear up around here. I think you should take a few days off and go somewhere on a short break."

"I'm not sure…," Aunty Hilda says. "We'll need to take care of Bubi. Besides, where for heaven's sake am I supposed to go?"

"Babu Siti," our housekeeper, "and I can take care of Bubi. Why don't you visit one of our fellow mountain hotels? I'll call up the Grand Hotel Sarangan to announce your visit as the co-owner of Grand Hotel Lembang. They will receive you with respect," Papi says.

Aunty Hilda keeps silent for a second and then answers, "I don't want to go all by myself. Bruno can accompany me and he can do the driving."

They leave the next day, in our red Chrysler convertible.

They've only been gone for two days when my father falls ill.

I sneak into Papi's bedroom. It takes some time before my eyes adjust to the lack of light. The room is soberly furnished. Papi and Aunty Hilda's king-size bed, which has a dark teak frame and a nightstand on either side, takes up most of the space in the room. On Aunty Hilda's small dressing table beside the window, there's an empty space where I'm used to seeing her makeup and perfume always neatly lined up in front of the oval mirror. Her stool has been pushed under the table. A sky-blue silk curtain covers the window, and a framed black-and-white portrait of Papi and Aunty Hilda hangs on the wall above the bed. Below the portrait, there's Papi, lying under a thin woolen blanket, his eyes closed. Uncle Ferdi is sitting right beside him on a chair. Apart from the sound of Papi's irregular breathing, the room is silent. I walk over to Uncle Ferdi. He looks worried and tense.

"It would be best to let your father sleep peacefully," he whispers in my ear. "He seems exhausted." I nod, place a finger on my lips for silence, and tiptoe out of the room. I start looking for Babu Siti. I find her cleaning the living room. Babu Siti is a little Indonesian woman. She has a warm, brown, round face, and black hair. She always wears a headscarf and a long batik sarong. She speaks Malay with me, teaches me the indigenous ways, and tells me about good and bad spirits. She feels like a mother to me.

"Bu Siti, what's wrong with Papi?" I ask.

"Your father has terrible cramps on his chest, Sinjo Bubi, and he's very tired because of it."

"Bu Siti, Aunty Hilda once told me that Papi has a heart disease."

"Yes, it's a disease with a difficult name, called angina pectoris. Your father is under the supervision of the cardiologist in Bandung for it. Uncle Ferdi has already called the doctor."

Uncle Ferdi walks by, and I jump up and follow him to the lobby. His face is sweaty, and he looks even more worried. He walks towards the telephone. Our telephone is made out of smooth, dark wood, and has a shiny copper dial. He picks up the receiver and dials a number.

"Good afternoon. Is this Grand Hotel Sarangan?"

Some crackling comes from the phone.

"Could I speak to Mrs. Treipl, please?"

More crackling and then it goes quiet.

"They're going to get Aunty Hilda," Uncle Ferdi whispers to me.

I move a little closer to him to try to hear the conversation on the other side.

"Hilda, I'm so glad to hear your voice. I have bad news. You must come back home immediately. Vickerl is seriously ill."

Papi's full name is Franz Viktor, but Aunty Hilda doesn't like the name Franz and always calls him Vickerl, an Austrian diminutive for Vick. Aunty Hilda talks, but I can't hear what she's saying.

Uncle Ferdi replies, "He's in bed and has chest cramps. We can't find his medication anywhere. Normally his bottles are always sitting on his nightstand."

Aunty Hilda's voice comes through the receiver again.

"Yes, I've already called the cardiologist in Bandung. Please come home as soon as you can, but drive carefully. I look forward to seeing you soon." He then hangs up, sighs deeply, and turns to me. "Go to the kitchen, and ask Babu Siti for your dinner."

The hotel kitchen is behind the dining room. The servants are setting the tables with white linen sheets, porcelain plates, wine and water glasses, and shiny silver cutlery.

I pass by, and they greet me with broad grins on their faces; they probably don't know yet that Papi is very sick. "Good evening, Master Bubi," they say in Malay.

"Good evening, sir," I respond politely to each one in Malay.

The dining room is large and chic and can accommodate at least a hundred guests in a single sitting. The walls are plastered white. Rays of sunshine come in through the tall windows, and in the middle of the room, wooden pillars reach all the way up to the ceiling. The floor tiles are large and smooth, and it's fun to slide in socks on them. I take my shoes off and hurry down the hallway. Babu Siti sees me coming and gestures me to our dining room. I sit down at the table, and she serves me my dinner: European food—potatoes, meat, and vegetables. My stomach is rumbling. That night, Babu Siti brings me to bed early.

I wake up to a hand stroking my cheek. It's Babu Siti.

Uncle Ferdi is also sitting on the edge of my bed. He whispers, "Bubi, Papi died last night."

I sit up and grab hold of Mr. Bear. Confused, I look at my uncle with a questioning glance.

"Why?" I stammer.

Uncle Ferdi nervously straightens his shirt, clears his throat, and his voice sounds hoarse when he says, "Bubi, Papi was seriously ill and his medication didn't arrive on time, and so he died."

Died? The word echoes through my mind. Papi died? It feels so strange. I know that word and see my mother, my magnificent Mami with her curly hair and the flowers on her bed. Babu Siti gently hums a song and strokes my head with her warm hand. It feels nice.

"Is Papi in his bed?" I ask Uncle Ferdi.

"Yes, Bubi. Would you like to go see him?"

I nod and crawl out from under the blankets. I walk in my pyjamas with Uncle Ferdi to Papi's bedroom.

Papi's lying in bed, under the blanket, his eyes closed, and he doesn't move at all. It's so quiet in the room. I walk towards him, take a seat on the edge of the bed and stare at him. He's not breathing. What is happening here? Uncle Ferdi puts a hand on my shoulder while sobbing into his handkerchief. I get up and run out of the room.

"Bubi?" Uncle Ferdi calls after me.

But I don't want to be polite, so I just run into the garden looking for a place to hide. I don't want to talk to anyone anymore and clamber into my favourite ironwood tree, hoisting myself onto a large branch where I can lean my back against the thick old trunk, my legs dangling on either side of the branch, like I always do. I close my eyes and feel tears running down my cheeks. Papi, dead? Why? I don't understand any of this anymore!

Who knows how long I've been sitting here like that, when all of a sudden, tires are skidding on the gravel. I open my eyes and see our red Chrysler convertible in the driveway. Aunty Hilda jumps out and hurries towards the lobby, followed closely by Bruno. Uncle Ferdi comes out, and Aunty Hilda slows her pace. She looks up. Uncle Ferdi's head is slowly shaking no. He looks tense; he's wringing his hands.

From up in my perch, I hear him say, "We've searched everywhere. No trace of them! The hospital in Bandung sent new supplies, but they came too late."

"No! That can't be true. That's impossible. His medicine could've easily saved him," Aunty Hilda howls. Her face turns red, and the veins in her neck swell. Tears are running down her cheeks. She brings her hand and handkerchief to her forehead. She doesn't look stable on her feet. Bruno catches her and guides her inside while holding her by the shoulders. I can't stand seeing Aunty Hilda panic like that. I miss Mami. I sigh deeply and close my eyes.

After a while, I lower myself from my tree and hesitantly walk to the lobby. Aunty Hilda has recovered a bit. She's sitting in an armchair with a glass of water in her hand, drying her tears with her handkerchief. I walk over to her, and without saying a word, I wrap my arms around her neck. Aunty Hilda grabs me and pulls me onto her lap. She strokes my hair with her hand, whispering in my ear, "How's it possible, Bubi? Soma saw the disaster coming, and now we're in the middle of it."

Papi and Soma practiced astrology together—a strange twist in the personality of my otherwise phlegmatic father that also reflects the special bond he had with Soma. They used to hold special meetings, which Papi called seances. One day, during a seance, a vision came to Soma: he saw Papi being carried out of the house horizontally. Soma knew it meant that things would go wrong one day, and Papi was shocked. "That means I will die soon," he told Aunty Hilda. Aunty Hilda dismissed the idea, but thereafter, Papi had been worried about the future, about Aunty Hilda, Mami, and me. Shortly after that séance, being the ever-prudent businessman that he was, he started buying gold bars at the the Java Bank. "I want to leave all of you well off when I die," he had said to Aunty Hilda.

Papi passed on December 19, exactly one week after Mami's death. His death doesn't stop the holiday season from coming, though. The hotel is packed with guests, who are all in a festive, Christmassy mood. Aunty Hilda works from the early hours until late at night. I admire her strength and try not to bother her. I spend most of my time with Babu Siti. She's very kind to me and takes care of me.

Aunty Hilda also arranges the funeral. Here in the Dutch East Indies, people have to be buried quickly because the temperatures are so high. Papi is buried next to Mami and Opapa at the large European cemetery in Bandung. The funeral is sober, just like Mami's and Opapa's. Only our family members are present.

Six Indonesian men carry Papi's coffin on their shoulders out of the funeral home. They set it down on beams above the grave that's been dug for Papi. Aunty Hilda is dressed in a black dress and wears a black hat with feathers and a short transparent black veil in front of her face. She has her eyes closed. She's praying. We were here only a week ago, but then, Papi was still here, and we were speaking our kind words to Mami.

The pastor blesses the grave, and the men lower Papi's coffin into the ground with the ropes. Then we all walk back to the funeral home. The grown-ups drink coffee and eat sugary cake and talk to each other in hushed tones. I get cake and lemonade.

All the family members—Uncle Ferdi, Bruno, Aunt Lintschi, and Uncle Pepi—pitch in as much as they can at the hotel. The new Dutch manager, Mr. Versteegh, who was hired by Papi a few months ago, also helps, but I don't like him very much.

I move to a new bedroom, Opapa's old room, next to Aunty Hilda's. We celebrate Christmas with the family in Papi and Aunty Hilda's large living room. A giant Christmas tree with glittering decorations has been set up beside the grand piano. The Christkindl—Christmas Child—brought us presents and everyone is being very nice to me.

After Christmas, Aunty Hilda and I visit the small church near Dursasana street in Bandung. After the service, we buy fragrant carnations in different colours and visit our three graves. Mami's tomb is an earthen mound without any kind of marker, while at the head of both Opapa's and Papi's graves are tasteful stones carved with an inscription. Papi's stone reads:

HERE RESTS
MY DEAR HUSBAND
FRANZ VIKTOR TREIPL
DURING LIFE
DIRECTOR & OWNER OF GRAND HOTEL
LEMBANG
VIENNA 1–4–1889
LEMBANG 19–12–1939

"Why doesn't Mami have a nice headstone, Aunty Hilda?" I ask, upset. But Aunty Hilda doesn't answer, and my thoughts soon stray. It's so serene at the cemetery, and I like to visit the graves, although I don't know what to say to the deceased.

"What shall I say to Papi?"

"Pray for him, Bubi. Papi will go to heaven, and when you pray, you'll go to heaven one day too, and you'll meet him there again."

I don't feel like praying, so I just think of Papi and Mami in silence. I'd rather do what the Chinese Indonesian people do. Their family members are buried in imposing tombs with Malay writing carved into the grey stone. There's a special day when they sit with the whole family on top of the grave while they eat, talk and laugh, and tell each other stories. It's as if the people underground still belong to the family.

Aunty Hilda prays while we're standing at the graves. "Lord Jesus Christ, bless this grave and send the holy angel to guard it. Free the soul of my beloved Vickerl, who is buried here, from all ties to sin, so that his body can rest in peace. Amen."

Then I place the red carnation in its vase on Papi's sparkling new gravestone. The white carnation, I lay on top of Mami's earthen hill.

On January 19, my birthday, Aunty Hilda presents me a gift-wrapped box. "It's an exceptional gift," she says.

My slow smile builds with curiosity.

"Open it, sweetheart."

I pull the wrapping off and throw it on the floor in a crumpled ball. A wooden box appears. "ROYAL TALENS" it says on the lid. I open it to reveal a sleek pen and heavy matching inkwell, and a small note next to it, which I unfold.

January 19, 1940

My dear son,

Happiest birthday wishes to you on this special day. I couldn't be prouder of the remarkable learner and writer you're becoming. It fills my heart with immense joy to watch you grow. To mark this occasion, I'm delighted to gift you this pen and inkwell. I hope they'll inspire you.

With all my love and admiration,
Papi

A handwritten note from Papi. I get tears in my eyes.

"He bought this gift for you a long time ago," Aunty Hilda says in a soft voice.

I'm amazed by Papi's foresight—he'd clearly been thinking about my birthday long before he died. I hold the little box against my chest. The tears run freely down my cheeks. I'm nine years old today and realize that this is the very last gift I will ever receive from my Papi.

Chapter 8

SELAMATAN

On January 28, 1940, forty days after Papi's death, Aunty Hilda has a selamatan prepared to involve the staff in the well-being of our family, in accordance with Javanese tradition. A selamatan is a celebration of happiness and prosperity, a religious feast, in this case, to give Papi's soul the chance to leave the earth, allowing him to reach the eternal realm peacefully. All the hotel staff and our family members are present. We often celebrate selamatans together for important events such as special staff birthdays, or the birth of a child, and we also had one once for the Susuhunan of Solo, the sultan, who came to stay at our hotel.

It's two p.m. and the lunch for the hotel guests is over, the tables have been cleared and set for dinner, and the floor has been polished. In the wide hallway between the dining room and the kitchen, family members and staff are starting to gather. Low tables have been placed on the floor, on which Indonesian dishes will be displayed. There's a plate on the table for Papi and next to it a framed photo of him, along with a candle burning.

I walk into the kitchen and watch the cook, who's busy pressing yellow spiced rice into a large pointed cone. Shortly after that, she dumps the rice into the middle of a large round dish, then decorates the top of the cone with banana leaves. The kitchen staff arranges all kinds of delicious dishes around it: sambal goreng telor, hard-boiled eggs in a spicy sauce; tempeh; sate ajam, chicken satay; rendang, stewed beef; fresh vegetables; and a lot of other scrumptious dishes. For decoration, they sculpt blossoms out of radishes and cucumbers. It all looks gorgeous.

"Bu, could I please have a piece of chicken?" I ask the cook.

"No, Bubi, the dishes prepared for a selamatan may not be tasted beforehand. They can only be eaten when we start the celebration."

"Why are you building that tower of rice?" I'd never seen anything like that before.

"The rice tower is only for a selamatan in the event of death. One of our rituals is to divide the rice cone in half, representing the separation between the deceased and the bereaved."

"The bereaved?" I ask.

"The ones that stay behind, the family members who are still alive, like you."

"Oh yes…," I mutter. "You're preparing a lot of food."

"Yes, that is to make sure that everyone present gets their share, and gets to try a little bit of everything. All the leftovers will be handed out to the hotel guests, to share prosperity and spread happiness."

The cook and her kitchen staff have completed their cooking tasks and now carry the large round platter with the rice cone and various other dishes into the hallway. Everyone is looking for a place on the floor mats. I'm sitting next to Babu Siti, my legs slightly under me, just like her. Soma lights some incense.

Aunty Hilda stands up and opens the ceremony. "Dear family and friends, thank you so much for coming. We are gathered here in memory of Franz Viktor Treipl, my beloved Vickerl. The head of our family has passed away."

She tries to catch her breath, her face filled with sorrow, and fiddles uncomfortably with the paper in her hands. She then turns her gaze to Papi's picture on the table and continues even as her voice breaks, "Dear Vickerl, you devoted yourself to this hotel with tremendous dedication. This was our shared dream. You were always strict with yourself, and yet you had a caring nature. You wanted to do well for our family, our community, and the village of Lembang. You were a fair man. Although you have passed away, your legacy will live on in all of us. I see you in the face of Bubi, and I find comfort in that. We will miss you terribly. May your soul find peace and happiness in the eternal realm. Amen."

Aunty Hilda dries her tears with her handkerchief. Babu Siti stands up and puts an arm around her. Soma starts praying and singing in the Sundanese language, and various other staff members follow his example. The ceremony deeply moves me, but I'm a little upset too. Aunty Hilda said such great things about Papi. I looked up to him, but he was never really that concerned with me. I loved him, but I was not that close to him. "I see you in the face of Bubi, and I find comfort in that," she had said. But everyone always tells me I look like Mami. I miss Mami more than Papi. That bothers me some. *Would he feel that? Here, during the selamatan? Could he know?*

The cook hands a silver knife to Aunty Hilda, who cuts the rice cone in half. Soma solemnly says, "Boss Franz, may your soul go to the hereafter in peace, and may there always be a strong bond between you and your loved ones."

The cook carefully fills Papi's plate. Several others offer sacrifices of food on banana leaves to the ancestors, spirits, and gods.

After that, these offerings are distributed. One of them is handed to me. I hesitate to accept it. Soma sees the doubt on my face.

"The spirits just eat the aroma," he explains with a broad grin. "We get to eat the food."

I smile back at him and bow slightly, as a greeting and to show respect, as is essential in Indonesian culture, and I take the food with both hands. The others also receive their share, and we eat with our fingers. The delicious smells and an atmosphere of hope and love fill up the hallway. People talk, laugh, and reminisce.

I look at Papi's plate of Indonesian food, and I look at his picture. All of a sudden the outlines of his face are hovering just above the picture frame.

He looks peaceful.

"He's only leaving now," I mutter to myself.

I smile at him.

Chapter 9

ONRUST ISLAND

Since my homeschool teacher Missy got fired, I've been attending the Dutch school in Lembang. I now have a ton of friends and I love going to school. But this Friday morning, May 10, 1940, when I walk into the building for my regular school day, I'm immediately taken aside by the principal, Mr. Banning. I like him. He always gives me a pat on the back and makes me feel good.

"Unfortunately, Victor, I have to expel you from school," he says.

I look at him in surprise. "But, why?"

"Because you're German."

"But, Mr. Banning, I'm not German. I'm Austrian."

"Yes, I know. But it's a complicated matter. Come on, you better go home. I'm sorry. I can't do anything about it."

I don't understand any of this, but I do as he says and take off. At first, I just wander around the schoolyard, my bookbag under my arm. Expelled from school...What is this all about?

I don't feel like going home immediately, so I decide to visit my friend Reggie. He's an Indo, like his mother, who is of mixed Dutch and Indonesian descent. His father is an Englishman. They live in a large white house with a wooden fence around it, opposite the market. Reggie was sick yesterday and not in school. His mum is standing in the front yard. In one hand she's holding a pair of garden scissors and in the other a large bouquet of white Indian jasmine.

"Good morning, Mrs. Lambert. Is Reggie feeling better today?" I ask, throwing my bookbag on the ground.

"Much better now than yesterday. He'll go back to school on Monday. He's outside, somewhere in the backyard."

I'm already on my way to the back porch when she shouts after me, "Hey, why aren't you at school?"

I find Reggie in the backyard playing with his marbles. He grins when he sees me.

"Shall we play hide-and-seek?" I ask.

He nods yes, and a few minutes later, we're climbing trees and crawling behind bushes, and behind the garage and the outbuildings, taking turns to find the best hiding place. Now it's my turn to seek, again, and I have to count to ten. I cover my eyes with my hands, but I listen extra carefully. "One, two, three, four...," Reggie giggles as he scampers across the yard. "Five, six, seven, eight..." The radio in the kitchen is turned on loudly. It's the NIROM, the Dutch East Indies Radio Broadcaster. "...nine, ten! Ready or not, here I come!" I take my hands away and take a quick look around.

Suddenly Reggie's mother shouts, "Bubi, where are you?"

I emerge from behind my tree.

"I'm here, Mrs. Lambert!" I call back.

"You better go home," she tells me.

I raise my eyebrows then furrow my forehead. "Why's that,

Mrs. Lambert?"

She turns around in the doorway and repeats in a stern voice, "It's better that you go home. Reggie, come on inside." She disappears into the house.

Reggie appears from behind the garage. He shrugs his shoulders at me. "I don't understand either," he says.

Our game is over. I stroll reluctantly to the front yard, grab my bookbag, and run for home.

I rush into the dining room and start chattering to Aunty Hilda. "Mr. Banning expelled me from school because I'm German. But I'm not German at all. And then I went to play with Reggie, and I was sent home again by Mrs. Lambert. What is going on?"

"There's a lot of commotion in Europe."

"But what does that have to do with me, and with Reggie and school?"

Aunty Hilda doesn't answer. She gets up from her chair, turns the radio on, and tunes into the NIROM. "Good morning, ladies and gentlemen, here's Bandung's general program. Radio Hilversum in the Netherlands tells us the following: 'Proclamation of Her Majesty the Queen of the Netherlands. My people, our country has observed strict neutrality all these months with meticulous care. And while it had no other intention than to maintain this attitude rigorously and consistently, last night, the German Wehrmacht launched a sudden attack on our territory. This notwithstanding the solemn promise that our country would be spared as long as we maintained neutrality ourselves.

"'I hereby raise a fiery protest against this exemplary violation of good faith and damage to what is decent between civilized states. My government and I will do our duty now too. Please do yours, everywhere and in all circumstances, each in his place, with the utmost vigilance and with that inner peace and surrender that a clean conscience enables!'

"The general headquarters message reads: 'As of three a.m., German troops have been crossing our borders. They've attempted air attacks at some airports. Resistance and defence have been ready. Our onslaughts are progressing according to plan. As far as known, at least six German aircraft have been taken down.'"

Aunty Hilda turns the radio off. She has a serious look on her face, and she looks a little pale too.

"They've been broadcasting this news all morning," she says.

"But what exactly is going on?"

"War has broken out in the Netherlands. Two years ago, the Germans marched into Austria and conquered the country by force. Today they invaded the Netherlands, and the Netherlands has now declared war on Germany. Because the Dutch East Indies belong to the Netherlands, we are now also at war with Germany, if you understand what I'm saying."

I feel dazed. "But…It's all so far away. We have nothing to do with that war, do we?"

"I don't know that yet. We'll have to keep an eye on the news. But come, you better go play outside. Stay close to home, though. I have work to do."

It's busy in the hotel because of the spring break. Several guests are clumping together in groups in the hotel garden and the lounge. There's a lot of tense discussion going on.

When I come back in for lunch, Aunty Hilda is agitated. "I just heard on the news that all Germans in the Dutch East Indies will be arrested and interned, as they are now considered dangerous to the Dutch state. And with the term 'Germans,' they mean all Germans and Austrians, all German and Austrian Indos, and all Germans and Austrians that have previously been naturalized to Dutch citizens."

I don't understand much of the excitement. My classmates

come from all different backgrounds. I have Dutch, Indo, English, Austrian, and German friends, and we all get along very well, but it seems that the radio thinks that my family and I, all of a sudden, are monsters and spies.

"I wonder what's going to happen to us," Aunty Hilda says with a somber voice. She gets up and stalks away.

"Where are you going?" I call out.

"I'm going to call a few friends in Bandung and Lembang to see if they know more than we do."

I catch up with her and follow her to the lobby. After a few phone calls, it becomes clear that nobody knows anything.

"Bubi, can you find Aunt Lintschi, Uncle Pepi, and Bruno and ask them to come to the family dining room, please?"

I run around the hotel to gather everyone up, and moments later, we're all together. Aunty Hilda takes the floor. "Maybe you've all heard it on the news too. We Austrians in the Dutch East Indies have been declared dangerous to the state by the Dutch government. This morning Ferdi drove to Bandung by car to run a few errands for the hotel. It's well past noontime now, and he's still not back."

Aunty Hilda walks around feverishly.

"I'm crazy worried. Ferdi should have been back a long time ago. This is not like him. I'm afraid he may have been arrested."

Aunt Lintschi and Uncle Pepi are mumbling something and move uncomfortably back and forth on their chairs. Not Bruno, who takes charge and says resolutely, "I'll go see where he's hanging out, and I will bring him back home."

Aunty Hilda nods in agreement. Bruno immediately jumps up and is already on his way out of the room.

"Be careful," Aunty Hilda calls after him.

He tears off the gravel path in our red Chrysler convertible.

Two hours later, we're gathered in our family dining room again,

Aunt Lintschi, Uncle Pepi, Aunty Hilda, and me. Neither Uncle Ferdi nor Bruno are back yet. Aunty Hilda is walking around in circles again. Aunt Lintschi's fiddling nervously with the edge of her skirt, and Uncle Pepi is biting the nail of his index finger. Nobody says a word. The air, heavy with their emotions, weighs on my shoulders.

Uncle Pepi gets up. He's all jittery: stretching and flexing in the doorway. His fingers are shaking and his lip is quivering when he says, "I'll go find Bruno and Ferdi."

I jump up. "Can I come?"

"No, absolutely not," Aunty Hilda growls. Her stern tone frightens me. "You stay right here, Bubi. It's way too dangerous out in the street."

To Uncle Pepi, she says, "Thank you, dear. I'm afraid there's no way around this. But if you sense danger, come back home immediately."

Aunt Lintschi starts to hyperventilate. Uncle Pepi grabs both her hands and talks to her, which seems to calm her down. Together, the four of us walk outside. Aunt Lintschi kisses Uncle Pepi. He then gets into the car and we all wave goodbye. Aunt Lintschi's face pinches with worry. Aunty Hilda puts an arm around her shoulder and talks softly to her.

Both women go back to work.

It's already nearly six p.m., and now Uncle Pepi hasn't returned either. Only the three of us are sitting at the table in the dining room. Aunty Hilda is grinding her teeth. Her neck tightens because of it. Aunt Lintschi looks as pale as a ghost. She stares blankly ahead, her hands in her lap, fiddling with her apron.

I'm getting nervous just looking at them. Sitting still like this is the worst. I push the chair back and stand up, leaning against the table. Aunty Hilda takes action too; she turns the radio on again.

"Today all German men in the Bandung area were arrested and

interned. They will be transferred to Onrust," the newsreader says.

The women stare at each other in shock.

Aunty Hilda stammers, "This can't be true."

I hold my breath and slowly sit down again.

Aunt Lintschi starts sobbing; her shoulders are moving up and down.

"Where is Onrust?" I ask.

"Onrust is the name of an island off the north coast of Batavia," Aunty Hilda says.

"What's so bad about it?"

Aunty Hilda doesn't answer. She gets up, turns the radio off and starts walking in circles. Aunt Lintschi's moaning softly, her head in her hands. I jump up again from my seat.

"Aunty Hilda, you're making me awfully nervous," I cry out. "What's so bad about that island?"

"Onrust has a horrible reputation," she says. "It's a prison island, where Indonesian smugglers and thieves have been locked up in barracks for years. They've taken our men out there now. It looks like all three of them have been put in jail."

Upon hearing the words *prison* and *jail*, a feeling of shock comes over me. "But Uncle Ferdi and Bruno and Uncle Pepi haven't done anything wrong," I exclaim.

"You're right, honey, but it's wartime now, and justice has gone out the window. I fear there's worse yet to come." Aunty Hilda sighs deeply.

Poor Aunt Lintschi is still sitting at the table with her head in her hands, producing long, low humming sounds of pain.

That night I lie awake for a long time. My bedroom is dimly lit, with a soft glow coming from a small night light. The moonlight filters through the curtains. Freshly folded clothes for the morning rest on the chair. My toy cars are nicely parked in one corner, providing a small sense of comfort amid the uncertainty. But various questions are buzzing in my mind. *More bad things coming? But what does that mean? Is something bad going to happen to us?*

I wrap my arms tightly around Mr. Bear. I think of Onrust and imagine its hot, moist, dirty prison barracks, cockroaches crawling over each other. A shiver comes over me and I close my eyes. Poor Uncle Ferdi, Uncle Pepi, and Bruno. Will they be able to sleep tonight? Are they scared?

Chapter 10

EVICTION

The next morning, I find Aunty Hilda and Aunt Lintschi engaged deeply in conversation in the family dining room. They're seated at the table, as always elegantly set with crisp white linens. The morning sunlight streams through the window. Their faces reflect worry and concern, however. Aunty Hilda whispers, "We can't ignore this, but we have to find a solution, even if it means carrying on as if nothing happened."

Aunt Lintschi nods. "You're right. The guests mustn't know."

They exchange a determined look before slowly rising from the table.

Mr. Versteegh, the tall, Dutch manager, is standing by the large window in the smoking room, next to the lobby. He takes a long drag from his cigarette, his behaviour dripping with arrogance. Aunty Hilda approaches him, her quick footsteps echoing in the room. I follow right behind her.

"Mr. Versteegh, could you please take over Ferdi's tasks as the head of the dining room?"

To me, it seems like a reasonable question to ask, but the Dutch manager blows out a cloud of smoke, stubs out his cigarette in an ash tray with a forceful gesture, and raises his voice to Aunty Hilda.

"I no longer intend to follow your orders," he says and strides into the lobby, leaving Aunty Hilda standing there.

For a moment, she wears a blank, flabbergasted expression, but then Aunty Hilda presses her lips together, narrowing her eyes while mumbling "For crying out loud…," and walks briskly after the manager.

I'd rather not be part of the escalating situation, so I run outside and sit down on the steps in front of the hotel, but I can still hear Aunty Hilda and Mr. Versteegh quarreling in the lobby.

Aunty Hilda tries to reason with him. "Mr. Versteegh, we need your cooperation to keep things running smoothly. Please understand the situation we're in."

Mr. Versteegh dismisses her. "I don't care about your situation. Find someone else to handle your mess."

Aunty's quick footsteps fade away.

I'm watching two cars arrive. It's a Dutch police officer, dressed in uniform, the mayor of Lembang, and two other men. I've met the mayor before. His name is Mr. Widargo. He was a good friend of Papi's. The police officer and the two men jump out of their cars and march into the hotel lobby. Mr. Widargo's demeanour sets him apart. He follows them hesitantly. I hurry inside.

In the lobby, an extremely amiable Mr. Versteegh welcomes the men. The police officer introduces himself as Van de Wetering, and he presents the assistant resident of Bandung, the highest Dutch civil servant of the local government, Mr. Velthuizen Weil; the mayor of Lembang, Mr. Widargo; and a Mr. Drijfhout, head of the Orphan Chamber of Bandung and surrounding area. The latter has the face of a bulldog.

They request to see Aunty Hilda, who just happens to walk into the lobby. I hide behind her because it feels like disaster is about to hit. The assistant resident takes the floor. "Mrs. Treipl, the Kingdom of the Netherlands is officially at war with the German Empire, which includes Austria. For that reason, you and your family have been declared dangerous to our state. On behalf of the Kingdom, we claim your original bookkeeping and the keys to your safe."

"What did you just say!" Aunty Hilda exclaims in Dutch with her heavy German accent, staring the man down. Then she slowly turns her gaze to Mr. Widargo. The mayor of Lembang is trying to stay invisible; he looks ready to jump out of his skin, he's so jittery.

Mr. Versteegh quickly steps forward and, oozing charm, says, "Please follow me, gentlemen. I'm at your service."

Aunty Hilda's anger is so intense it seems like her head might explode.

"Wait a minute," she shouts. If looks could kill, the manager would have dropped dead right there. But Mr. Versteegh doesn't hesitate for a single moment—he leads the men to the office, straight to the safe. Now, in the midst of our crisis, he flaunts his true character.

The assistant resident, in full regalia, stands pontifically in front of little Aunty Hilda. He holds up his hand and says, without blinking, "Mrs. Treipl, the keys to your safe please."

Aunty Hilda reluctantly removes the ring of keys from her pouch and hands it over to him. As the heavy vault door is being opened, Mr. Versteegh, that nosy villain, pushes himself to the front row to see what the assistant resident takes out of the safe. Securities, jewelry, Soma's handwritten bookkeeping, and various other valuable documents and belongings appear. Mr. Drijfhout has taken a seat behind Papi's desk and is taking notes on a sheet of paper.

"What exactly are you planning on doing?" Aunty Hilda snaps.

"I'm going to register all your belongings, after which they will be confiscated."

"This is daylight robbery," Aunty Hilda exclaims. "With what right are you doing this? We have owned this hotel since 1922. Can you please show me a search warrant?"

Mr. Drijfhout, seemingly unperturbed, continues to record our assets, ignoring Aunty Hilda's outburst. I glare at Mr. Versteegh, who's watching the scene with a sly smile on his face. Eventually, Papi's gold share certificates are taken out of the vault. The gold bars that he had bought to protect us from Soma's foretold doom are neatly numbered and stored at the Java Bank. They confiscate the certificates, along with everything else from the safe.

I stare agape at Aunty Hilda. "Das ist so schrecklich unfair! Papi hat das für uns gespeichert!" I blurt in German. This is so incredibly unfair! Papi saved those for us!

The Dutch police officer gives me a nasty look and says in a hostile tone, "We no longer want to hear one single word of German. Dutch is the only official language in this country."

I'm shocked into silence. My face turns red and hot, and tears are welling up in my eyes. I feel like screaming out my anger. How dare that man say this?

"I see what's going on here," Aunty Hilda hisses. "You're expropriating all our possessions."

The assistant resident raises his eyebrows and takes a confrontational stance. "Mrs. Treipl, you are German, and you have been declared dangerous. From now on, your assets will be controlled by the Dutch state and managed according to their guidelines."

Aunty Hilda straightens her back, places her hands on her hips, and tilts her head back. "Which guidelines exactly?"

My cheeks are burning and it's all going way too fast for me for me to follow. German? But we're Austrians. What do they mean by managing our assets? This is our stuff, right?

The assistant resident continues, "Your Dutch manager will act as the operational director of this hotel. His appointment is effective immediately. You and your family will be allowed to pack a suitcase, and you can take two hundred guilders each. We will take you to Bandung, and you must report to the Orphan Chamber every week, starting next Monday."

"Where in Bandung?" Aunty Hilda asks. The assistant resident scratches his forehead. Aunty Hilda gazes at him. He turns his head towards the police officer. The police officer shrugs his shoulders. No one seems to have an answer.

"Would you allow me to call friends who can accommodate us?" Aunty Hilda asks.

After some hesitation, the assistant resident answers, "Yes, you may."

Aunty Hilda leaves the office and walks briskly towards the lobby. I run after her. She picks up the phone and, after a few attempts, manages to get a room with Mrs. Kelsen in Bandung. I remember her husband, Mr. Kelsen. He was friends with Papi. He was a Danish painter who had made a long wall of three-dimensional paintings of the Borobudur-temple in Hotel Homann, in Bandung. I remember visiting him with Papi, when we got to see his work in progress.

After ending her phone call, Aunty Hilda walks back to the assistant resident and tells him, "Under no circumstances do I want to be removed in front of my hotel guests. We can leave with you at noon, when all the guests are having lunch in the dining room."

He gives her a decisive nod and responds calmly, "As you wish, Mrs. Treipl."

The men shake hands with Mr. Versteegh and then leave. The manager turns to Aunty Hilda with a roguish grin on his face.

Aunty Hilda is on fire. "I strongly suspect you've been working behind my back with the police in Bandung for months. You also knew exactly how to get to the vault. You've scammed us. May you perish in agony and your soul roast in hell!"

Mr. Versteegh produces a superior whistling sound between his teeth. "Tssssss. Choose your words carefully, Mrs. Treipl. I'm the one who'll be running this hotel from now on."

Stomping her feet in anger, Aunty Hilda takes off in the direction of our private rooms. I rush after her. Once inside the living room, she slams the door behind us.

"For crying out loud, how is this possible?" Her fists are balled tight. "Yesterday, we were prominent members of the Lembang community. Highly respected citizens, who were consulted when important decisions had to be made for this town. The Dutch have mercilessly declared us 'hostile subjects,' robbed us of all our belongings, and appointed that crook as the operational director." Aunty Hilda is now red-faced and furious, gesticulating wildly as she speaks. "If Papi had been here, he would've taken that guy by the scruff of the neck and thrown him out onto the street. Now, we're to be deported from our own hotel, treated like scum. Where is their sense of decency? I'm going to challenge this decision."

I've never liked Mr. Versteegh, ever since the very first moment I met him. I didn't know why. But now I do. I'm trying to picture what it would have looked like if Papi had grabbed him by the neck. Papi was not that tall. It might have been a better idea if he'd taken out his shotgun.

Aunty Hilda sits down at the table and sighs deeply. "Bubi, think about which things are dearest to you then choose what you want to take with you. I'll collect some clothing for you. It must all fit in one suitcase. But first, let's inform Aunt Lintschi. She's coming with us."

Aunt Lintschi paces around her apartment while Aunty Hilda gives her a full and vivid update.

"Ach Himmel, Herrgott, Maria und Joseph!" Aunt Lintschi moans. Jesus, Mary, and Joseph! "When I saw those cars drive in, I ran straight to my room. I had no idea what to do."

"You should have seen it, Lintschi, how our manager was laying it on thick with the assistant resident. The hypocrite. It's all a deliberate game. He's been working on having us expelled from the hotel for months."

"Ach Himmel, Herrgott, Maria und Joseph!" Aunt Lintschi mumbles again.

"Yes, if they could ever help us…," Aunty Hilda snarls. "But I will find a way to challenge this. I wonder where they would've taken us, if I hadn't arranged for a place to stay in Bandung myself. A camp? Just like Bruno, Pepi, and Ferdi? It's all so unfair."

"Ach Himmel, Herrgott, Maria und Joseph!" Aunt Lintschi sighs deeply.

She's not nearly as eager to fight as Aunty Hilda.

Around noon we say goodbye to Soma and Babu Siti and some other loyal staff members who have become friends over time. They all look worried and have tears in their eyes. It makes me want to cry too. I cling to Babu Siti.

"Bu Siti, why aren't you coming with us? I will miss you so much," I sniffle.

She pats me on the head. "I can't come with you, Sinjo Bubi. I have a job here at the hotel. But I'll be looking forward to the day you return."

"Come, we have to go," Aunty Hilda says, gently pushing me towards the car. The driver opens the doors. Aunty Hilda takes a place in the front seat, and Aunt Lintschi and I take the back. I'm sitting facing backwards on my knees so I can look out the rear window. As we drive down the gravel path, I wave sadly to Babu Siti and Soma.

"Farewell, Grand Hotel Lembang. Farewell," I mutter.

Aunty Hilda has fixed her gaze on the road ahead of us and does not look back. Her face looks pale and grey.

The driver takes us, under police surveillance, to Mrs. Kelsen's house. Upon arrival, the agent hands Aunty Hilda the Orphan Chamber's address, where we'll have to report on Monday. The driver unloads the suitcases, politely bows and shakes hands with Aunty Hilda, wearing his white gloves.

"I wish you a lot of strength, Madam Treipl. We will miss you terribly," he stammers with tears in his eyes.

Aunty Hilda takes both his hands in hers, gently squeezing them. Then he gets in the car and drives off.

Three small suitcases sit on the ground in front of us. After all those years of hard work, her suitcase is the only thing Aunty Hilda has left.

All the while, Mrs. Kelsen has been standing in the doorway, watching this scene unfold. Silently she hugs my aunts and puts a hand on my shoulder. We go inside and she shows us the bedrooms. I put my suitcase down and sit on the bed while the women talk in another room.

"They've just imprisoned Mr. Kelsen in Ngawi, in the lowlands near Madiun," Aunty Hilda whispers to me when she comes back into the room. "He too has been declared dangerous to the state— all because his wife is of German descent. It's such a shame."

"Really? What are they going to do to Mr. Kelsen?"

"I have no idea. But I do know that we'll have to stay strong together and that I want my hotel back."

Aunty Hilda feels like a powerhouse, as if she's drawing energy from a secret source. Then I suddenly remember that I also have a secret. I open my suitcase and take out my piggy bank, a square steel box with a combination lock. I set it on the bed, in front of Aunty Hilda, and look at her proudly. I had stuffed the piggy bank with socks so that the money didn't rattle. I dump the contents on the bed.

"Bubi, that's a lot of money," Aunty Hilda stammers.

"Yes," I smile triumphantly. "Just over twenty-five guilders. Saved with my pocket money and collecting empty bottles. It's for you."

"Oh my goodness, you're an angel." Aunty Hilda's eyes brim with tears of bliss. "We can eat for three months with that money."

I blush and feel light inside.

That evening we have schnitzel and boiled potatoes with butter, perhaps the tastiest I've ever had. I try to store the taste in my memory. After dinner, Aunty Hilda brings me to bed. She kisses me on my forehead and leaves the room.

The door stays open a crack, and the warm yellow light from the hallway shines inside. Aunty Hilda's footsteps pad away. I think of everything that has happened today. Will I ever see the hotel again? And Soma and Babu Siti? The lush gardens? And Fieps? I often bullied him, but now, I miss him. I wrap my arms tightly around Mr. Bear. The women's voices echo in the kitchen. Then the persistent murmur of water falling on the roof. A tropical rain shower. I fall asleep.

Chapter 11

THE ORPHAN CHAMBER

On Monday, we report to the Orphan Chamber and are taken directly to Mr. Drijfhout's office. He sits tall behind his desk with his back straight and looks at us over the top of his thick glasses. He has a puffy, wrinkled face, a slightly flat nose, and large fleshy ears. The corners of his mouth slant down towards his hanging jowls. It's dim in the room, and it smells terrible, like cigars. The atmosphere feels unfriendly and uncomfortable.

"Take a seat," he commands, pointing to the two chairs opposite his desk. Aunty Hilda sits down on the edge of her chair, like she always does when she's excited or tense. Mr. Drijfhout asks her all sorts of questions while he nonchalantly takes notes on paper. Aunty Hilda answers and asks questions in her best Dutch.

"What are your plans with Grand Hotel Lembang?" she asks.

"Your manager will be running it for the time being," Mr. Drijfhout replies.

"Yes, I know that. But what will happen in the longer term?"

"We have no plans other than to manage it."

"May I conclude that it will remain my property?" Aunty Hilda asks.

"Yes, you can." Mr. Drijfhout carelessly scribbles circles on the paper on his desk.

"So it won't be sold."

"No. We have confiscated it on behalf of the Dutch state, and it is being managed," repeats Mr. Drijfhout.

My eyes roam the room: dark brown teak furniture, a small window, a bookcase with drawers underneath.

"How old are you exactly, Victor?"

I startle, my quiet examination of the premises interrupted. "Nine years old, Mr. Drijfhout," I answer politely.

"He was born on January 19, 1931," adds Aunty Hilda.

"Victor is registered as the sole heir," Mr. Drijfhout remarks.

"Yes, that's correct," says Aunty Hilda.

"What are we doing here anyway, Aunty Hilda?" I whisper to her in German.

"Shut up," Mr. Drijfhout snarls at me.

His sudden outburst takes me aback. I shrink on my seat and keep silent. My face turns hot. Why does everybody have to be so cruel to us?

Aunty Hilda jumps up and bangs her flat hand on the desk. "How dare you speak to my son like that. He's only nine."

It surprises me she's calling me her son, but there's no space for me in the conversation.

"Watch your temper, Mrs. Treipl," Mr. Drijfhout roars. "I'm in charge of things here."

Aunty Hilda gives him a vitriolic look and sits back down on the edge of her chair.

"You're now completely dependent on me," Mr. Drijfhout continues. "The Orphan Chamber will pay you a monthly allowance. For that, I'm going to refer you to the officer of legal rights in times of war."

"Legal crime in times of war, you mean. What gives you the right to confiscate our hotel? It's my hotel. We bought it in 1922, and we've worked tirelessly for years. This is not yours to claim. I demand justice."

Mr. Drijfhout lights a cigar and blows a large cloud of smoke towards us. The explosive atmosphere in the office is frightening to me. Who knows what could happen? Then Mr. Drijfhout suddenly stands up, unruffled, opens a drawer behind him, and takes out a bill of fifty Dutch East Indies guilders, which he disdainfully thrusts at Aunty Hilda.

"Here is your justice, Mrs. Treipl," he says in a harsh tone. "Your monthly allowance. This conversation is over."

It's an embarrassing moment for Aunty Hilda. Taking money from this odious individual, when, only a week ago, she was the owner of the chicest hotel in and around Lembang. She stands up and looks furiously at the man, snatches the bill from his hand, and puts it away in her purse. Then she turns around resolutely and gestures at me to follow her.

Once outside, she says under her breath, in German, loud enough only for me to hear, "From now on, Bubi, I will refer to you as my son. That'll be safer for you. It has become dangerous to speak German openly. As young as you are, you are now also an 'enemy.'"

"But, my family speaks German. Why does Mr. Drijfhout have to yell at me?" I whisper grimly, grinding my teeth. "At school, or when I meet a Dutchman, I speak Dutch. With Babu Siti and at the pasar I speak Malay. And I speak German with you. What's wrong with that?"

She lays her hand on my shoulder. "Under normal circumstances, there's nothing wrong with that, but these are different times. It's wartime now, and the Dutch are in charge. They don't want to hear German anymore, because Germany has occupied the Netherlands. I agree with you, Mr. Drijfhout is a horrible man, but he has power. We have to watch out for him and other people like him. I think we're better off, from now on, when Dutch people are present, to no longer speak German with each other, okay?"

"But how can I just switch to only speaking Dutch with you? I'd rather keep my mouth shut," I sulk, my arms crossed. "Why exactly do we have to go to that Orphan Chamber anyway?"

"The Orphan Chamber normally manages the property of under-aged orphans. Now that there's a war going on, they also manage the confiscated properties of 'hostile citizens,'" Aunty Hilda replies, spitting those last two words out contemptuously.

I barely understand a word of what she's saying.

She holds out her hand to me. "Come, give me your hand."

I place mine in hers, and we start walking back home together. I look up at her as I'm walking. Aunty Hilda walks proudly, with a straight back and small, sturdy steps. I try to do the same.

Suddenly she stands still and turns towards me.

"You know what I find so unfair?"

"What?"

"I've heard through the grapevine that our German acquaintance Annie Meister, who owns Pension van Hengel, hasn't been evicted from her home and hotel at all. But our hotel and all our belongings have been stolen. Why? I think because our hotel is one of the nicest hotels in all of West Java. That's why they wanted it. It's completely arbitrary," Aunty Hilda says fiercely, with a flushed face. "I'm absolutely convinced that manager Versteegh worked hard at this behind our backs. We're now receiving money from the Orphan Chamber to live off, but it comes out of our own pocket, like they're offering us one of our own cigars."

Aunty Hilda suddenly increases her pace and I need to do my best to keep up with her. I hate cigars. They stink. Just like Mr. Drijfhout's office. Ugly Mr. Drijfhout, who told me to shut up, and says I'm not allowed to speak German any longer. I think of Papi and how hard he worked to take care of us. All his gold bars are gone, and Papi is dead. What was the purpose of working so hard?

Chapter 12

POOR AUNT LINTSCHI

We now report to the Orphan Chamber every week, to the officer of "legal crime in times of war," and I learn to keep my mouth shut. Once a month, Aunty Hilda receives fifty guilders, and with these, we pay the rent and our food. Mrs. Kelsen is grateful for every penny Aunty Hilda can spare.

Mrs. Kelsen also has a daughter, Evi. She's already in high school and cycles every day to the Christian Lyceum, on Dago Street in Bandung. I guess at her school they think she's Danish, like her father, and they didn't send her home because of that. I like Evi very much. Finally, I have a big sister. I would love to go to school too, but no school wants to accept a "German" child. The result is that I get bored and often hang out in the street. I have to be careful, though, because the outside world is becoming increasingly unfriendly. The Royal Dutch East Indies Army has called on the Dutch people to participate in the City and Country Guards Committee. They are given guns and being trained, so there are soldiers everywhere now.

One day our beautiful red Chrysler convertible drives by with the Dutch army commander at the wheel. Seeing my father's old car like that is like getting a kick to the gut. I stand, stupefied, on the side of the road, and watch him drive by majestically. The commander is treated like a kind of god in Bandung. His palace is an impressively large white building with towers and a wall around it. It's heavily guarded. The car is shining in the morning sun and looks well polished. "Hey, that's our car," I shout, but nobody hears me. Dejected, I watch as my favourite car slowly disappears into the distance.

That Sunday in the Catholic church, Dutch people are sitting in our seats. Our usual spots have been given away to prominent Dutchmen, or so we are told. We end up in the back. I don't really mind sitting in the back because at least we don't stand out, but it hurts to see the pain on Aunty Hilda's face.

My aunts and Mrs. Kelsen now often listen not only to the Dutch broadcaster NIROM but also to Radio Zeesen, the German channel. It's prohibited. Whenever they listen to Radio Zeesen, they put Evi and I on the lookout. The volume is turned down low, and the three women sit with their ears glued against the radio. They are told that the German war machine is marching forward, that Hitler occupied Denmark and Norway in April and May, that the Netherlands and Belgium fell in May and that France is soon to follow. A catastrophe of major proportions is in the making.

Through the grapevine we hear that all the arrested "German" men will be transferred from Onrust Island to Kutatjane, a Dutch internment camp in the Alas Valley, in the Atjeh province in North Sumatra. Not long after that, we receive a card from Uncle Pepi via the Red Cross. The card has been censored; a lot has been scribbled over in black ink. There's hardly anything left of Uncle Pepi's note to read, but at least it's a sign that our men are still alive.

We receive a letter from the Orphan Chamber stating that Aunt Lintschi will be interned in Banju Biru, a women's camp in Central Java. This can't be true. My dear little aunt is going to be locked up in a camp. A shockwave goes through the house. Despair grips us all, and chaos ensues. My aunts and Mrs. Kelsen engage in endless discussions, but their words offer no solace. At times I escape the house to avoid the constant talking, but just like them, I am tormented by questions. Why Aunt Lintschi? Why her and not us? Why not Mrs. Kelsen? What will they do to her? Nobody gives us any answers.

On the designated day, Royal Dutch East Indies Army dump trucks arrive, and Aunt Lintschi is taken away. Big, thick tears roll down my face.

"Write as often as you can, Lintschi, send us cards through the Red Cross," Aunty Hilda says, her voice quivering in her throat. "Stay strong. We will see each other again."

I wonder if that's even true. Uncle Ferdi, Uncle Pepi, and Bruno disappeared one by one, and we haven't seen them again. Aunt Lintschi climbs into the open flatbed of a truck, her little suitcase in her hand, and takes her place on a bench. She's being transported the same way Dutch soldiers are. Her face is tight with anxiety. We all cry, and we wave until she becomes nothing more than a tiny dot in the distance.

I'm standing as close as I can to my Aunty Hilda, crying, gripped by a fear that I might lose her too.

Chapter 13

SKYPE CONVERSATION

Birgit Treipl, Nelson, BC, Canada
Victor Treipl, Loupiac, France

March 13, 2017

"Lately, I've been thinking about how the war in the Dutch East Indies began," I say, "and I'm amazed at the rapid pace at which the Dutch people labeled other Europeans as 'hostile citizens.' How they arrested all men, imprisoned them, and confiscated their property. It almost seemed like an organized robbery."

"Yes, it did indeed look like that, and it was. I once read a book called *Batavia seint: Berlijn—Batavia Signals: Berlin*—written by Dutch author Cor van Heekeren. He was a civil servant in the Dutch East Indies at the time. His story showed that this campaign had been meticulously prepared months in advance and that all governors and mayors of the larger cities had orders from the Dutch government in their vaults, just in case."

"Just in case?" I ask.

"In case the Netherlands should go to war with Germany. On May 10, 1940, immediately after the German invasion of the Netherlands, Dutch civil servants throughout the Indonesian archipelago—which is large—were instructed via the code 'Berlin' to arrest anyone suspected of being 'German.' Almost three thousand people were arrested and interned. Most of them men. They were arrested and interned preventively, not because they had done something wrong, but because they were considered German. After the war, the Dutch governor-general indicated that it should all be interpreted as a 'security measure' and no different."

"But many of those people had lived in the Dutch East Indies for years. They had lived an honest life and had built up a pension."

"That's right. They didn't have a criminal record, and many Europeans worked for the Dutch East Indies government—engineers, doctors, missionaries, you name it—and were therefore naturalized as Dutch citizens. But on May 10, 1940, they were all fired and interned on the spot," Dad says. "The Dutch government thought it better to arrest everyone right away and then investigate who could be released later. But what they hadn't foreseen was that the Dutch public's reaction in the Dutch East Indies, after those arrests, was so fiercely anti-German that releasing once-interned people was virtually impossible. Upon release, they were no longer accepted in the small, white top layer of colonial society."

"Hmm…Imagine having been a doctor, who had worked for the Dutch East Indies government throughout their whole career," I respond.

"Yes, those people were certainly around. And several of them had already been retired for years."

"Your uncles and cousin were interned right away, and a little later, Aunt Lintschi. But not Aunty Hilda and you, not Mrs. Kelsen, and not Mrs. Waldstein, Helga and Jutta's mother, who lived in the hotel. It seemed to be—at least in my perception—an arbitrary decision. The Dutch seemed to be doing whatever they wanted, particularly regarding the confiscation of possessions. What's your opinion on that?" I ask.

"About eight hundred interned German men, including Uncle Pepi, were married to German women. On Java, about one hundred and fifty of those German women were listed as National Socialists, who, according to the Dutch, were expected to act as spies for Germany. They were locked up in barracks in Banju Biru and guarded by female members of the Dutch Salvation Army. The German women were treated well in general, but they remained imprisoned there until the Japanese released them.

"Life got harder and harder for the women who remained free. Many were evicted from their homes by their Dutch landlords, and most of them were in financial trouble because the Dutch had confiscated their husbands' possessions."

"Some of your German acquaintances, such as Annie Meister, the owner of Pension van Hengel, did not lose their properties, but the Dutch confiscated Grand Hotel Lembang and all your family's possessions. Why was Annie allowed to keep her hotel and not you?"

"I think I do have an answer to that. Annie Meister managed to navigate through the war years in a lucky way. She was from Merano in Southern Tyrol. When the war broke out in 1940, she was married to a Dutchman, so she bore a Dutch surname. That allowed her to keep Pension van Hengel. When the Japanese invaded the Dutch East Indies in 1942, she had just divorced her husband and had adopted her German surname again. So, luckily for her, her hotel was again left alone," Dad says. "But unfortunately, we saw our assets all go up in smoke…"

Chapter 14

LANKY DUTCH BOYS

Aunty Hilda has been quiet since Aunt Lintschi's departure. We try to make the best of our situation, but there is uncertainty regarding just about everything. I'm going stir-crazy because I have nothing to do—and Mrs. Kelsen and Aunty Hilda talk all day long.

But then, after Aunty Hilda's many efforts, I'm finally admitted to primary school. I will be starting in the fourth class, which has five other students, at Friars School Saint Joseph, on a side street off Riouw Street in Bandung. I'm bouncing with happiness.

The school principal is a nice man, but unfortunately, I have a mean teacher, Brother Simon. Almost every day, he has me raising to the third power, make cube numbers, such as 34,562 x 34,562 x 34,562, and sometimes six of those stupid operations per afternoon. Why don't the other children have to make those? It's so unfair. But I don't dare open my mouth. It's not just Brother Simon who bullies me—my Dutch classmates are starting to as well. After school, just as I'm about to jump on my bike to ride home, the five boys appear in front of me. They're your typical lanky Dutch boys with unmanageable hair of an indefinable yellowish colour. Suddenly, they pull my bookbag off my bike and throw it on the ground.

"Hey vuile mof," they all shout. You filthy German. I try to pick up my bag, but before I can do anything, they've surrounded me. One of the boys grasps my upper arm firmly. He's much taller than me and is tanned and muscular.

"Stay away from me," I shout.

"Stay away from me," the boy parrots in a high, whimpering voice. His friends burst out laughing. Immediately after, they whack me on the jaw. I stumble and fall to the ground. They all start kicking me: my side, my butt, my back. A stabbing pain shoots through my stomach and I instinctively pull my knees up.

"German! Asshole! You don't belong in our school," the tall blond boy shouts.

I start screaming at the top of my lungs, "Help! Help! Help!" and they scurry off.

I'm lying on the ground, rolled up in a ball on my side. They've knocked the air out of my lungs, and I'm in a lot of pain. Nobody is showing up to help me. Slowly I stretch my legs and scramble up. I rub my arm against my face and wipe away snot and tears. I dust off my clothes while looking around timidly. Quietly, I pick up my bag and tie it to the rack of my rickety bicycle. I rub my cheek and my aching arms and notice that both my right knee and elbow are scraped.

As I cycle home, tears of frustration start running down my cheeks. What can I do about being German? I'm not even German. I'm Austrian. That's something entirely different. And besides, I didn't ask for this rotten war. I wish I still lived in Grand

Hotel Lembang. I wish I could hide up in the trees like I used to. I wish Babu Siti would sing songs for me. I wish Mami were still here. And Papi...

I'm always alone, too, damn it. Nobody ever backs me up. Nobody's kicking those boys' asses, for once. All of a sudden, I start feeling very sick. I get off my bike, sit down by the roadside, and pull my knees up. I begin to drool and have to gag. I turn onto my hands and knees. My stomach cramps up, and then I start really salivating and need to throw up. I vomit until all that comes up from my throat is bile. It's almost a relief. I turn around and lie down. I let my tears run wild. My body is shaking.

As the minutes slip by, my breathing gets calmer. I get up, grab my bike, and mount my seat. I'm utterly depleted, but at least I'm not far from home. I wipe my face dry with my sleeve before I go inside. I'm so embarrassed about being bullied and don't want to talk to Aunty Hilda about it. She tried so hard to get me into that school...

But before I've even entered the house, Aunty Hilda has noticed. She spreads her arms, there, at the door.

"What happened? Come here, sweetie. Where did you get those bumps and bruises?" she asks me.

"I fell off my bike...," I lie.

She looks at me with a penetrating gaze—I didn't sound very convincing. I start crying again. Aunty Hilda wraps her arms around me, so I bury my face in the warmth of her chest. She holds me close and rocks me back and forth.

"Tell me what happened, Bubi."

With downcast eyes, I tell her the whole story. About Brother Simon and the math, the boys beating me up in the schoolyard, and then me throwing up by the roadside. Aunty Hilda is furious. Her nostrils go up and down when she's outraged.

"I'm going to request a meeting with the school principal tomorrow."

I shrink. "Oh no, please. Brother Simon will hate me even more, and the boys will keep on bullying me."

"Don't be scared. It's not your fault that you're being bullied. Those boys are cowards. And Brother Simon is the instigator. He leads by example. Trust me. I'm going to talk to the principal, and if Brother Simon doesn't immediately change his behavior, we'll look for another school."

She sounds so determined that I have to believe her. Then she goes and gets iodine and cleans and bandages my elbow and knee. The iodine stings. I groan.

That evening I tell Evi my story, and she promises to help. The next day, she comes to pick me up from school. As the boys approach, already jeering, Evi appears with a raised hand and slaps every bully she can get her hands on in their face. Bang! Bang! Bang! They pull back like whipped dogs.

"You better not touch my brother ever again," she calls after them. I jump up and down, cheering. How wonderful to have a big, strong older sister. Not to mention, Aunty Hilda went to talk to the principal, and I don't have to calculate cubes anymore either. This day can't be ruined.

My happiness is short-lived. A few days later, when I come home from school, Aunty Hilda tells me, "Mrs. Kelsen is going to Shanghai by boat and then back to Denmark from there."

I'm stunned. "Will Evi leave together with her?"

"Of course."

Tears spring to my eyes. I clench and unclench my fists. "Why do I have to stay here? There will be nothing and nobody left. I want to leave by boat too."

I run to my room and slam the door behind me. I fall on my bed and let my tears flow while beating my fists wildly on my pillow.

"How am I supposed to live without my big sister? I'm always and forever alone."

Two days later, the dump trucks arrive again, benches mounted in their open flatbeds. History starts to repeat itself.

Evi hands me a picture of herself and says, "Here, Vicky, it's for you. It will remind you of me. Don't forget me. I am and will always be your big sister. When the war is over, you must come visit me in Denmark."

It's the first time anyone has ever called me Vicky. We say a tearful goodbye. Then Evi and her mother climb into the back of the truck. I hate dump trucks.

Chapter 15

THE LETTER

After Evi and her mother's departure, Aunty Hilda manages to find a new place to live for us, a small house in Lembang, our hometown, on Crater Avenue, the main road to the north. The Orphan Chamber agrees to it on the condition that we continue to report to them in Bandung.

Outside Lembang, the war is raging, but our tiny home feels like a safe haven. It looks cozy and has white plastered walls, a red-tiled roof, light blue doors and window trim. Concrete steps lead up to the front door, with six window panes in it. Even though there is only basic furniture inside, we have everything we need. The house is surrounded by a bountiful, overgrown garden with bougainvillea, many fruit trees, a lawn, and a wooden fence, defining the boundaries and offering a sense of security. I can climb trees and eat fruit from the boughs like I used to.

After a few conversations with Aunty Hilda, my beloved old principal, Mr. Banning, has allowed me back in the Lembang school again, and Helga and Jutta Waldstein are my classmates again too. They now have a little sister, Gudi, and live with their mother—I call her Aunt Doris—in a house near the edge of the canyon, behind the market. Their father has been interned in Ngawi, like many other men.

One day, I come home from school, throw down my bike, burst into the kitchen, and holler in my usual way, "Aunty Hilda! I'm home!"

But the familiar echo of her reply remains absent.

Curiosity and worry propel me into our intimate living room. My eyes land on the batik-covered coffee table, a white piece of paper lying on top of it like a story waiting to be told.

Aunty Hilda is standing there as though nailed to the floor. All the colour has disappeared from her face. She looks at me in dismay, picks up the letter, and starts reading in a monotone.

Bandung, December 2, 1941

Dear Mrs. Treipl and young Mr. Treipl,

With this letter, we would like to inform you that Grand Hotel Lembang has been at a loss for some time. We have fired Mr. Versteegh, your manager, because of the misappropriation of funds, and we immediately appointed a new manager who has taken cost-saving measures in the business operation. However, last Monday, after careful consideration, it was decided to accept a generous offer from a Mr. Schalks to take over Grand Hotel Lembang for the sum of one hundred thousand Dutch East Indies guilders. The court in Bandung has since ratified the purchase.

The purchase price is registered in a bank account with the Java Bank in your name and will be managed by the Orphan Chamber during wartime. Your monthly allowance of fifty guilders will be deducted retroactively from this amount. At the end of the war, the

*remainder, insofar as this is the case, will be made available to you
as a whole.*

We trust to have provided you with sufficient information.

Yours sincerely,
J. Drijfhout, The Orphan Chamber

I lay my hand upon my mouth and stare at Aunty Hilda in
astonishment as I try to absorb what I've just heard. The hotel sold?
To Mr. Schalks? I do remember him. Before the war, he was one
of our competitors, a Dutchman. He was a pastry chef and owned
holiday homes on the Tangkuban Perahu volcano.

"Bubi, those officers at the Orphan Chamber assured me
time and again that they wouldn't sell the hotel, and now
they've done it anyway. In a backroom deal, without involving
me. They sold it to Mr. Schalks, of all people, who knew our
hotel well. They gave it to him for next to nothing," Aunty
Hilda yells and screams, filled with impotent rage, pain in her
eyes. "The hotel was worth well more than nine hundred thousand guilders before the war."

She raises her arms, palms up, and the letter swirls down. She
runs to her bedroom, and her door slams shut. The letter stays on
the floor in the middle of the living room.

For a moment I am frozen, but then I run after her to the bedroom. Standing in front of the closed door, I press my forehead
against it. The door feels cold. On the other side, Aunty Hilda is
crying uncontrollably. Her intense sorrow flows right through the
door. Only once before in my life have I seen her this upset. That
was when Papi died.

I turn my back against the door and let myself slowly slide
down to the floor. I place my elbows on my knees and lower my

head into my hands. Mr. Drijfhout's puffy face and his ugly cigar come to my mind and his fancy, worthless promises. Aunty Hilda's dream is shattered. What the hell are we supposed to do now? I'm really worried about her.

I don't know how long I've been sitting here against her door like this, but it has become quiet in the bedroom. There's some rumbling and movement from behind me, and I raise my head. Suddenly the door opens, and I roll backward.

"Oh, sorry," Aunty Hilda says, and a faint smile appears on her face. A smile like Mami's, when she was in pain, yet laughing at my silliness anyway. I jump up and put my arms around her.

"I can't stand it when you cry so hard," I say.

Aunty Hilda strokes my hair and kisses me on the cheek, but she hasn't yet lost her anger. "Mr. Drijfhout is one of the greatest hypocrites I've ever met, along with that manager, Versteegh. Last week we were sitting at Mr. Drijfhout's desk, and he never mentioned a single word about a sale." The rage shows up in her eyes again. "He confiscated all our assets 'to manage them,' then sells our hotel for a ridiculous price and pretends like everything is normal. I put my heart and soul into that hotel for crying out loud. My entire pension is invested in it. The money needed for my old age and your school education, it's all vanished into thin air." She stops talking abruptly.

Then she continues in a softer tone, "I shouldn't get so mad. But it brings me some relief, to scream and shout, and cry. The tears seem to soothe the pain."

"What are you going to do about this?"

"I don't know yet. I need time to think. There must be a way to challenge the sale."

But Aunty Hilda would not get the opportunity to challenge the sale anytime soon because before she could get a chance, the Japanese intervened.

Chapter 16

THE RISE OF THE JAPANESE

It is Monday, December 8, 1941. In our cozy kitchen, Aunty Hilda and I are sitting side by side at the wooden table, which is covered with a worn yellow tablecloth, and we're reading the Dutch newspaper *Java Bode* together. That is, I'm reading the children's page, my eyes dancing across funny black and white illustrations, while Aunty Hilda reads her section—the real news. Her fingers are tracing lines of text that carry a weight of significance and her brow is furrowing occasionally.

The warmth of the room, the rhythmic rustle of turning pages, the faint clicking of cups as we sip our tea, and the aroma of freshly baked bread create a delightful sense of routine. I love reading the newspaper with Aunty Hilda.

I read aloud snippets from my children's page and Aunty Hilda listens attentively. Her kind eyes meet mine, she smiles, a silent exchange of connection that bridges our worlds. She then reads from the news and explains to me what it means.

The newspaper has brought only bad news today. Japan has joined in the war and is striving to eliminate the European colonial administration throughout Asia. Japan wants to take over the leadership. "Asia for the Asians" is their opinion. Because Japan has announced that it also wants to "liberate" the Dutch East Indies from its Dutch rulers, the Dutch government declared war on Japan today, just as the Americans have done.

"There's a lot of oil in the Dutch East Indies. That must be the real reason behind it," Aunty Hilda growls. "The newspaper also says that the Dutch fear Japan will free all German men from the Dutch camps."

"Why would the Japanese do that?" I ask.

"Japan is fighting on the German side in this war. The German men had good jobs here before the war. Men like your uncles, and Mr. Waldstein, and Mr. Kelsen. Their knowledge can be of great value to the Japanese."

I wonder how our three men are doing. They have been imprisoned in the Kutatjane internment camp for over a year now. And ever since Aunt Lintschi was locked up in Banju Biru, we haven't received any cards from Uncle Pepi.

"Here!" Aunty Hilda exclaims, pointing out a paragraph in the newspaper. "Listen to this: 'the Dutch and British governments have agreed to relocate all German men from Kutatjane as quickly as possible to the English camp Dehradun, in the north of the British Indies. They will be shipped according to their level of threat; apparent Nazi supporters will be transported first.'"

She turns her face towards me. "We'll need to find out more about those transports. Our three men will be on them."

I now browse the newspaper daily, looking for news about our family members. On December 29, 1941, the *Java Bode*'s big headline reads: "First ship with German men leaving for the British Indies." The ship is called the *Ophir* and carries 975 prisoners on board.

The front-page headline for January 3, 1942 reads: "Second ship with German prisoners en route to Bombay." The *Plancius* has 938 prisoners on board.

When Aunty Hilda investigates, she is referred to the Red Cross, where lists of names are to be made available.

Java Bode's January 7 headline reads: "The *Ophir* reaches the port of Bombay."

The Red Cross indeed has more information. Bruno, Uncle Ferdi, and Uncle Pepi are on their lists, but it is unknown who is being transported on which ship.

In the newspaper January 18, we read the following: "The *Van Imhoff* leaves from Sibolga, Sumatra." The third Dutch steamboat is en route to Bombay, with the last group of 478 German men on board.

Aunty Hilda hears speculations that they transported Bruno on the *Ophir*, and that the ship has arrived in Bombay, but there is no news about Uncle Ferdi or Uncle Pepi.

The *Java Bode* January 20 headline reads: "*Van Imhoff* bombed by Japanese bomber."

As if struck by lightning, I read the article: "None of the bombs struck the ship, but one torpedo came so close that it tore the ship's bulkhead under the waterline. The Japanese action has claimed a large number of victims." It happened on January 19, 1942, at ten a.m.

Why did the Japanese fire that torpedo? Has the ship sunk? Were there any lifeboats? Were Uncle Ferdi and Uncle Pepi actually on that ship? And if so, did they survive the disaster?

Aunty Hilda takes a deep breath and gloomily says, "I fear the worst."

"What do you mean?"

"That they're dead."

Chapter 17

THE CANYON

On Crater Avenue, military columns pass by our little home day and night on their way to the front. The threat of war is at our doorstep. One loudly roaring plane after another flies over. The Japanese have been conquering more and more territories in the Dutch East Indies and now have landed in northern Java. The British have also come, to support the Dutch, and one of their generals and his men have taken over Grand Hotel Lembang.

Unexpectedly, the Dutch released all German women from the Banju Biru camp, and my Aunt Lintschi has found her way back home. I'm incredibly attached to both my aunts, and I'm glad we're back together again, but one thing really annoys me: my aunts delight in endless gossip.

While I'm lying in bed, something that sounds like Mami's name, Mary, catches my attention. I press my ear against the closed bedroom door and listen over the loud thumping of my heart.

"Sometimes Mary really didn't know her place…"

"...bossed me around in the linen room..."

"...constantly ill and absent..."

"Vickerl spent too much money on her..."

"...tried to lure him in..."

"...wrapped him around her little finger..."

Why are my aunts gossiping about my mother? She was an essential member of our family. She was, after all, Papi's wife. Shall I go inside and ask Aunty Hilda for an explanation? No...I can't do that, because then I'd have to admit that I was listening at the door. But wait, I have nothing to lose. They are wrong, not me.

I take my time to find the guts to open the door, but finally I charge into the room.

"Why are you gossiping about Mami?" I yell.

My aunts look at me in shock and immediately shut up. Their faces speak more than words can describe.

"How dare you speak ill of her. She was Papi's wife. What could she have done about being sick all the time?"

"I'm sorry, Bubi, it won't happen again. But your mother wasn't innocent in every way," Aunty Hilda stammers.

"I don't want to hear anything about it. It is not fair. I wish Mami were still here. Then at least she could defend herself."

I turn around and head back to my room. I slam the door behind me and go back to bed. I hate my aunts. I miss my mother. I lie awake for a long time.

The next morning, I keep my distance from my aunts. There's not much to do, so I just stare out of the living room window. All of a sudden, a fighter plane plunges noiselessly from the sky, black smoke coming from its right wing. What follows is a colossal explosion up the hill near the old fort, where Aunty Hilda and I usually turn around when hiking.

I jump up from the couch. "That plane was shot down," I holler, completely forgetting my anger at my aunts.

I run into the front yard. Thick grey clouds of smoke are rising into the sky. A tiny dot, high up in the air, is slowly floating down. A truck rushes by. Dutch soldiers are marching along the road. I run to the fence, pointing to the hill. "Sir, was that a Dutch plane that crashed?"

"Yes, it was a Dutch reconnaissance aircraft that unfortunately got knocked down by our own anti-aircraft guns," the soldier replies. "The para is descending." He nods and walks on.

Aunty Hilda is standing in the doorway. "Be careful about addressing soldiers," she warns.

"But, I spoke Dutch, didn't I? He doesn't know that I'm German," I answer.

"Yes, you speak Dutch very well, but I don't want you to get in trouble unnecessarily."

Late morning, the Japanese begin to bomb the town of Lembang.

"We are far too vulnerable here. All traffic to the north passes by our house," says Aunty Hilda.

"Where would you want to go, then?" I ask.

"We can hide in the canyon."

The canyon. A fluttery feeling of nervous excitement arises in my stomach. How many times have I stood there as a six-year-old boy looking over the edge? I firmly believed that alligators lived deep down there and never before dared to go in.

We pack our suitcases and walk to Aunt Doris's house. She and Helga, Jutta, and Gudi are also going to come. As we go all down into the canyon, we encounter dense bamboo forests—a great place to hide. No alligators in sight.

Three women and four children sit in silence on their little suitcases, packed together amongst the bamboo stalks. We listen to every bomb hit and hear them getting closer and closer. Our hiding place is, of course, not bombproof. All my muscles are tense and my heart is pounding so loudly and fast that I wonder if the others can hear it.

All of a sudden we see the bamboo leaves around us slowly moving, as though being pushed aside. I hold my breath. Eyes partially covered in camo rags are staring at us. We're all frozen with fear—nobody says a word. Then the bamboo leaves slowly slide back, and the faces silently disappear. It becomes quiet around us. We sit there watching and listening for a long time, without saying anything. We realize that we've seen the Japanese soldiers. And that they've left us alone.

The bombings end in the afternoon. We crawl out of the canyon and go to Aunt Doris's house to have a bite to eat. The street is swarming with soldiers, soldiers, and more soldiers. Dutch army officers knock on every door.

"The Japanese are coming! They're coming with an army of Indonesian robber gangs that are plundering and vandalizing everything," they tell us. Europeans, white or Indo, we're all instructed to stand along the road with our belongings to be evacuated. We will be picked up by army dump trucks driving us to Bandung. They're giving us no choice. We have to leave.

A whole row of dump trucks arrive and it's chaos. Soldiers are hoisting mothers and children into the back of the vehicles. Kaspar, Aunt Doris's shepherd dog, is not allowed to come. I'm hoisted onto the first truck. The others are behind me; they get on the second truck. Kaspar whines and barks desperately as the trucks start to move. A stabbing pain pierces my heart. Who is going to take care of him? How will he survive?

Three wounded soldiers are sitting in the back of the truck with us. They all have blood on their clothes. One has his right hand in a bandage and another one a bandage around his thigh. They have hollow eyes. But not all the soldiers we encounter are so morose. While we are driving down the hill to Bandung, we are cheered on by trucks full of young Dutch soldiers driving in the opposite direction, uphill, on their way to fight the Japanese.

We arrive in Bandung. Roaring planes are flying low over the city in the pitch dark. Bombs explode. Shots are fired. There's shouting. Everyone jumps off the back of the trucks. There's a massive crowd of women and children. I start wriggling through the throng in search of Aunty Hilda, holding my little suitcase in front of me like a shield. Pushing and pulling. People, people, people everywhere.

An elbow hits me in the face. Then another. I get irritated and push on. But after half an hour of shoving my way through, I still haven't seen Aunty Hilda, and now I can't breathe. I start to jump up and down, trying to see over the crowd. I don't see her. A wave of cold sweat engulfs me. What if I don't find her? With that thought, my throat squeezes tight. My body's shaking, and I want to scream. I open my mouth, but no sound comes out. I throw down my suitcase and jump on top of it. I stretch out my neck, as far as I can, to catch a glimpse of my little aunt.

Then I take a deep breath. "Aunty Hilda, Aunty Hilda," I scream at the top of my lungs, and my voice sounds hoarse. "Aunty Hildaaaaaa!"

Suddenly, it sounds in the distance, "Bubi! Bubi! I'm here!" The sound is coming from somewhere behind me. I turn around and see her waving fiercely. Distressed and flustered, I run towards her. Tears are streaming down my cheeks.

"I couldn't find you anywhere," I cry. "I couldn't find you anywhere."

She takes me in her arms.

"I know, I was so worried. I've been searching all over the place for you."

It takes a while before we both calm down again. We find Aunt Lintschi, Aunt Doris, and her children not far from us.

A Dutch officer brings us to their Salvation Army, where we receive an extremely unfriendly reception.

"These women have a much too distinct German accent. The Salvation Army is not here to support the enemy," snaps the Dutch woman behind the counter.

But the officer insists, "These are innocent women and children. They need a place to sleep and some food."

He has to promise that he'll come back the next morning to personally pick us up again, otherwise, we're not allowed to stay. We get a cot and a bowl of soup. With the airstrikes continuing throughout the night, we can't catch a single hour of sleep.

The Dutch officer proves himself to be a man of his word. Halfway through the next morning, he arrives as he said he would, accompanied by an Indonesian driver operating a three-wheeled rickshaw. The cacophony of bombing and gunfire from outside is overwhelming, filling the air with a deafening roar. The Indonesian rickshaw driver appears in doubt, his hesitation clear as he contemplates driving a group of white individuals through the ongoing bombings. However, the officer's determination shines through. He points his loaded revolver at the hesitant driver, a gesture that overcomes any objections. Despite the perilous circumstances, with the Japanese airstrikes painting the sky, the Dutch officer takes on the responsibility, risking his own life, and ensures our journey to the relative safety of Bandung's city hall.

There, a civil servant assigns us a garage within walking distance, on the Dagoweg. The officer arranges mattresses for us. This man is a hero. In one of the outbuildings, we find a toilet and a kamar mandi, a tiled room with a cold water basin. It's rudimentary, but we're grateful despite our misery.

After the sleepless night and continuous bombing and gunfire, the garage feels relatively safe, and exhaustion settles over us all. I lower myself onto the bare mattress, wrap my arms around Mr. Bear, close my eyelids, and start drifting off. But just before I sink into sleep, a sudden jolt courses through my limbs, bringing me back from the brink of unconsciousness. Blinking groggily, I take in my surroundings, but a haze of confusion clouds my senses. It is dark in the room. Where am I?

I sit up, and the room gradually takes shape. Aunty Hilda is lying on the mattress beside me, her snoring a sign of the depth of her exhaustion. Aunt Lintschi, Aunt Doris, Helga, Jutta, and Gudi sleep on the mattresses next to us.

The Dutch officer's face and friendly demeanour come to mind. He was the one who guided us to the safety of this garage. Outside, bombings rumble in the distance, a reminder that danger still looms just beyond these four walls. The Japanese are coming.

Chapter 18

THE JAPANESE

Three weeks pass living in the garage. Its confines, housing seven of us, are so cramped we mostly spend our days outside, seeking space and fresh air.

The transformation that has ravaged the once luxurious resort city of Bandung is impossible to ignore. The elegant hotels, chic restaurants, cozy cafés, and upscale European boutiques that once defined the city's identity as the Paris of Java have borne the brunt of the bombings. We watch the first Japanese trucks driving through Bandung.

While we're buying a small meal at a warung, a mobile food stall in the street, a gaunt German shepherd comes running towards Helga, yelping and barking exitedly. Kaspar! How has he tracked us down, from Lembang all the way here? It's a miracle. Helga wraps her arms around his neck. The dog licks her face and cries and whimpers. She takes him back to the garage with us, and after ten days of feeding him scraps of her own food, he's almost back to his old self again.

The Japanese are clearly prevailing; we now see them everywhere. Rumour has it that they're opening up the Dutch camp in Ngawi, in the lowlands near Madiun, East Java, and releasing German men. There's been a great commotion amongst the women. Which men have survived? How will they know where to find us?

To our great surprise, Mr. Waldstein, Aunt Doris's husband, appears in our midst, and Uncle Pepi shows up a few days later, extremely skinny and weak. How is this at all possible? Hadn't they transported him from the Kutatjane camp to Bombay? Will Uncle Ferdi come back to us as well? We have countless questions.

Gently, we assist Uncle Pepi onto a mattress, carefully arranging so that his back rests against the wall. We all gather around him. Even though he's weak, he manages to talk. "When everyone was shipped to Bombay," he begins, his words punctuated by pauses as he conserves his energy, "I was so gravely ill that the Dutch authorities decided to leave me at the Fort de Kock hospital." He draws his breath, his gaze distant yet focused. "Then the Japanese recently took over the hospital and liberated everyone."

There is a fraught pause as we absorb Uncle Pepi's story of survival. Kaspar, the dog, stirs, and his whines and laboured panting produce a restless undertone. Helga makes him sit and soothes him, laying her arm around his shoulders. And then, with visible effort, Uncle Pepi shifts his attention. "Any word from Bruno?"

"I heard that Bruno would have been transported on the *Ophir*," says Aunty Hilda. "And that the ship has arrived. That's all I know. What about Ferdi? Have you heard anything?"

"No," Uncle Pepi replies, his voice heavy with concern, "but we were both in Kutatjane. The last I knew, before I went to the hospital, was that he was supposed to leave with the last ship."

The room seems to hold its breath, each of us caught in the gravity of the moment. We're all staring at Uncle Pepi, now so thin and frail. His physical fragility is in stark contrast to his once vibrant personality. No longer the tough and energetic man with chubby cheeks. Aunt Lintschi doesn't seem bothered by this. Her constant smile radiates her inner happiness.

"What is it? What's wrong?" he asks.

Aunty Hilda's answer holds a sobering truth. "That's not very good news."

"Why not?"

"Well, if that is the case, he must have boarded the *Van Imhoff*, and the Japanese torpedoed that ship."

Uncle Pepi drops his shoulders and looks at us in disbelief.

"How can this be…" he stammers. "Are there any survivors?"

"We don't know," Aunty Hilda replies. "The Dutch aren't providing any information. All we know is that the disaster has claimed a significant number of victims."

We sit together, each in our own thoughts and with unspoken emotions. We share a collective sense of uncertainty.

On March 9, 1942, the Royal Netherlands East Indies Army surrenders, and Japan now occupies the entire Dutch East Indies. All Europeans are instructed to register, and they've opened the *Deutsche Geschäftsstelle*, the German office, for the German community. We have to register there, and we don't know the danger that entails, but once we do, we get food rations and a little money to live on.

More and more Dutch people are losing their jobs and are only allowed out on the street with a special pass. Dutch citizens who own weapons must hand them all in to the authorities. European schools and government buildings are closing. Guilders become rupiahs. The Dutch language is banned and replaced by Malay. The

Japanese calendar and time system are introduced; the clock moves forward by an hour and a half. It's forbidden to listen to foreign radio stations. Only Japanese propaganda channels are allowed.

The Japanese still tolerate us "Germans," but the full-blooded Dutch are disappearing one by one. We don't immediately hear where they're taking them, but over time it becomes clear that the Japanese are in the process of interning them. Dutch men are the first to disappear—locked up in the internment camps that they themselves previously set up for the Germans. Dutch soldiers are put to work as forced labourers. Police barracks and city districts are fenced with barbed wire, and soon the Dutch women and children are imprisoned also. Most Indos are seen as Asians and aren't locked up.

We hear talk that the German Office has released the Red Cross's lists with the names of the German prisoners who were shipped to the British Indies in January. Aunty Hilda and I immediately go to their headquarters to find out about Bruno's and Uncle Ferdi's fates. Many others in our community do the same—we are not the only ones to have had a family member taken away by boat.

We see so many emotions in the faces around us, from relief and joy to dismay and consternation. It seems to take forever in this anxious swarm before we can get close enough to see the lists.

We scan the first ship's list—the *Ophir*—and see Bruno's name written on it. Aunty Hilda takes a deep breath, and her shoulders relax a bit.

We diligently continue our search for Uncle Ferdi. His name is neither on the first nor the second list. Aunty Hilda's face darkens, and she grabs me by the arm. A cold shiver runs down my spine.

I briefly scan the third list of the *Van Imhoff*, and all of a sudden, at the "S" under "Missing persons," it says: "Seiferth, F.F., Grand Hotel Lembang, Java." I point out his name to Aunty Hilda, and with tears in our eyes, stung with dismay, we shuffle aside to make room for the people behind us.

Slowly I begin to realize what this means: Uncle Ferdi is gone. He was Mami's only brother. The last time I saw him was when he drove to Bandung to run errands for the hotel.

"I can hardly imagine that he'll never come back," I say. "Missing, that means dead, I suppose? The idea that he's lying somewhere on the bottom of the ocean…If only I had said good-bye to him."

"Don't blame yourself for anything, sweetheart," Aunty Hilda whispers. "This is very depressing news, but it is not your fault."

"I'd like to know what exactly happened on that ship," I say.

"Maybe it's better not to know," she replies.

Dejected, we return to our garage.

The situation in the garage—living in close quarters with nine people and a dog—is becoming increasingly unbearable. There aren't enough beds for everyone, so Mr. Waldstein and Aunt Doris are now sleeping on one mattress. Helga and Jutta also share one so that Uncle Pepi, whose health is still delicate, can have a bed to himself. Kaspar sleeps on the incredibly dusty floor between everyone. Every morning he steps over our mattresses with his dusty body and dirty paws and licks our faces to say hello. During the day, it's crazy hot. Nobody has any clean clothes, and we smell of sweat, even though we take what Aunty Hilda calls "bird baths" and occasionally rinse our shirts in the bathroom sink. We decide that it's high time to find a new home, so Uncle Pepi and Mr. Waldstein start looking for possibilities.

Many houses in Bandung have been sitting empty since the Dutch were interned. Most have been trashed, plundered, or burned out. But Uncle Pepi and Mr. Waldstein manage to find us a vacant home that is still reasonably intact, in the Zorgvliet district, at the end of the Nijland Street, where the road to Lembang starts. The house has four bedrooms—enough space for all of us—and in the garden grows a papaya tree covered in fruit.

Around midday, we start moving. A sense of purpose binds us. Helga, Jutta, and I hoist a mattress, its edges firm in our grip, our hands cradling the corners. Atop the mattress perch our three little suitcases. Kaspar, with his tail wagging, trots alongside Helga. We start heading west from Dago Street, through DeRuyter Lane and Van Bevervoorde Street, to Nijland Street. The journey is not without challenges, as we are missing a fourth person, and the mattress, weighty and unwieldy, slips out of our hands from time to time.

In the midst of our struggle, Helga turns to me and says, "You know, I always dreamed of joining the circus. Who knew my acrobatic skills would come in handy for mattress transportation."

Jutta chuckles.

The absurdity of our situation hits me, too, and I giggle, "Well, if this is a circus act, I demand applause. Maybe we should start charging admission for our next move."

Helga grins, "Brilliant idea. We could be the first-ever travelling mattress circus."

Our laughter echoes through the neighbourhood as we continue our journey. The thirty-minute walk takes us twice as long, but by the end of the afternoon, all mattresses and suitcases have been moved to our new location, and we've installed ourselves in our rooms. Aunty Hilda and I share a room, as do Mr. Waldstein and Aunt Doris, and Aunt Lintschi and Uncle Pepi, and the largest room of the house is shared by the three sisters—Helga, Jutta, and Gudi.

The next day Aunty Hilda and I decide to look for our belongings on Crater Avenue, so we take the bus to Lembang, a little over half an hour's drive. But as we get closer to our hometown, as we pass endless rows of sad-looking houses with broken windows and open doors, our hope dwindles. Stark reminders of lives interrupted. Our little home has been wrecked and ransacked too. Without exchanging a word, we enter and stare at the ruin. There is nothing we can salvage.

We wander over to Grand Hotel Lembang. It looks ravaged, just like all the houses, but here, the Japanese seem to have occupied the space—their crimson-sun flag is flying at the main entrance. With much trepidation, we dare to walk onto the property, but nobody pays attention to us, and we walk straight into the backyard. The gardens have been neglected. Fieps's cage is open. I only hope he has escaped to the jungle of Tangkuban Perahu and found some friends up there. He was always all by himself, just like me. The giant birdcage is also empty, as are the rabbit cages, and the water in the pool is green with algae.

"Hey, what are you doing here?" a Japanese soldier yells in Malay, his rifle raised.

"We used to live here, sir," Aunty Hilda replies. "This hotel is our property, our home."

"Get out," the soldier commands, waving his rifle menacingly in the direction he wants us to go. "This place is off-limits to civilians."

Obediently, we turn around and start walking off the hotel grounds, down the gravel path towards Lembang Street.

"What will happen to the hotel, sir?" Aunty Hilda dares to ask.

"We're turning it into a food factory for the Japanese army, madam," the soldier replies.

We return to Bandung somber and empty handed.

I have a hard time getting used to our new home. Mr. Waldstein is always looking for an argument with Aunt Doris and yet, they still seem to want to be together. Aunty Hilda explains to me that, out of necessity, the women have become very independent in recent years and that they no longer wait for their husbands' permission or rely on their instructions.

Mr. Waldstein is also very curt to me. As the new man in the house, he's decided he's running the show. He comes up with all kinds of new rules. He interferes with my daily routine and how I interact with my "sisters," his daughters. I'm no longer allowed to walk in and out of their room like I always have. "Because you're a boy," he says. I'm not too fond of these developments, and so I do my best to stay outside all day.

The imperative task is to find money and food. The Orphan Chamber is now closed, and we don't have much money to live on. The Japanese soldiers like children and often give out food, but Aunty Hilda doesn't want me to talk to them.

"Beware," she warns me, "the Japanese are ruthless."

I ignore her warnings because the soldiers are kind to me. They give me chocolate bars, and other delicious treats. With a sense of victory, I take these treasures back home. I don't tell anyone where I've gotten them, and nobody asks any questions. Everything is shared and enjoyed equally.

Japanese armed guard posts have been installed throughout the city. The Japanese officers are easy to identify, wearing single-breasted dark green tunics, five buttons running down the front, four scalloped pockets, long pants along with puttees, and leather ankle boots. On their heads, they wear cloth field caps with flaps to protect their necks from the sun. I try to avoid them by moving through the backyards. Every time you pass a guard post, you have to stop and bow to the guard on duty. If the bow is not sufficient, you must redo it. Sometimes they make you repeat the bow ten times, just as often as the guard thinks is necessary. Everyone must bow, Europeans, Indos, and Indonesians. It's humiliating.

One day, as I'm walking by, I watch a Dutch lady on a bicycle being stopped by a Japanese officer, who orders her to get off her bike. The officer wants her to bow to him and the Japanese flag, but the Dutch lady refuses. So the officer slaps her in the face, grabs her roughly by the hair, and shoves her face into the dirt. Her bicycle falls on top of her. Only then does the man let go of her.

Appalled as I am, I try not to stare at the violent scene. I've never seen anything like this before. We may be considered "enemies" of the Dutch, but we're still white Europeans just like them. The Japanese brutalizing the Dutch isn't something to celebrate—it means danger for us too.

All of a sudden, the officer turns his face towards me, and reality hits—I recognize him. He was one of the salesmen at Toko Tjijoda, the Japanese department store in Bandung, where we used to shop before the war. Then it dawns on me. The Japanese salesmen must have been army officers in real life, spies actually, well before the war began. Thanks to their foresight, they speak simple Malay and know the area well.

I turn around and start running home. Aunty Hilda was right. The Japanese are ruthless.

Chapter 19

TO SARANGAN

In December 1942, when I'm almost twelve years old, the German ambassador comes to visit from Tokyo and demands that all German children in Java receive education in the German language and traditions. He also makes it clear to the Japanese that they must treat us well. That's an assignment from Berlin.

After that visit, things change quickly. The German Office draws up a list of names of German mothers and children and a few fathers. There are hardly any fathers because most of them are imprisoned in the British Indies. Everyone on the list will be taken to Sarangan, a remote mountain village in East Java, on the volcanic slopes of Mount Lawu, where the children will be taught at the German School.

Whether German, Hungarian, Czech, Austrian, Dutch, or Indo, everyone tries to get their name on that list at all costs. Anything better than a camp. People who have never spoken a single word of German but who have a German family member try to quickly learn the language. "High German" and "Indo German" are both spoken in our communities. Those who are unable to master either of them will have their names removed from the Sarangan list. The Japanese will likely take them to an internment camp.

Whispers of the Japanese soldiers' cruel treatment of Dutch prisoners tell of a grim and scary prison where people have to stand still for hours in the blasting sun, where they get far too little food and water, no medication, and where contagious diseases run rampant. I believe the stories. I remember how hard the officer raged against that Dutch lady.

During the first two years of the war, when the Dutch were in power, Dutch became the only accepted language, and I was no longer allowed to speak German. Now that the Japanese have taken control, the roles have been reversed; speaking Dutch has become a life-threatening offence. If you're Dutch, you'll be interned.

In preparation for what's to come, Mr. Waldstein has started to teach his daughters and me how to read and write German. Even though I'm already fluent, I'm learning to write German for the first time in my life, the old Sütterlin way, with those beautiful, big strokes. Helga and Jutta get the hang of it much faster than me. My handwriting is a disaster.

In the meantime, the German mothers are buzzing with rumours. What will we be up against in Sarangan? How will they take care of their children? Where will the Japanese accommodate us? What are we allowed to bring?

I have no idea where Sarangan is or what it looks like, but Aunty Hilda does. She's been there before: on vacation to Grand Hotel Sarangan with my cousin Bruno in our beautiful red Chrysler convertible. If only she had never gone, she often says, because then Papi might still be alive. She tells me Sarangan is an isolated village, high up in the mountains, on a gorgeous lake called Telaga Pasir. Before the war, it was a tourist destination, but now it will be guarded by Japanese soldiers.

We've started packing our belongings. They don't tell us how much we can take with us, but we do know we'll have to carry everything ourselves. Aunty Hilda and I each have two small suitcases. At six a.m. on the day of departure, at the Bandung railway station, we await the train to Madiun. The sun has just risen, and bright rays are shining through the station entrance's high windows. Our train is already waiting alongside the platform. It's a steam locomotive pulling a long row of metal wagons with seven double, glassless window frames on either side of each one; women are leaning out on their elbows.

The platform is jam-packed with people saying their goodbyes and mothers and children boarding. Indonesian children in shorts wearing trays strapped to their shoulders are selling fresh food rolled up in banana leaves. Aunt Lintschi and Uncle Pepi have come to send us off. They have no children, so they're allowed to stay in Bandung. Uncle Pepi has found a job at a factory.

Japanese soldiers with rifles on their shoulders order us to board. We squeeze ourselves onto the train with our suitcases, and I manage to claim a seat for Aunty Hilda. I stack our suitcases in the aisle and sit on top of them. Finally, our wagon is loaded. Many children are sitting on luggage in the aisle, just like me, the wee ones on their mothers' laps. Some are crying. We hear the shouts of soldiers outside, the driver blowing the horn, and with a lot of hissing and pounding, the train starts inching forward. Aunt Lintschi and Uncle Pepi are weeping and waving their handkerchiefs. And as I watch the train station glide by, I can't help but feel empty inside.

Chapter 20

HOTEL BEAU SITE, ROOM NUMBER 4

The train is travelling southeast. From my spot on top of the stack of suitcases, I swivel my head left and right to look out the windows. Not far from Bandung, we go up the mountain towards the Nagreg mountain pass. The pass is so narrow it feels more like a cavern. Then the train moves at a walking pace over a vertiginous steel railway bridge. I stretch out my neck as far as I can and see the rice paddies and small villages far below. Nature around us is green and exuberant. It's monsoon season, warm and muggy. From time to time, a thundershower batters the roof of the wagon. Then, when the rain stops and the sun comes out, we drive through a steaming rainforest.

The train chugs along all day, from Tasikmalaya to Djokjakarta, where we buy rice wrapped in banana leaf and my favourite drink, tjendol dawet, made of coconut milk, containing droplets of green rice flour jelly that look like worms, and Javanese sugar. Then we continue on to Madiun. The heat and the cries of babies on the train are wearing me out. I lean against our suitcases on the floor, listening to the sound of the wheels on the rails, and slowly fall asleep.

I'm sitting next to my father in our beautiful red Chrysler convertible, and we're driving to the mountains south of Bandung, in the Pengalengan region. High against the mountains, there are lush green tea gardens, and my father says, "They grow tea of the best quality here, Bubi." Then we descend and drive past rice paddies of ethereal beauty. Standing in long rows with their backs bent, women wearing large hats plant tiny little rice plants. Everything is light green. I look at my father. He's smiling at me. The sun shines on my face, the wind plays with my hair, and I feel light and happy. We drive south towards the lowlands, through black forests and along vast rubber plantations, and finally, we arrive at the Indian Ocean.

The ocean is a deep turquoise blue, and along the coast, tall trees are growing. I run onto the beach. It's delightful to feel the hot sand between my toes. I roam around and find large conch shells, the size of my hand, pearly pink and smooth on the inside and white and rough on the outside. We walk along the beach and arrive at the mouth of a river. An estuary. The water entering the sea is very clear but yellowish brown. "Why is the water in the river brown, Papi?" I ask. "That is because branches, leaves, seeds and nuts fall to the ground and come into contact with the creeks and rivers, turning the water yellow-brown. They are called blackwater rivers and are one of the cleanest natural waters." My Papi sure knows a lot about everything.

I splash around in the surf, and suddenly, I'm startled by a gigantic mouth opening right in front of me. I'm standing face-to-face with a larger than life crocodile. I start screaming.

"Bubi, Bubi!" It's Aunty Hilda's voice. Where the heck did she suddenly come from? I start running away from the humongous crocodile. I run, and run, and run. I'm too scared to stop. The Ursone family farm, called Baru Adjak, shows up. I run past the cows in the tall, sharp elephant grass, and my legs are starting to bleed. I run straight through the kina plantation to Lembang Street, where I live, in Grand Hotel Lembang, at number 272. I rush into the high hotel lobby and see Mami standing there. She's wearing a fancy suit, and her curly hair is stunningly combed. She must be going to the Social Club in Bandung.

"Mami, Mami, I was chased by a crocodile," I shout.

She looks at me with compassion but starts floating away. I reach out to try to grab hold of her, but I can't get to her.

"Mami, Mami, no, don't leave," I yell, but my voice gets stuck in my throat. A hand touches my cheek. I open my eyes.

"Bubi, darling, you had a bad dream," Aunty Hilda says. "You were screaming and your little legs were kicking all over the place."

I look around, feeling confused. Women and children are staring at me. I'm sitting on the floor in the train, my back leaning against our suitcases. Slowly my thoughts come back to reality. Grand Hotel Lembang is gone. I don't have a home anymore. No Mami, and no Papi either. I'm all alone with Aunty Hilda. It's wartime, we've been exiled to Sarangan, and I'm sitting on the train to Madiun.

The fog in my head clears, and in that moment, just like when I saw Papi hovering above his picture during the selamatan, I realize that I "see things." And that my dream has a purpose. What I get from it is that my old life has ceased to exist. Everything is gone. The crocodile attack stands for the threat of death and war. I'm on my way to a new world. This is a test, and only the strongest will survive. I'll have to be strong.

"No, it wasn't a bad dream," I respond, feeling strengthened by my new resolve. "And I'm no longer a little boy. I don't want you to call me Bubi anymore. My name is Vicky."

It's late in the afternoon when we finally arrive at Madiun Station. We're ordered to get off the train, and the Japanese load us onto buses that take us to Ngerong. Once there, they tell us to find transportation to get to Sarangan. Everyone has to figure out their own way, depending on whether they have money to spend or not. So, we walk.

It's a long, steep hike uphill. There are Indonesian carriers carrying the luggage, balancing it on their shoulders. I'm glad they've taken charge of our suitcases, because I'm tired. I dawdle and need to take a break about every ten minutes. Aunty Hilda is getting impatient with me.

"Come on, we don't have forever," she says. "It'll be dark before you know it."

I suddenly think of the vision I had. I walk up to the carrier who's carrying my luggage and ask him to please give me back my suitcases. I want to carry them myself.

With a suitcase in each hand, I start walking up the mountain at a steady pace. I can do it. I'm not a kid anymore. I can do it. I repeat to myself. Aunty Hilda looks amused while I walk past her. But half an hour later, I'm hitting a wall: the suitcases are too heavy, and the mountain is too steep. I stumble and, because I have a suitcase in each hand, I fall flat on my face on the dirt trail. I start to cry and wail, and Aunty Hilda comes running to comfort me. But this time, I don't let her.

"No, I don't want to be comforted," I shout, stomping my feet on the ground. I wipe my face with my forearm. It hurts, there's blood on my arm—I've scraped my cheek.

Aunty Hilda shrugs and says, "Well, good, then," and continues her journey up the hill. Somewhat stunned, I remain standing in the middle of the path. I secretly expected that making a scene would garner me some loving attention and that Aunty Hilda would suggest that the carrier take my luggage again. But she's done none of that.

I pick up the suitcases again. *Geez, these things are heavy*, I sigh. I don't want to be a pushover though, so I start walking. Aunty

Hilda's diminutive frame is steadily ascending the mountain ahead of me. I can't possibly keep up with her.

But this time, I'm not giving up, and with the occasional stop, I finally reach the top. I'm exhausted. I set the suitcases down and sit on them, and try to catch my breath.

"That was quite the climb, wasn't it Vicky? Are you tired, my boy?" Aunty Hilda asks.

"No, I'm not tired at all," I lie and jump up.

Aunty Hilda grins and starts a conversation with the Japanese soldiers. Everyone who's expected gets accommodation some-where. We get our address: Hotel Beau Site, room number 4. It is March 1943, and this is our new world.

Chapter 21

THE NEW WORLD

The Japanese flag and the swastika fly above paradisiacal Sarangan. How frightful the contrast between freedom and the lack of it. This village, once a popular tourist spot, has been repurposed as a German "protection camp." The Japanese guard the camp, and we have to abide by the Führer's guidelines. We are tolerated by the Japanese only because of the alliance between Berlin and Tokyo, but the Japanese still consider us "unwanted Europeans."

We are housed in the hotels, inns, and detached houses of Sarangan and in the Eagle's Nest Hotel, located high above the village. The view is much freer here than from the houses below. One has the feeling of floating above the world. Separate from our residences is the old settlement, where the Indonesian and Chinese people reside.

Aunty Hilda and I have been living in room number 4 of Hotel Beau Site for quite some time now. The room is small, but we've managed to make it work. Hotel Beau Site, located right on the lake and owned by the Swiss Sonnhofer family, is managed by Mr. Quidort and his wife. Willy Quidort is actually a visual artist, a painter, who lived in Bali for a number of years. In hearing of the arrival of the former director of Grand Hotel Lembang, he received Aunty Hilda with great respect and even asked if she could offer him some advice on hotel management. Mr. Quidort speaks French and Swiss German, and he's not a friend of the Nazis. Aunty Hilda isn't either, so they get along very well.

Every day I attend the German School. The building is made out of woven bamboo and lessons are led by several mothers who teach us all they know. A handful of mothers are certified teachers, but most aren't. At first, we had few textbooks or school supplies, so our teachers had to improvise a lot. Our lessons focused mostly on the German language. But over time we received a number of textbooks from Germany, and now we are also learning Japanese, French, English, arithmetic, geography, and history. I particularly like making calculations and writing, as part of the German language classes.

We have an inspiring gymnastics teacher, Mr. Hupfer, a German who lived in Tokyo for years. He's taught me a lot. I love track and field; I often compete in tournaments against other kids. Long-distance running and kayaking have become favourites in my repertoire as well. I've become skilled in gymnastics on the horizontal and parallel bars and on the pommel horse, and I excel in the shot put and javelin. I always get A+ for gymnastics on my report card, and I'm quite proud of that.

Before I arrived in Sarangan, I was a skinny little boy. I was always out of breath and a very slow hiker. I have since developed into one of the best students in sports, and I'm only getting stronger.

I feel as free as a bird here, much like in Lembang. And though I'm getting taller, I don't have the concerns the adults have. I have many friends and am no longer as lonely as before. After school, we often play outside, and we work out a lot. Sometimes we'll roam around, looking for fun, or stuff we can steal, but the residents of the houses always chase us away. Our mothers have forbidden us kids from entering the old Indonesian settlement. They don't want us to interfere with the native inhabitants or steal from them. The Indonesians collaborate with the Japanese. They are used to dealing with Europeans, and the women used to work as babus and cooks in the surrounding hotels and family guesthouses when Sarangan was still a holiday destination. They grow vegetables and sell them to us in shops and street stalls, and they rent out small horses, palanquins, and boats to take out on the lake. In the middle of the village is Toko Asia, a small department store where—according to Aunty Hilda—you used to be able to buy anything, but now the shelves are pretty empty. When we first arrived in Sarangan, the village people thought we, like the tourists, had money to spend, but they quickly found out we don't own much more than they do.

The landscape around Sarangan reminds me of Lembang. On the opposite side of the lake, the volcano, Mount Lawu, towers ten thousand feet into the sky, even though the lake and our houses are already at an altitude of four thousand feet. Next to the town stands another amazing volcano, Kukusan, with its distinct cone shape and impressive height of 8,800 feet. The vegetation around Sarangan is green and lush, and the lake sparkles like a blue gem nestled in the heart of the earth. There's a tiny island in the middle of the lake, with tall pines growing on it. Temperatures are just as cool here as in Lembang, August being the coldest month. We sleep under a wool blanket at night and burn log fires in our fireplaces and kitchen stoves.

It can get rough here when the storms come from out of the gorge behind the island to roar and rattle the houses and hotels. We've made bamboo wickerwork to protect the front of Hotel Beau Site so that we can at least get out the door when the wind is tearing at the buildings. The Indonesian settlement, much older than our modern houses and hotels, is better protected. The storms bother them less there.

During the wet monsoon season, it rains a lot. The rain pelts the windows of our small room. The water in the lake is high and crashes over the top of the timber retaining wall. There's a large lock near the other end of the lake that regulates the water level. When the rains stop, the lock is opened to supply the lowlands with water, where the rice paddies of the indigenous population grow.

In the dry season, many children play in and around the water, as do me and my friends Otto, Dieter, Guido and Günther. We're allowed to use kayaks from Hotel Beau Site and a sturdy metal lifeboat that we named *Kahn*, German for sloop, but we often lose the battle for the boats—the older boys like to get out onto the lake too.

The lock is a massive attraction to us. We usually play warrior there: if you don't want to be tagged, you have to jump off the lock. When the lake water is high, it's a jump of only six feet, but when the rice paddies are being irrigated, it can be a thirty-five-foot jump into the water. You have to aim the jump precisely so as to not end up on the walls of the funnel-shaped lock. Bruises, scratches, and scrapes are inevitable, but luckily none of us has broken a bone so far.

Of the four friends in my group, Otto Müller is my best friend. He's two years older, slightly taller than I am, has dark-blond hair, and wears glasses. In general, Otto is decisive and adventurous, and I like that about him. He and his father hike a lot, so Otto knows the mountains quite well, and he's actually a wizard when it comes to starting a campfire. He often takes the lead when we're doing things together, but I'm determined to catch up to his adventurous spirit. He was born in Palembang, on the island of Sumatra, and grew up in Batavia, West Java. Both his parents are German. Otto has an older sister, and the family lives in House Irene in Sarangan.

Aunty Hilda often worries. "Our stay here is no picnic," she likes to point out. She emphasizes that we live in captivity.

"There's a difference between feeling free and being free," she says. "It's not because you feel free that you are. You must remain on guard, Vicky."

She's right about that. We're completely cut off from the outside world and are only allowed to leave the village in exceptional cases and with a special pass. We are being guarded with a heavy hand by the Japanese and the Indonesian police, and we have great respect for them. It's a respect born of fear. Now and then, the police beat up boys for doing (in my opinion) rather innocent things, like stealing corn on the cob from the local Indonesian farmer's field. Me and my friends have stolen a few cobs as well, but we haven't been caught. The other boys did recover after these assaults, but every time it happens, it leaves us in shock for a while.

Our German community consists of around three hundred people, with two hundred children, ninety-three mothers, and seven fathers. Our community is led by Dr. Johanson—the community doctor we call "Dr. J"; our school principal, Mrs. Bode; six female teachers; and Otto's father, whose name is Otto Müller Sr., who used to be the head of the Dutch Police Academy in Sukabumi before the war. He had been stationed in Japan when he was a young man and therefore speaks Japanese as well as German and Dutch. Our German community must adhere to the Japanese guidelines. If we don't, men are physically punished, and then the Japanese tighten the rules for all of us Germans.

Aunty Hilda and I had to register again with the local German Office. They created two groups, the Reichsdeutschen, citizens of the German Empire, people holding German or Austrian passports when they emigrated to the Dutch East Indies, and the Volksdeutschen, people without German citizenship but of German ancestry living outside of German. Aunty Hilda registered with the first group, and since I'm a minor under her care, I was also registered in the same group. The Indo Germans born here, and the Germans who were naturalized as Dutch citizens because of the government jobs they had, and anyone else calling themselves German, belong to the Volksdeutschen. This division causes no noticeable difference in the interactions between the people, but the German Office surely makes a distinction, mainly in the amount of support they offer: as Reichdeutschen, we receive twice as much as the Volksdeutschen.

No one, except maybe the Japanese, realized that Sarangan would become a closed camp. In the first two months, we were still able to buy all the food we needed, and it was all very cheap. You could buy a sandwich with ham, cheese, and a fried egg for only two and a half cents. But it wasn't long before the gates were closed, and food became scarce. Now we're all on food rations, and the quality of the food has gone down significantly. Any kind of meat, even chicken, is a rarity.

Aunty Hilda often shares her food ration with me. She has little money, and she doesn't have any items to trade. Yet, she never complains. So, I started lending her a hand. I "source" things from all over the place for her—and by that, I mean, I steal. The difference between *mine* and *yours* doesn't count so much in wartime. The only thing that matters is getting something to eat. The cornfields and the local planting of lobak, large beet-like radishes, take a hit. And whenever I'm able to steal something from the Japanese, I do. My friends and I spent hours figuring out how to make a lock-pick out of pieces of metal and wire. No Japanese storage shed is safe from my homemade lock-pick now. I can jimmy any lock—even padlocks—in a matter of seconds. Otto and I often wander around the barns and warehouses the Japanese have taken over, scouring the place for things we can trade for food. We're becoming savvy and, simultaneously, more careful to avoid being arrested and beaten.

Due to the shortage of food, with the local police's permission, a lively barter system has developed between the German mothers and the Indonesian market vendors. These women travel long distances with their merchandise over the mountain, all the way from Tjimoro Sewu, a region near the town of Solo. They often bring fruit and vegetables. They carry baskets of merchandise on their heads and walk straight up the mountain, majestic and graceful, talking and singing. Sometimes they have an urgent need to go to the bathroom. That's an entertaining scene. The women come to a standstill, spread their legs, and seconds later, a river of pee pours on the ground. Then they continue walking, with straight faces, as if nothing ever happened.

A lot of time here is spent on "the development of the German youth's body and soul." Boys and girls both must learn how to march, do drills, and sing German and Japanese songs. Every week we meet under the leadership of our captains, eighteen-year-olds who report to Mr. Schmid. He's a little man who proudly walks around in exquisite, shiny black boots and who does his very best to be a good "youth leader." We call him Puss in Boots. Under his supervision, we've learned to shoot with real bullets.

Several times a week, we have to work for the Japanese. We plant djarak trees that produce castor oil for the planes. There's also labour service for the local community. A few mothers who know a lot about gardening are in charge of the vegetable garden of Hotel Beau Site; I work in the garden and chop wood for the kitchen. At Eagle's Nest Hotel, a few dairy cows provide milk for the sick. We have to feed the cows, which is a time-consuming job. We take turns cutting grass with a sickle, which we bring to the cowshed, where it's weighed by the cows' caretakers, boys only a year or two older than me. If you don't bring enough, they make you start all over again. Sometimes we try to outsmart the caretakers by wetting the grass so that it weighs more, but we haven't fooled them yet. Senior Japanese officers regularly come by to monitor our work, which certainly makes us take our job more seriously.

On Emperor Hirohito's birthday, Sarangan turns into a sea of Japanese flags. All children at the German School receive a flag in their hands—the red circle, symbolizing the rising sun, against a white background, and we march around the lake singing Japanese songs. We also get to see open-air films of Japanese victories projected onto a large, white screen.

I think it's great fun that they organize all these activities for us, but Aunty Hilda doesn't like "the Führer's business," as she calls it. Not at all. She especially disapproves of the propaganda films, the marching, and the shooting. She'd rather see me running track.

Even though Sarangan is a closed camp, the Japanese allow us to explore the natural surroundings. Most hiking trails loop back to Sarangan. Those extending over the mountains end on bridges and at posts guarded by the Japanese.

On a crisp but sunny Sunday morning in July 1943, Aunty Hilda (an avid hiker) and I set out to conquer Mount Kukusan, accompanied by my four eager friends—Otto, Dieter, Guido, and Günther. It is to be my first serious mountain climb. Aunty Hilda believes I'm strong enough, at twelve years old, to hike all the way up.

After an hour's journey, we reach what Aunty Hilda fondly refers to as "the Fairy Tale Meadow," a serene valley with a flower meadow and a clear stream flowing gently through. We drink water and take a short break here, while we marvel at the natural beauty surrounding us.

Suddenly, Otto grins. "Keep an eye out for snakes, guys. I heard there are some cool ones in these parts."

Dieter looks horrified. "Snakes? Seriously? I hope they're friendly, the non-venomous kind."

Guido laughs. "Yeah, like the ones that just want to have a friendly chat and share their snake tales."

I remember overhearing a story between the older boys at school earlier that week. "Someone actually caught a triangle keelback snake on the mountain. One of the most dangerous snakes around."

Otto nods in agreement. "One day, I'd love to catch one too, just like the older boys."

"How do they manage to catch them?" I ask.

"A strong branch with a fork on the end. They press it just behind the snake's head. It paralyzes the snake," Otto says.

The thought of catching one makes me feel a little uneasy. What would Otto actually do if we encountered one?

Aunty Hilda urges us to continue the climb. "Okay, enough of this, boys. Let's get up this mountain." She stands up, shoulders her backpack, and wields her wooden hiking stick, leading the way.

The path becomes steeper, and we traverse through a dense, dark forest, the air thick with the scent of earth and trees. Further up, the trees separate, and the tall undergrowth disappears. The arm-thick trunks and trees curve strangely, like living creatures suddenly frozen into position.

Aunty Hilda teaches us the art of maintaining a consistent, sustainable pace. But even without wasting our energy, the climb to the top tests our resilience. When we finally reach the conical summit, it reveals a breathtaking vista—the shimmering lake, our humble village, and the majestic Mount Lawu standing tall in the distance.

In the fall, Otto and I, fueled by our newfound adventurous spirit, hatch a plan to explore the Banju Urip water wells and camp overnight. It's a first for us—going without the company of elders, spending a night under the open sky. Thankfully, Otto's parents and Aunty Hilda approved of the idea.

On a sunny Saturday afternoon, we load our backpacks with blankets, food, water, and matches. I bring along my favourite old slingshot, just in case we encounter any intimidating animals.

Although the journey to the wells is only a short walk through the woods, it feels to us like we're embarking on a grand expedition.

Under the tall trees, the water from the springs flows directly from the mountain, splashing on the rocks and producing a refreshing mist. We rest on a moss-covered rock, absorbing the serenity of the moment. Suddenly a doe emerges from the woods, walking in our direction. She's an elegant, slim, reddish-brown creature. Upon noticing us, she raises her head, and we stare into her large brown eyes. Startled by our presence, she darts away, her little black tail slapping up and down on her bum. Otto and I exchange smiles; we've never before seen a deer in the woods around here.

Just before sunset, we kindle a small campfire. "Start with dry mosses and bark from the trees in the middle," Otto instructs, his eyes gleaming with the knowledge of a seasoned camper. "Then build up a little triangle with small branches around that. Light that with a match. Like so." With a swift strike, he lights the match, and the little bundle catches fire, the flames dancing and crackling. "Then you keep feeding bigger kindling to the fire and bigger pieces of wood after that. You need to create a solid base of hot coals underneath."

Otto's method proves effective, and as the night settles in, we find ourselves enveloped in the warmth and glow of the campfire, wrapped in our blankets and savouring the sandwiches we brought. The crackling flames paint shadows on our faces.

Curiosity takes hold of me, and I turn to Otto with a question that carries the weight of our uncertain future. "What do you think you want to be in the future, Otto? I mean, what kind of job do you want to do?"

"I'm not sure," he says, his gaze fixed on the flickering flames. "But my dad says that if I pursue higher education, I'll have a better chance of finding a well-paying job. In my free time, though, I'd like to live in a place just like this, where, on my time off, I can hike the mountains, make campfires, swim in a lake, and fish."

His vision resonates with me as we continue building up our little campfire. "And what kind of future do you see for yourself?" Otto turns the question back to me.

"I'm not sure yet either," I confess. "But I know that I love this land I was born into: the mountains, the lakes, the ocean, the people, the food, the smells. My Aunty Hilda wants to try to get our hotel back in Lembang. I love it there. But I'm not sure yet what I would be doing…Maybe a swimming champion?" I laugh. "Impress the girls?"

Otto bursts into laughter, and the night unfolds with the exchange of stories, jokes, and more laughter. Without a tent, we nestle in the grass, the vast expanse of the night sky above us.

I cherish a million things about this night, and above all, the sounds of nature lulling us to sleep, the warmth of the fire, and our friendship flourishing in the midst of the uncertainty we live in. As we drift into a peaceful slumber, I yearn for these adventures to last forever, hopeful for a future where laughter and dreams replace war for a brighter tomorrow.

Chapter 22

MR. FISCHER

In January 1944, a high German embassy figure from Tokyo comes over unannounced to inspect our school. He's part of a committee that will determine whether we meet the German criteria established in Berlin. The adults in our community are nervous. And with reason. The inspection's outcome is that most Reichsdeutschen and Volksdeutschen may stay, but any children and adults with a partially Dutch background must disappear. Even our beloved school principal, Mrs. Bode, has to leave Sarangan because she's married to a Jewish man; it's deemed unacceptable for her to lead German children as an educator. Where they're taking these people and what will happen to them, we don't know.

Around this same time, new people are admitted to the village. Our former Hungarian barber from Bandung joins us—as does the Waldstein family. Helga, Jutta and Gudi are here. Aunt Doris and Mr. Waldstein seem to have settled their disagreement because

Aunt Doris is near the end of her pregnancy. She has her fourth child in Sarangan, a son, and she calls him Peter.

Also among the new people are Ernst Fischer and Albert Vehring; two of the very few survivors of the torpedoed *Van Imhoff* disaster. The news of their arrival is spreading like wildfire. Everyone wants to hear their story firsthand. Mr. Fischer introduces himself directly to Dr. J and the leadership of our German community. He appears to be a great negotiator and has many connections with political leaders here and abroad and in civil life, and is appointed mayor right away. At the insistence of many, a meeting will be held where Mr. Fischer will tell his story. Children aren't allowed to attend.

It's dark out, but there's a tiny bit of moonlight. Otto and I are hiding in the bushes behind the dining room of Hotel Hansje. As usual, I'm wearing my shorts, and squatting there, the imprint of the scratchy branches hurts my knees and shins. I'm uncomfortable, but I don't dare to move.

The dining room window is ajar, and we hear a man's voice say, "My name is Ernst Fischer and I'm Austrian. Like so many other German men, I was held captive by the Dutch in Kutatjane, a camp in the Alas Valley, in North Sumatra.

"In December 1941, through the grapevine, we heard that Japan was threatening to invade the Dutch East Indies, and not long after that, the leaders of the Dutch camp announced that we would all be shipped to Bombay, in the British Indies, for further transport to Dehradun, to a British camp at the foot of the Himalayas, near the Nepalese border.

"They divided us into groups. Two ships had already left, and the camp felt deserted when, on January 18, 1942, I was transported by truck to the port of Sibolga, Sumatra, along with the last group of German men. The Dutch merchant ship, the *Van Imhoff*, was already waiting for us there.

"Most of us were malnourished, and many were in poor health. At the last moment, the Dutch decided to leave the weakest behind in a hospital. There were missionaries among us, as well as merchants, farmers, artists, scholars, and the elderly. All innocent people."

Mr. Fischer pauses for a second and we can hear people sigh and whisper to each other.

"My Uncle Pepi was one of those weakest ones," I whisper in Otto's ear. "He should have been on that ship as well, but they brought him to the hospital in Fort de Kock. He was very ill, but at least he survived. He's in Bandung now, with my Aunt Lintschi."

Otto looks me in the eye and gently nods his head.

"We were told that there were eighty-four Dutch crew members on board, and sixty-two officers and soldiers from the Royal Netherlands East Indies Army to guard us," we hear Mr. Fischer say. "We were brought on board, then packed below deck, behind barbed wire, on wooden bunk beds that seemed more like cages.

"The circumstances were shocking. We received very little food and water, and there were no sanitary facilities whatsoever. There was a disgusting human smell, and it was hard to withstand the heat."

A nervous wave is going through the room.

Mr. Fischer continues. "The ship sailed out of the harbour, and I fell asleep from exhaustion. One night passed, and another hot day arrived. The loud roar of planes overhead startled us. Shortly after that, a deafening blow followed, then another, and another. About five or six massive explosions.

"Nobody knew what was going on. At first, we thought some of our people had started to revolt, but it turned out to be a bomb striking the starboard side. The ship swept wildly back and forth, and we tumbled over one another in the hold. Water started pouring in, and panic broke out. Many were trampled in the frenzy to escape.

"We shouted at the crew to free us, and some of us tried in vain to break open the metal gates and the barbed wire fencing with their bare hands. But instead of releasing us from the hold, we heard the officers calling out orders to the crew to prepare to abandon ship.

"The entire Dutch crew, including the captain and the officers, sailed away in liferafts, leaving us behind in the hold behind barbed wire. As you know, the captain should be the last to leave a sinking ship. What's worse, just before they left, they destroyed the radio and freshwater containers."

Ohs and *ahs* go through the room and women are moaning softly. I sigh deeply and look at Otto. He holds a hand over his mouth and his eyes are as big as saucers.

"Why did the Japanese destroy an unarmed transport ship?" one of the women is asking.

"I'm not sure, but I later heard that the ship didn't carry a Dutch Red Cross flag," Mr. Fischer replies. "The Japanese must have thought that the ship was transporting Dutch war material instead of German prisoners."

"But how could they knowingly let people drown behind barbed wire?" someone shouts, bewildered.

"I completely agree with you," Mr. Fischer responds fiercely. "Not even in times of war is one allowed to let this kind of thing happen. It was inhumane. The captain should have known better. One of the guards at least had thrown a bunch of keys down the hold before he abandoned ship. A few of us managed to get free in time, and every one strong enough ran upstairs to the deck."

My thoughts go to my Uncle Ferdi. I can still picture him in his handsome suit, directing the servants and serving guests in our hotel's dining room. He was a soft-spoken man. Then, in a flash, I picture him, huddled up, locked behind barbed wire in the ship's hold, weak and thin and dressed in rags. I witness the harrowing sight of prisoners in a frenzied struggle, crawling wildly over each other, fueled by fear and panic as the water floods their confined space. Yet amid this chaos, Uncle Ferdi isn't fighting—he remains oddly still. Why isn't he moving? What is going on in his mind? Is he too weak? I'd like to shout, "Uncle Ferdi! You have to get out! Get off the ship and fight for your life!" But my voice is stuck in my throat, leaving me a silent observer of the unfolding tragedy. Uncle Ferdi doesn't do anything. I swallow a few times against my rising nausea. Mr. Fischer's voice pierces my thoughts.

"The ship was sinking rapidly. Various men jumped overboard, desperate, and tried to grab hold of floating debris. The sea was full of sharks; we all knew that.

"The Dutch left behind one lifeboat, but it was stuck to the davit. We managed to pry her loose and lowered her onto the water. It was a mad dash fighting to get on that boat. We were heavily loaded and had no oars, so with only our bare hands and pieces of driftwood, we started rowing towards land. The seawater came up nearly to the edge of our boat. It had to be just after six, because the sun was setting on the most gruesome scene: people swimming and drowning all around us.

"To make matters worse," Mr. Fischer continues, "there was another Dutch ship nearby, called the *Boelongan*. Seeing that we were in distress, it approached us, but when the captain realized that we were all Germans, he turned the boat around and left us to our own devices.

"One of us, a jeweler, his name was Arno, wriggled out of our boat and swam towards their ship, wailing and calling for help. When he tried to pull himself up one of their ropes, he was ruthlessly knocked off. We couldn't get to him with our lifeboat. We were powerless to help—if he were to climb on, our sloop could turn over. We didn't want that to happen. He drowned before our very eyes."

A painful moan goes through the room. Sitting in the bushes, Otto and I quietly absorb the terror of these events. I feel paralyzed, defeated, and sad.

But Mr. Fischer keeps going. "Ultimately, a week after the disaster, we washed ashore, dehydrated, on the island of Nias, delirious from the tropical sun. We were with more than sixty survivors. The vast majority of prisoners on the *Van Imhoff*, more than four hundred men, did not survive the disaster. If the Dutch crew had valued our lives as they did their own, if they'd used the lifeboats to capacity and shared them with our men, nobody would've had to drown."

There's a deafening silence in the room. Followed by soft sobbing. It's getting too much for me too. I let my head hang and feel warm tears streaming down my cheeks. I'm not sure if I should have heard this disgusting story. It's just too painful. Too unjust. Poor Uncle Ferdi.

Otto lays his hand on my shoulder, and I raise my head.

"Let's go," he whispers.

I stand up and rub my hands on my throbbing knees to brush off the twigs stuck there. Slowly we start walking back home.

"I saw Uncle Ferdi sitting in the hold," I say softly. "He was skinny and dressed in rags. I have a feeling he drowned in the hold."

"It's sickening how they left them locked up down there," Otto whispers. "The Dutch should have at the very least released the prisoners."

"Yes, I agree. And why did they have to destroy the radio and water containers?" I respond.

"And that other ship…," Otto says, "That came to the rescue and then just turned around. They deliberately let them drown."

"It's a miracle that Mr. Fischer and those other men survived. I'm glad that he has become our mayor," I say.

Back home, I light a little bundle of dried pine needles with resin on a small dish in front of our window, a makeshift candle, and I think of my Uncle Ferdi, who is now in heaven.

Chapter 23

SKYPE CONVERSATION

Birgit Treipl, Nelson, BC, Canada
Victor Treipl, Loupiac, France
January 1, 2018

On New Year's Day, I call my parents to wish them a happy New Year. They're recovering from their usual festivities, during which they partied into the wee hours with the same group of friends that they celebrate with every year. I'm glad they're still enjoying life so fully, with such vigour. My parents actually stayed up much later than I did.

"Around Christmas," Dad tells me, "Episode One Productions broadcast a three-part documentary on TV, via the Dutch channel BNN/VARA, entitled *The Doom of the Van Imhoff.* Your Mum and I were glued to the tube."

It strikes me just how much the *Van Imhoff* disaster has been a foundational experience for my dad.

"Ahh, I would have wanted to watch that too," I say. "What was the title again? *The Doom of the Van Imhoff*, you said? I'll look it up online. But tell me: what stood out the most for you?"

"Well, just the intriguing opening sentence, to start with: 'This is a story that was never meant to be told.' The great-grandson of Doctor Heidt, one of the few survivors of the *Van Imhoff* disaster, was doing the talking. He's writing a book about his great-grandfather and is looking for answers. His name is Thomas Heindl, and he lives in Vienna. Heindl contacts the Dutch captain's granddaughter, Anouk Hoeksema, in the Netherlands. The contrast between the interpretations of those two! Yes, I think that's what has stayed with me the most."

"What was so different in their accounts?"

"Well, after Thomas read about the horrors of this disaster, he asked Anouk in a Skype interview: 'Have you ever heard of the *Van Imhoff*?' And she said that she only knows the romantic story her father told her. 'My grandfather was a captain on some sort of "love boat,"' she said. She was curious to find out what happened and thought that maybe it was a family secret. She knew nothing, nothing at all, about the atrocities that took place on the *Van Imhoff*. So, the two descendants take up this quest together, going back in time to search for answers that change both their lives considerably. Of course, what really stood out for me is how shamelessly people lied, especially the Dutch government. The Dutch government has covered up the horrendous truths all those years."

Dad leans forward, at his computer screen, and looks at me intently.

"Go on...," I say.

"Well, in 1965, the Dutch government imposed a ban to block VARA management and editor Dick Verkijk from broadcasting his documentary. Verkijk was fired with immediate effect. Then the tapes with the recording disappeared inexplicably. It took all these years, until 2017, before this story finally saw the light of day.

Believe it or not, Dick Verkijk was involved in the creation of this new documentary," Dad says.

"And that Mr. Fischer, who brought the story to you in Sarangan, did his story match what you saw in the documentary?" I ask.

"Yes, the stories completely corresponded. Episode One has done a terrific job putting the pieces of the puzzle together. The entire political playing field was also discussed. I found that very interesting. And, at one point, Thomas Heindl was holding the list of the deceased in his hand, and I could clearly see Uncle Ferdi's name on it. Amazing that he somehow obtained that list…Another striking detail is that Doctor Heidt, Heindl's great-grandfather, was a good friend of my parents. He came to our hotel numerous times. He survived the disaster but died a few years later, in Nias."

"Geez, it's all so close to home. I'm looking forward to seeing that documentary. The Dutch government has dropped the ball quite a bit in the time since, I'd say. How do you feel about that?"

"Yes, that's my opinion as well. The Dutch don't want to face the fact that there are war criminals in their ranks. I once read an article that stated that in 1953, a German survivor filed a complaint with the Dutch Ministry of Justice against Herman Hoeksema, the Dutch captain of the *Van Imhoff*. And although that complaint was processed in 1958, the Netherlands concluded that there were no reasons to lay criminal charges. They referred to Captain Hoeksema's statement that he, along with some of his officers, had given to the Harbor Master of Tandjong Priok, the port of Batavia, shortly after the disaster. Hoeksema claimed they left sloops behind for the German prisoners to use. But his statement raised prickly questions. If he had truly attempted to help the Germans, why were the Dutch first to disembark? Why leave the Germans imprisoned behind barbed wire while the holds rapidly flooded? And the Germans who managed to free themselves and jump overboard—why let them drown instead of pulling them into the lifeboats with the Dutch, where there was still plenty of space for more passengers? I'm glad that the case is in the news again," Dad says.

"Yes, the Dutch often say, 'Well, it was all so long ago,' when people talk about the war or colonial times," I answer. "But for the government to not even acknowledge these deaths with a simple apology…"

"Yes, indeed."

"What about Mr. Fischer? What kind of man was he? It was quite remarkable that he was immediately appointed as mayor of your community."

"Mr. Fischer was an Austrian from Vienna. He was the representative for Robert Bosch AG in the Dutch East Indies. You know Bosch, the washing machine company? Well, his skills translated well to politics and civil life, and he ended up working very hard for our community.

"When he washed up on Nias with the other survivors, they were captured on the spot by the Dutch. But Fischer and Vehring managed to win over the Indonesian guards and turned them against the Dutch. The Indonesians released the Germans and locked up the Dutch. Working with the Indonesian population of the island, Fischer and Vehring proclaimed the independence of Nias. That situation didn't last very long, but just imagine how that set an example of what was possible. When the Japanese came to power, Vehring and Fischer presented themselves as allies; they offered translation services and made their knowledge of the country and of the Dutch people available. Not long after that, they somehow ended up in Sarangan, which is when we learned of Uncle Ferdi's fate."

"Mr. Fischer proved to be politically strong."

"Yes, he certainly was. He spoke several languages and had connections at the level of government leaders."

Later that day, I watch all three episodes of *The Doom of the Van Imhoff*, and I recognize what a profound impact this story must have had on my parents, as they sat watching it unfold in their own living room in France.

Chapter 24

DR. JOHANSON

Sarangan, like Lembang, is a mountain resort town with a healthy climate. Perhaps partly because of that, I'm rarely sick. But I do have one sensitive spot: my eyes.

It's the fall of 1944, and I'm lying on Dr. J's hospital bed. He's a German doctor of the Evangelical Rheinland Mission, freed by the Japanese from the Dutch camp in Ngawi. He has set up a provisional "hospital" in Sarangan. My eyes are in great pain; my eyelids are red and swollen. Aunty Hilda is sitting next to me on a chair.

"What's wrong with him, Dr. Johanson?" Aunty Hilda asks.

"He has trachoma. An eye infection mainly caused by dust. He has bumps on the inside of his eyelids that are chafing his retina," the doctor says.

"Hmmm. This isn't the first time for him…"

"I'm sorry, Mrs. Treipl, but I will have to perform the treatment without anesthesia. We have no drugs here, nothing to ease the pain or his nerves," the doctor says.

"I guess we have no other option," Aunty Hilda sighs.

Before I get what's going on, the doctor has rolled up my right eyelid with a match and starts piercing the inflammations one by one with a needle.

I groan and cry at the same time.

"Good boy. I know. This hurts," the doctor says softly. "Crying helps; it will flush wounds' fluids from your eyes."

The tears do feel soothing. I imagine the shock on Aunty Hilda's face while she's squeezing my hand. It's probably no fun to watch this treatment either.

"Try to move as little as possible, Vicky. I'll have to treat the bottom of this eyelid and your other eye as well," Dr. J says. He continues his match-and-needle treatment with a steady hand while I cry and scream and cling to the hospital bed to keep myself from thrashing like a fish.

I stay in bed writhing in pain the rest of the day, as does Otto, who has trachoma too. A week after the treatment, the problem, unfortunately, hasn't disappeared, but I can't bear going back to Dr. J.

Luckily, Aunty Hilda thinks it was just as terrible an experience as I do. She wants to know how a follow-up treatment can be performed more effectively and less painfully. The doctor tells her that the Bandung eye hospital has an option for anesthetic treatment. Moreover, they'd have medication available for the aftercare. He gives me a referral to the specialist.

For such treatment outside of Sarangan, permission must be sought from the Japanese army commander; Aunty Hilda submits a request for a meeting. I'm only allowed to leave Sarangan with his permission and a surat idjin, a travel pass drawn up in Malay and Japanese, which permits free passage.

I'm just thirteen years old and will travel by train all by myself across Java, from Madiun to Bandung. Aunty Hilda somehow has arranged for me to stay with Aunt Lintschi and Uncle Pepi.

"Be careful," she tells me. "I have no idea what the world outside of Sarangan looks like now, but we know that the Dutch are locked up in internment camps, and the Japanese are in power. If they ask about your nationality, make sure you tell them that you're Austrian."

The journey spans fifteen hours one way on the very train we embarked upon from Bandung to Sarangan: a steam locomotive pulling a long row of metal wagons with seven double, glassless window frames on either side. The difference is that this train is bustling with indigenous people, from infants to adults. The benches on the train are hard and uncomfortable, covered with a nondescript canvas that bears the marks of wear and tear. Indonesians carry an astonishing variety of cargo with them on the train. Live chickens cluck and rustle within their enclosures, and bundles of wood, crates of vegetables, cuts of meat, and baskets teeming with fresh fish are piled up in the aisles. As the train chugs along and a gentle tropical breeze flows through the open windows, a silent camaraderie weaves between me and my fellow passengers. Seated amongst the Indonesians, the rhythm of their conversations and laughter creates the welcoming atmosphere I remember from visiting the servants' outbuildings behind the hibiscus hedges of our hotel.

Seated across from me is an elderly lady, her warm demeanour instantly evoking memories of Babu Siti. A smile brightens her round, wrinkled, brown face, despite the absence of a few teeth. Her friendly dark eyes twinkle, and her shiny black hair is neatly arranged in a bun, secured with a simple wooden peg. It's hard to tell how old she is because she sits with an effortless grace, her legs folded in a cross-legged pose and her sarong elegantly draped around her legs.

"Where are you going, boy?" she asks me in Malay.

My answer is as simple as it is obtuse. "I'm coming from over here and going over there," I say, pointing back and forth with my thumb. That seems to satisfy her.

She extends her hand to me, palm up, holding a rolled-up banana leaf treat, and moves her hand up and down a few times as if to say, "Here, this is for you, take it." I accept her gift with both hands and nod kindly to thank her. I open my shoulder bag, take out my sandwich and unfold the paper. I, in turn, reach out to her and hand her half of my sandwich. She tilts her head slightly and nods. We eat our lunch in silence. I inhale the scent and enjoy every bite of the warm and fragrant lontong—rice cake—she gave me, and she seems to relish my European sandwich.

Throughout the ride, I drift between sleep and wakefulness, I eat and drink some, speak Malay, and exchange food with the Indonesians next to me. I'm obviously a white European boy, but they don't seem to be annoyed to see me on their train. Instead, I am met with genuine acceptance and warm curiosity. Only two Indonesian boys, who are older than me and seated a little farther away, are eyeing me with a hint of dislike. I'm not sure what's on their minds, but I'm unconcerned. For as long as the journey lasts, I forget it is wartime, and I feel one again with the land of my birth.

People come and go at every train stop, and I get the same question time and again, "Where are you going, boy?" And each time, my answer remains, "I'm coming from over here and going over there," pointing back and forth with my thumb. It appears to please everyone along the way.

I arrive safely in Bandung. The eye doctor at the hospital gives me three treatment sessions that don't hurt, and I get an ointment for the follow-up. In between treatments, I accompany Uncle Pepi to work. His boss is a German Indo who owns a sausage and canning factory. He must be working for the Japanese army, I figure, since there's no way he could have kept his factory this busy and successful otherwise.

I stay with Aunt Lintschi and Uncle Pepi for almost fourteen days. The travel pass works well on the return trip too. In hindsight, throughout my journey, not one single white European got on the train. I sat amongst the Indonesians the whole time. They shared their food with me, and I shared with them what I had. I spoke their language and never felt afraid. I felt like one of them.

I immensely enjoyed my trip, but Aunty Hilda was anxiously waiting for me to return home safely.

Chapter 25

THE GERMAN NAVY

No sooner do I return from my trip to Bandung than we hear, through illegal broadcasts on Radio Zeesen, worrying reports about the war's progress in Europe. Germany is losing ground, and Hitler is turning to his last resort: using all the young boys he can find to survive. Boys sixteen and older are summoned for military service.

A delegation of German Navy officers from Surabaja pays a visit to Sarangan and informs us that our boys aged sixteen and older will be recruited. There appears to be a U-boat support point for Southeast Asia in Surabaja, where the boys will receive their training. They will be fully equipped, provided with all necessities. There's no escaping it, and the boys' mothers are desperate. Aunty Hilda is overjoyed that I'm not sixteen yet—though she makes sure to keep that between her and me.

The boys themselves are incredibly excited. There are ten of them altogether. The subject of the Navy has suddenly become hot. Otto, Dieter, Guido, Günther, and I discuss how we'd love to go because we'd get fine clothes and other equipment and be well trained too. But we're not allowed to join. I'm almost fourteen years old and seriously envious. Otto, the eldest of our group of five, will turn sixteen next year, so he misses being recruited only by a hair. I hate missing out on all the good opportunities just because of a measly two-year difference.

One day in December 1944, trucks arrive, and after the last roll call, in the presence of all the people of Sarangan, our heroes are taken away.

For us, those left behind, life continues with a certain uneasiness. It feels weird when a significant group of older boys all of a sudden disappear from your environment. They were the older guys I looked up to, who I saw and spoke with every day. Gone. When will we see them again?

The scarcity of food and other items is worse than ever. There's less and less bartering with the market vendors because people have nothing to trade. We still receive our monthly allocations of rice and other food from the Japanese, but it's very little.

Our everyday labour service continues. We have to dig, plant, chop wood, and cut grass for the two cows still living at Eagle's Nest Hotel.

We go to school as always, but everything is different now. With the older boys gone, the girls finally see us.

After their first four months of training, our heroes come home. This will be the last time before they go fight in the war. It's amazing how they've turned into real men. Well dressed, well fed, and strong. We can't get enough of their courageous stories. But their leave only lasts a short while, and before long, they return to Surabaja, where they become part of the U-boat crew. I can only dream of such a fate.

Chapter 26

TAWAR

In the spring of 1945, tensions in Sarangan rise to a boiling point. It becomes clear that Hitler is headed for defeat in Europe. There are keen supporters of the regime in our community but also many opponents, including Aunty Hilda. She prefers to stay away from any discussions of the war.

It starts with rumours, and then the official news reaches us: the Führer is dead. Adolf Hitler committed suicide during the Battle of Berlin, and Germany has surrendered. The war in Europe has come to an end.

Japan is still at war in Asia and here, they continue to control Sarangan, but we hear that its power is also declining. More and more Japanese generals are instructing their officers to commit harakiri, ritual suicide, their way of trying to escape the disgrace of losing the war.

The question that arises is what are the Japanese going to do with our community? Nobody knows what their plans are. The

German embassy in Tokyo and the German consulate in Batavia have been closed. And though Germany's subsidy for our school and community has dried up, the German School is still up and running, and our labour services continue as usual.

The Sarangan borders relax somewhat. German men appear in town, mainly ex-marines of the abolished German Navy, looking for a safe place to live.

In early August 1945 the Americans drop atomic bombs on the Japanese cities of Hiroshima and Nagasaki, after which, on August 15, Emperor Hirohito announces the capitulation of his country via radio broadcast. Two days later, Ahmed Sukarno and Mohammad Hatta proclaim the Proklamasi Kemerdekaan Indonesia, the Independence of the Republic of Indonesia.

The Japanese disappear from Sarangan, and the Indonesian police, commissioned by the Sukarno government, take over surveillance of our community.

Mayor Fischer, who speaks excellent Bahasa Indonesia and is a powerful communicator, negotiates with the Indonesian authorities on behalf of our community to put our knowledge and skills in the fields of sports and education to good use. He's highly successful at that. An institute is established in Sarangan that houses Indonesian police-in-training officers, who receive education and fitness training. Soon, future Indonesian Army and Navy officers will also come to the same institute. And though there is hardly any money, we are paid in other ways; food is extremely welcome. Our community can sustain itself through this barter with the influx of Indonesians.

There's a lot of movement going on, though. We hear that the gates of the internment camps are now open, and the Dutch, having regained their freedom, are attempting to reclaim their former positions and are refusing to accept Indonesian independence. Many mothers are leaving our community, accompanied by their children, destined for Bandung or Batavia. They hope the Dutch regime will be restored, and believe these urban areas will offer them greater security. Also, an increasing number of mothers and children are leaving for Europe under the protection of the Red Cross. About a hundred and sixty of our friends have already left Sarangan—more than half of our original German community—and many of the homes and hotels they lived in are now sitting empty.

But Aunty Hilda doesn't want to leave. She wants to try to reclaim Grand Hotel Lembang when these turbulent times come to an end. The heart of our community has been ripped out, but I'm glad that we aren't going to Europe. There's nothing for me there, I don't think. I was born and raised in Java, and I want to stay here.

Many of my classmates leave, though, and I lose my best friends Dieter, Günther, and Guido. Otto and I are the only ones staying behind, and we become unseparable. Willy Quidort and his wife have decided to return to Switzerland, and the hotel owners, the Sonnhofer family, ask Aunty Hilda to take over the management of Hotel Beau Site. She agrees to their offer of a small salary and an attractive bonus, with the understanding that she will only receive the bonus upon successfully guiding the hotel through these uncertain years. Our German community now has around fifty residents, and we do our best to keep up our daily routines. Most hotel residents have no money and pay for their food and lodging by performing duties for the hotel.

One day Aunty Hilda takes me aside.

"Vicky, I have a concern," she says. "It's come to my attention that the residents of Hotel Beau Site are beginning to grumble about you getting a free ride, since I manage the hotel and you get free food. They're saying you're doing nothing in return to earn your keep. I don't want our neighbours to bear ill will against us. It's time for you to take a break from school, start contributing, and earning your keep."

"But I work in the garden and chop wood for the kitchen," I say, resistant to the idea of giving up my freedom.

"There's nothing special about that. The other boys and girls do the same. No, we're going to do things differently. I have a plan. You will officially become my purchaser. I want you to start buying vegetables, fruit, and firewood for the hotel every day."

"But Aunty Hilda, the market vendors speak Javanese. I only know Malay and a few words of Sundanese. Besides that, I'm not good at tawar. How on earth am I supposed to negotiate with them?" Haggling, tawar, is commonplace over here, but you need to know the game and understand the language. I remember watching my father haggle at the Pasar Baru in Bandung, but I was little then.

"I don't want to hear any more excuses," Aunty Hilda says, her voice firm, waggling her finger at me. "From now on, you're my purchaser. I'll let you know what we need, and it will be your responsibility to buy it. You'll pay for the products with our community cash." Aunty Hilda looks at me with a smirk on her face, then turns around and walks away.

I stay behind, stunned. How can she do this to me? How am I going to tackle this?

When I awake early next morning, the pouch with the community cash is sitting on the table, with a little note next to it. *Firewood, vegetables, fruit, and eggs for two days. And soup chickens, if they have any.*

Aunty Hilda has clearly gotten word out about my new role as purchaser. She must have sent the market vendors over to me; I can hear the bustle and chatter of women waiting in front of our room.

I try to encourage myself, straighten my shirt, then step outside, trying to look as confident as I can. All the women immediately get up and begin to talk over each other, competing for my attention, just like at the market. I come closer and take a look at what they have in their baskets.

"What does this cost?" I ask in my pasar-Malay while pointing at the goods. The women mumble some and raise their fingers to indicate the price.

"Is that your lowest price?" I ask.

The women peer at me kindly.

We communicate with hands and feet and a smile. I find it challenging to choose—I want to buy something from as many women as possible because, after all, they've come a long way. In the meantime, Indonesian men have arrived, carrying heavy wooden rods over their shoulders with a basket of firewood hanging from each end.

After an hour, I sit down, exhausted, on our small patio next to a large pile of vegetables, fruit, and firewood. I stick the pouch in my pocket to gesture that I'm done shopping. The women understand the hint and sidle off. I walk over to the kitchen and feel quite proud of myself.

"Aunty Hilda, I did it," I shout.

"That's great. Would you mind bringing the food to the kitchen? And maybe Otto can help you split and stack the firewood."

"But…it's a lot…"

"Show me what you bought," she says. She starts walking towards our room at a fast pace, and I run after her. When she stops at the patio in front of my pile, I read the shock on her face.

"Vicky! You've purchased food for a football team! What did you pay for all this?"

"Oh, sixty rupiahs…" I say reluctantly.

"Sixty rupiahs?"

"I wanted to buy something from all the women because they had to travel at least two hours with their heavy baskets over the mountains, all the way from Tjimoro Sewu."

"Vicky, they're used to doing that. These women sell their goods to all the hotels and inns around here. They sure had a fantastic morning with you. You've spent way too much money.

The next time you'll have to buy less than half that amount and bargain much, much more."

My face turns red as I stare at my shoes.

"We'll skip shopping for the next couple days, and I'll teach you how to bargain. Come, help me bring the food to the kitchen. The staff will have to process it so it doesn't go to waste."

That evening, sitting in our cozy living room, the warm glow of our only lamp creating an intimate setting for our conversation, Aunty Hilda's eyes hold a mischievous twinkle as she leans forward.

"Now, dear, let's unravel the fascinating game of tawar with our market vendors," she begins. "In our world, haggling isn't merely a transaction—it's a dance. It's a rhythm where both parties sway, testing the waters of price and value."

I nod, my attention unwavering, as if I were learning a secret language only a few were privy to.

"Imagine," Aunty Hilda's voice lowers to a conspiratorial tone, "the market stalls at the Pasar Baru as a theatre stage. The vendors, the actors, and you, Vicky, you have the leading role in this performance."

I can't help but smile at the imagery, the pasar transforming in my mind's eye into a lively theatre.

"The first rule is to approach with a smile, a compliment perhaps. Establish that connection, let them see you as a person, not just a customer."

I lean in, absorbing every word, her words conjuring scenes of bustling stalls and charismatic vendors within my imagination.

"Then comes the game of numbers. They name their price, you name yours. Never show them the money. Start out low. You can't accept their first number. The dance begins." Her fingers move as if in a delicate waltz, mimicking the exchange.

"You see, it's not about undermining their worth. It's about finding that sweet spot where both sides leave feeling victorious."

As Aunty Hilda continues to speak, my perspective shifts. Haggling is no longer about giving them what they want, nor is it about getting the best deal. It is a form of communication where all of us are satisfied in the end.

I go to bed with a smile.

It takes a while before I get the hang of it, but eventually, I learn to understand the market vendors' language. Now when I approach them, I smile and give them a compliment or make a joke. I keep my money hidden. When the women give me their price, I counter it by half, and sometimes I even bluff and walk away.

I start to enjoy the haggling, and it sparks my interest in finding other ways to procure money and food. From the market vendors, I buy baby bunnies, chicks, and ducklings. I build a coop and a rabbit cage behind the hotel's outbuildings, and Otto and I start to breed them. We teach ourselves to slaughter as well. Under Aunty Hilda's supervision, the meat is prepared in Hotel Beau Site's kitchen by the Indonesian cook and served in our dining room.

An ex-marine, Hans, teaches me how to make cigarettes. Using a fretsaw to cut the wooden parts, I fashion a device made of wood, glue, and wax cloth, and with that, he teaches me how to roll cigarettes with Virginia tobacco and cigarette paper. I follow his special recipe and treat the tobacco with a sauce of honey and licorice-flavoured alcohol, after which I dry the moist tobacco under a fan. I fashion the cardboard package myself as well; it can hold twenty cigarettes. Then Hans and I determine a price. They sell quickly in our community to the smokers that still have the money for it.

One fateful day, I use my lock-pick to venture into the dim corners of a warehouse and stumble upon a hidden trove. A stash of lightbulbs—shimmering, fragile orbs of potential. A thought ripples through my mind as I trace my fingers over them. In a world where even the most mundane commodities are scarce, where does Aunty Hilda get lightbulbs for the hotel? These bulbs will be worth money someday, so I steal a box of six and store them under my bed. Aunty Hilda's watchful gaze expresses her tacit approval. She lets me do my thing and never asks questions—a silent bond forged in our struggle to survive. In the same dim corner of the warehouse, I also find a His Master's Voice record player and a whole stack of records with classical music, completely covered in dust. I bring it home, together with the records.

After some thorough dusting, polished wood and brass emerge. I turn the lever on the side of the record player several times to bring tension to its spring, then lower the needle onto the record, and a lovely sound comes out of the massive horn. Aunty Hilda loves it. Sibelius is our favourite. When Aunty Hilda listens, it's like she absorbs the music. She sits on the sofa with her eyes closed, her hands folded, her head tilted slightly back, and a peaceful smile on her face.

The lightbulbs soon come in handy. Both Otto and I have been afflicted with a toothache for some time now, and the Indonesian police have given us permission to go to the Chinese dentist in Madiun. I bring Aunty Hilda's ring with me as payment for the gold crown and dental work, and Otto has one of his mother's golden earrings. I also carry a backpack full of lightbulbs with me. It is twenty-seven miles to Madiun. We take a seat on a tottering bus, and for a few rupiahs, we travel most of the way then walk the rest. In Madiun, we visit the Bombayers, East Indians, who specialize in fabrics. They sell the most exquisite materials, even Bemberg silk. The East Indians show great interest in my lightbulbs. I trade them for silk, fill up my backpack, and return with it to Sarangan. Some ladies in our community still have money, and the silk sells in no time.

The dentist isn't done with Otto and me in one sitting, and we will need to come back three more times. Each time, I make it a point to barter items, usually with Otto as my audience. On the second visit, I load up my bag with lightbulbs again, which

I exchange for fabrics I then sell to the German ladies. With the earnings from that, I buy a backpack full of Virginia tobacco and cigarette paper and roll cigarettes I sell to the smokers in town. The next time we go, I come home with a special gift for Aunty Hilda: an elegant golden watch, bartered at the pawn shop, that still ticks when you wind it up.

My trading success fuels my ambition, but despite having witnessed Aunty Hilda lose the hotel and all our worldly possessions, I'm only vaguely aware that ambition is a sibling to risk. Those who chase good fortune are often sorely humbled.

Chapter 27

BERSIAP

It is mid-November 1945 when Otto and I are back in Madiun for our fourth and last visit to the dentist and the Bombayers. By the time we're finally done with our business, it's already late in the afternoon. We can't find a single place to sleep in the city, and the next bus doesn't leave until the morning.

"I don't feel like spending the whole night in this bus shelter," I say.

"No, neither do I," says Otto.

"Maybe we should just walk to Sarangan," I suggest.

Otto nods. We split the weight between both our backpacks and start our journey. At six p.m., the sky darkens, but the night is clear and the moon is full, so it isn't pitch black. But of course, even in the dark, anyone could tell that we're white. Nine miles down the road from Madiun, we're stopped by a couple of Indonesian police agents. Their presence makes us feel uneasy; their questions are sharp and probing.

"What are two European boys doing out here in the middle of the night?" one of them asks.

"We're on our way to Sarangan, sir, and the busses aren't going until the morning," I answer in Malay.

"Sarangan. Hmmm. That's a long way off," says the officer. "You'll be coming with us to the lurah," the term referring to a position combining elements of the local mayor and the chief of police. He opens the door of the police car and points at the back seat. "Get in," he orders.

As he's driving, Otto and I glance nervously at each other.

"Do you think the chief will even be working this late?" I whisper to Otto in German.

Otto says nothing; he's busy biting his nails.

When the car eventually stops, the agent gets out. Peering out the window, I perceive the outline of a small, white building and a solitary light persisting against the darkness. Unmistakably the police headquarters. The agent opens the back door and orders us to step out of the car. We follow his lead towards the building, where a small plaque on the wall reads, "Pejabat Polis Maospati"— the police headquarters of Maospati. We then follow him inside, through a long hallway, and finally, to a closed door. The agent knocks with a measured sense of respect. In response, another agent opens the door from the inside, and we see an indigenous man sitting behind a desk. As he rises, he introduces himself as the village chief, his presence commanding authority. He then submits us to a strict interrogation. He wants to know who we are, what we do, where we come from, where we're going, and why two white European boys are walking the streets alone at night. What brought us to Madiun? Who are our parents? What's our nationality? He also wants to see our travel documents. The itch of sweat pearls on my forehead, and my shirt is wet. I wipe my forehead with my wrist and run my hand through my hair. Otto looks pale. He lets me do all the talking. I tell the village chief we had to go to the dentist, but I keep silent about our barter business.

"Do you realize that it's bersiap?" the village chief asks with a deep voice. Otto and I exchange a bewildering glance.

"No, sir. What do you mean by that?" I ask.

"Bersiap is the battle cry of the Indonesian freedom fighters. They seek death and destruction of the white Europeans," the village chief explains. "It's very dangerous what you're doing. You can't just walk the streets at night. The revolution is extremely violent. The gangs will rob and kill you if you cross paths with them. I'm going to call the police in Sarangan to verify things."

Call the police in Sarangan? We didn't even know they had a working phone. The village chief picks up the receiver and dials a number. A conversation ensues in rapid Javanese while Otto and I sit there like two sheep; their raised voices unnerve me.

Questions are preying on my mind. Do the Sarangan police know who we are? What could the village chief be discussing with them? If only I had been honest. We went to the dentist, yes, but that doesn't explain why we were in Madiun this late. If only I had told him that we went to the Bombayers. A little bit of trading isn't against the law. But now that I've lied, surely we look suspicious.

The village chief nods to one of the agents. The officer gestures to us to follow him into the long hallway. He opens a door, and behind it, we see a cell and bars. I startle, and Otto starts to whine softly.

"Are you going to lock us up, sir?" I ask in a small voice. "What's going to happen to us?"

The agent doesn't answer, just opens the cell door. There are two narrow bunks placed opposite each other against the walls of the cell.

"You will stay here until further notice," he says, and the bars clang shut. The agent takes a seat by the door. Otto is sobbing, and I feel guilty. How long will they keep us here?

We've been in jail for over an hour when the village chief final-ly arrives. We look at him tensely.

"I believe your story, and the police in Sarangan has confirmed you're harmless," he says.

I sigh deeply, and my shoulders relax. Otto's doing the same.

"You can continue your journey," he says with a serious voice, "but only on one condition: you will wait here for a ride home."

Otto and I are ecstatic with cheer and the village chief starts laughing.

"And you must promise me," the chief says, invoking a sense of urgency, "that you will never undertake a trip at night like this again—the police won't always be around to vouch for your lives."

We nod obediently.

We are taken back to the office, where the village chief offers us teh manis, very sweet black jasmine tea, and ginger cookies. The nervousness in our bodies finally ebbs away.

We sit around until five a.m., when an ox cart comes by. After some negotiation with the village chief, the driver is willing to take us to Mount Lawu. We take turns falling asleep on the bumpy cart, and eventually, we arrive at the bottom of the mountain in Ngerong. From there, it's still a good hour of hiking up until we get home. Otto's parents and Aunty Hilda haven't slept all night; they're beside themselves with worry.

In retrospect, I've realized that it was sheer luck that we didn't bump into any gangs of freedom fighters. The intervention of the police officers escorting us to the Madiun chief might have been a fateful twist. Against the backdrop of our current knowledge about the bersiap, with already around twenty-five thousand Dutch and Dutch Indos killed, being two white European boys travelling in the dark unaccompanied, we probably wouldn't have survived the night on that long road back home.

Chapter 28

SKYPE CONVERSATION

Birgit Treipl, Nelson, BC, Canada
Victor Treipl, Loupiac, France
April 9, 2018

"Dad, can you tell me more about that period immediately after Japan surrendered? So many parties were fighting each other: the government of Sukarno and Hatta, the freedom fighters, the Dutch, and the English. There was bersiap, and the Dutch Police Actions…With all this going on, why did you continue to live in Sarangan after 1945? Europe was free by that point. When Japan surrendered, didn't that mean you were free to go where you wanted to?"

"It was more complicated than that," Dad replies. "We felt anything but free. Remember that we were classified as Germans, the enemy. Yes, the war was over, but we were now the losers. Moreover, we were white. The Indonesian radical freedom fighters were in the process of killing white settlers in their country. We had no idea what would happen to us after the Japanese left Sarangan. And two days after the capitulation, Sukarno proclaimed Indonesia independent."

"So, let's revisit that. August 17, 1945, right? What happened?"

"That was the start of a dangerous and chaotic time. Sukarno proclaimed the independence of the Indonesian Republic in Batavia that day, and immediately renamed the city Djakarta. But the Dutch government wanted to kill the coup and reclaim the colony. The Dutch continued to call the city Batavia well into 1949.

"The Dutch did not see themselves as colonial 'oppressors' but rather as an 'educator' and even the bearer of God's message. They did not acknowledge President Sukarno as a legitimate leader but rather painted him as a rebel and troublemaker who deserved imprisonment. Personally, I felt drawn to Sukarno. He was an intelligent man, fluent in several languages, educated through the Dutch schooling system, and he had become a civil engineer. His yearning for an independent Indonesia resonated with me. But for the Dutch, his position as the figurehead of a 'free' Indonesia was a source of considerable discomfort.

"In August 1945, the Dutch had just come out of the camps, and the weakened Dutch army found themselves dependent on their allies. The British had taken strategic positions in Malacca, Singapore, and the Dutch East Indies, and the Allies appointed them to restore order to Southeast Asia. But initially, the British focused their attention on their own colonies, and prevented the more than 125,000 Dutch soldiers shipped from Holland to the Indies to 'restore order' from landing in Java and Sumatra. It took some time for the Dutch to get support from British forces and their Gurkhas, who were Nepalese soldiers employed by the British army."

"So, there was more or less a power vacuum on Java," I note.

"Yes, indeed, and the Indonesian freedom fighters cleverly made use of it," Dad continues. "They were resourceful. With all the means they had—bamboo spears, machetes, axes, krises, clubs, and stolen Japanese guns—they attacked the British. Countless bloody battles took place."

"What side was the Sukarno government on in all of this?"

"Sukarno and Hatta tried to negotiate in a diplomatic way. They called for peace but failed in that; they couldn't control the radical youth. Passions were high. The Indonesians fought en masse in their battle for Merdeka—freedom—while the Dutch were hoping to reinstate their halcyon pre-war idyll. Several women and children from our community decided to leave for Europe at that time, under the Red Cross's protection, but Aunty Hilda didn't want to go to Europe. She had her heart set on Grand Hotel Lembang."

"And when exactly did the bersiap start?" I ask.

"The bersiap officially lasted from October 1945 to March 1946. But it's easy to tell you that now, in retrospect. At the time, we didn't know. Living in isolation on the mountain in Sarangan, cut off from the outside world, we were always lagging, and badly informed about world news. Years later, we heard that our boys who had joined the German Navy and were missing after the war had been captured as prisoners of war by the British and the Dutch. And when the bersiap was going on, the village chief was the first to let me know," Dad grins.

Chapter 29

REBELLION IN MADIUN

On our mountain in Sarangan, we try to lay low. The ongoing political upheaval seems to be happening far away. The presence of Sukarno's soldiers, sanctioned by Mayor Fischer, lends our small community an atmosphere of relative safety.

I have to quit barterering, though, because Aunty Hilda absolutely refuses to let me outside of Sarangan. She wants to keep me off the streets but doesn't want me idle either.

That's how we find ourselves sitting at the small table at the back of the pastry chef's kitchen. The three of us—Aunty Hilda, Meiners the baker and pastry chef, and me—discuss my employment.

"He must start at the bottom of the hierarchy, and he needs to do all the work that the Indonesian servants do. They've been working for me for over a year and know much more than Victor," says Meiners.

I nod timidly.

"What will he earn, Mr. Meiners?" Aunty Hilda asks.

"The wage consists of a hot meal and a loaf of bread per day. Victor will have to swear an oath of confidentiality—all our recipes are secret. These secrets must not leave our kitchen."

Meiners looks intently at me and asks, "Can you agree to this, Victor?"

"Yes, sir," I answer wholeheartedly.

"Excellent," he replies, shaking my hand. "You start tomorrow at five-thirty a.m."

I have a lot to learn. I'm working full time; my only day off is Sundays. I carry bags, wash dishes, tidy up, clean and scrub floors. As the jack of all trades, I'm assigned all the dirty work. It's hot in the bakery, and I have to struggle out of bed before the sun's even risen; those early mornings have me yawning through my work. But I'm not complaining, and I come home with a loaf of bread every day, to Aunty Hilda's delight. I get along well with the two Indonesian servants, who are much older than me. One is twenty and the other twenty-two. I'm only sixteen. I try to be as helpful as possible, and it works: after two weeks, I get more interesting tasks. Slowly but surely, I learn from my colleagues, and the less-fun tasks are now shared among us. I knead dough for the bread, operate the oven, make marzipan, ice cream, pastries, and meringues. Under Mr. Meiners's watchful eye, I learn to prepare the daily lunch we eat together in the kitchen. Over time, I also learn to slaughter pigs and to smoke ham, bacon, and sausage.

I don't know how he does it exactly with the scarcity around us, but pastry chef Meiners has an extremely busy store. Indonesian and German customers both flock to our bakery—we end up sold out almost every day. I'm proud of the work I do and start to enjoy it more and more.

On Sundays, I often mess around at home, practicing everything I've been taught. I get my hands on a "belly bottle," a bulbous wine bottle, and strawberries, and I make strawberry wine according to Mr. Meiners's recipe.

Sometimes I do gymnastics or go for a run around the lake. One loop is three miles. I'm not allowed to go on anymore hikes into the mountains because it's far too dangerous in the woods. Once in a while, when I can get tobacco, I roll cigarettes and sell them to anyone in our community who still has money for it. They bring in quite a bit of cash, and from time to time, I buy a meal for Aunty Hilda and me at the local Indonesian food stall: nasi goreng, fried rice; ajam-kuning, chicken in a turmeric-coconut sauce; sambal-telor; rendang; or any other delicious Indonesian dish they have going.

One morning in September 1948, I come across a group of Indonesians in the street on my way to work. They're all squatting together, gripping the handles of their machetes, holding their sharpened bamboo spears across their laps. Their grim expressions make me nervous. I pull my pockets inside out and put on my most innocent face to let them know I'm harmless.

"Selamat pagi," they mumble. Good morning. I hurry past them while Mr. Meiners and his wife crane their necks from their window. I reach the bakery unscathed, and Meiners puts me to work.

An hour later, we learn what this is all about. An Indonesian man in a khaki uniform bursts into the bakery with some of the men I saw this morning and introduces himself as the unit commander.

"Line up," the commander barks at us while his men start combing the building. He informs us that Madiun has been taken over by the communist party PKI, led by their commander Musso, and that the surrounding villages will now also be taken over by Musso. We've never heard of this guy Musso before.

Mr. Meiners whispers, "Yesterday morning, a Sukarno soldier buying pastries told me they were called away, so we are now unprotected."

I'm starting to feel uncomfortable. What do these communists have in mind? The commander reappears in the kitchen and declares that they've completed their search. But this is only the first of several days of house-to-house inspections sweeping through the village and also at Hotel Beau Site. The rhythm of our life changes and we receive conflicting messages about what's going to happen to us. Over the course of several days, we all have to participate in the communists' farming activities, like cutting grass for the cows, tillage, and chopping wood, much like the labour service the Japanese imposed on us before. We have no choice but to follow their orders, though we watch with sadness as these events unfold.

The situation lasts no longer than a few weeks.

"I see Indonesian flags, and I hear shooting," shouts a resident from the upper floor of Hotel Beau Site as he runs down the hallway and past all the rooms. What follows is a cacophony of shuffling feet and muffled exclamations. The residents of Beau Site dive for cover inside the hotel and along the garden walls outside. Aunty Hilda and I huddle underneath the window sill of our room, our fingers grazing the worn surface while we lift our heads up to peek out the window. I recognize the Sang Dwiwarna, the red and white flags of the Indonesian Republic. My eyes, wide and alert, scan our village and the lake. "Look, Aunty Hilda, the guard posts are deserted," I whisper. Everywhere I can see, the communist guard posts stand empty.

Shortly thereafter, in the distance we watch a group of men in uniforms come up from the canyon. I can hear the rhythmic thud of boots against the earth echoing through the air, punctuated by the occasional command. Someone outside the hotel recognizes the uniforms—the distinct insignias of the Siliwangi division, Sukarno's elite army unit, renowed for their unrelenting discipline and steely resolve. My heart beats a little faster as they come closer and I recognize a familiar face, Sukarno's adjutant, known for his severity.

Fortunately, the first encounter with some of our people passes without victims on our side and the soldiers understand who we are. Once again, we are under the protection of Bung Karno, Father of the Indonesians, 'our' president.

After Sarangan has been recaptured from the communists and the Indonesian Army has reestablished itself in our community, the Siliwangi troops move on. We hear they arrest anyone even remotely linked to communist activities. Musso, the elusive communist leader, escapes.

Only a few days later, the Siliwangi troops return and march into Sarangan. The barrels of their guns cast long shadows, pointing at a procession of stumbling prisoners whose hands are cuffed behind their backs. There are acquaintances from Sarangan's Indonesian settlement among them, including the chief of police.

Otto and I stand frozen, our gaze fixed on the unfolding scene. The chief of police, who had once shown us kindness, his actions etched in our memories—the passes for the dentist, the phone conversations with the lurah in Madiun to prove our innocence—now stands in the ranks of the 'communist prisoners', his hands bound and his fate sealed.

The procession is brought to a halt in the open field next to Hotel Beau Site. It all happens very fast. Orders are called in Malay, and I only understand half of them. The prisoners are lined up, and the soldiers line up opposite them, their guns at the ready. I hold my breath. Someone shouts a command.

I will never forget the deafening bang or the splashing of blood. The bodies bend and tumble to the ground, where, to everyone's horror, they lie under the burning sun all day. Both Otto and I are sick to our stomachs.

Chapter 30

SCORCHED EARTH

Outside of Sarangan, Operation Crow—the code name for the Second Dutch Police Action—is in full swing. Agresi Militer Belanda II, the Indonesians call it. Their name, Dutch Military Aggression II, feels more like a war initiative than a police action. Operation Crow began on December 19 in Djogjakarta when President Sukarno was arrested, along with nearly his entire government. The United Nations and America have demanded the withdrawal of Dutch troops and President Sukarno's immediate release, but the Dutch continue to resist Indonesian independence.

Around noontime on December 24, 1948, the Indonesian Army commander shows up in our neighbourhood.

"On the lawn," he shouts.

Feverish, I jump up and run to the kitchen.

"Aunty Hilda. You have to come out *now*," I shout.

Aunty Hilda is overseeing the work of the kitchen staff, who are preparing Christmas Eve dinner for tonight. She sees that I'm serious and walks with me. I'm seventeen years old now and a head taller than she is.

People are coming out of their houses, bewildered; we gather on the field, muttering nervously to each other.

The commander's voice booms out, "We have no time to lose. The Dutch troops are advancing, and I can no longer guarantee your safety. I advise you to leave immediately. My army will apply scorched earth tactics. We will set all the buildings on fire so that the Dutch will not find houses, people, or animals in Sarangan."

We stare at the man open-mouthed. Then, everyone starts to shout at once. It's chaos. Leave? Where to? Into the woods? Our houses set on fire? Mr. Hupfer, our gymnastics teacher, is the first to gather his wits.

"You say we have to leave, sir, but where to?" he asks.

"Unfortunately, I can't help you with that," the commander replies. "There is fighting going on everywhere, and you are white and German. I don't know what the Dutch will do to you, and the Indonesian freedom fighters can't see from your faces that you're not Dutch. You may choose to stay here, but we can't guarantee your safety."

Aunty Hilda takes me by the arm. "I have no intention of leaving. It's too dangerous. We're in the middle of the battle line. And I promised to run the hotel. If they set it on fire, I will not receive my bonus and we will be destitute."

Aunty Hilda is determined as always. I nod in understanding.

"And what if we want to stay here? Will you also set fire to our houses?" she asks the commander.

"If you decide to stay, we will set all buildings on fire, except for the buildings you live in. I'd like to hear from all of you, right now, what you're going to do," the commander says. Many houses and hotels now sit empty, a somber testament to the decimation of our community after the departure of mothers and children to Bandung, Batavia, and Europe.

There's a buzz.

Mr. Hupfer retakes the lead. "Who's planning on staying?" he calls. "Raise your hand, please."

Aunty Hilda resolutely raises her hand, and I follow her example.

There is doubt in the air. People glance around and, hesitantly, raise their hands. I twist around to see Otto. He raises his hand also. I'm grateful he did. One by one, more people join in. Everyone chooses to stay.

"I respect your choice," the commander says. "Your homes will not be burned. I ask you to return to your homes and stay inside. I wish you all good luck!" He salutes and turns to leave.

We stand together, uncomfortably. Although I support our choice, my stomach is churning and tension building in my chest. How will we defend ourselves? What will the Dutch do to us? When will they arrive?

Suffocating black clouds churn skyward into the thick white fog that descended on Sarangan this morning. I watch desperately as roaring flames flare and spread. Hotel Lawu, Fujiya, Eagle's Nest Hotel, and Oma Petsch Inn are on fire. My eyes are tingling, and my lungs ache with smoke. I double over in a coughing fit. Windows shatter, roofs and walls collapse. The buildings where my friends once lived transform before my eyes into charred, smouldering heaps. As the fire licks its way close to Hotel Beau Site, I raise my arms in despair and lower myself to my knees.

Memories flash vividly in my head like bursts of light: Dieter, Günther, Guido, Otto, and me. Out on the water with Hotel Beau Site's kayaks, or the sturdy metal lifeboat we named Kahn. Playing warrior jumping off the lock. Joking about snakes while climbing Mount Kukusan. Rummaging through the Japanese warehouses

that we opened with our lock picks. The German School, the bustling athletics field. Otto and I sprinting through the woods to
the water wells of Banju Urip. No tents, just lying in the grass,
our faces radiant with smiles. How those days felt wonderfully
carefree.

The pop of distant gunshots and the roar of planes interrupt my
boyhood memories, which shrivel and char. Of our group of
friends, only Otto and I are left. It is Christmas Eve 1948, and
Sarangan is on fire.

Chapter 31

MELANCHOLY

In the pitch dark, a loud tumult startles us awake. Shots ring out, accompanied by flashes of light, and yelling and screaming. I jump up and run to the window. I can't see but someone's kicking hard at our door. Aunty Hilda goes to open it and finds herself face to face with a Dutch naval officer who towers high above her.

"In the name of the State of the Netherlands, we've come to liberate you," the man proclaims.

"Free us? From what? And who do you think you are, kicking down our door?" Aunty Hilda shouts in her very best Dutch.

The officer, visibly surprised to hear his mother tongue, stands briefly stunned. It's so ridiculous, it's hilarious, and I barely hold back my laughter.

But he recovers quickly and returns a stern command, "Tomorrow morning. Eight a.m. On the lawn. In front of the hotel."

Now, in daylight, all fifty of us are outside. It's Christmas Day, the rain is driving down on our heads, and we're soaking wet. The air is heavy with the smoldering fumes. More than half of the hotels and houses have gone up in smoke. Aunty Hilda is standing next to me, shivering. A rather hostile Dutch officer addresses us.

"Do you still have food for a few weeks?" he roars.

I nod. Yes, we do. I learned at Mr. Meiners's bakery how to preserve eggs and other foods, and I've built up an excellent stock in our closet.

"You will be picked up by trucks and taken to the Chassé camp in Batavia. Each person is permitted fifty-five pounds of luggage. Pack your bags and be ready to leave at any time. Your rooms will be locked, and we will send the rest of your belongings to Batavia."

The officer salutes, turns around, and walks away.

We return to our room.

"Those Dutch Marines who came to supposedly 'liberate' us— what the hell are they talking about?" I say, irritated. "Liberating us from the Indonesians? We lived in harmony with them here. The Dutch want to lock us up in their camp in Batavia. With what right? The war has already ended."

"I don't know," Aunty Hilda commiserates. "There are mainly women and children here. What harm can we do? Why don't they just leave us alone?" She hurls her suitcase on the bed while I pace restlessly, swinging my arms.

"I wonder why that officer asked us whether we still have food for a few weeks?" Unease floods my belly like a cold current and I open the closet doors. My fingers trace the contours of the jars before me, settling on one filled with pickled eggs. My preserves are way too heavy to take with us. I consider sadly how much dedication I've put into preserving sustenance for the days ahead. I imagine how delicious these eggs will taste, then realize I don't have to imagine and I twist the lid of the jar. The pungent aroma of vinegar and spices wafts up, tickling my senses. I pluck a single egg from the jar and put my teeth in it. The taste that floods my mouth is nothing short of delightful—a harmonious blend of sweet and sour, and the natural richness of the egg.

A bittersweet smile graces my lips. "Bastards," I grumble.

Aunty Hilda's busy packing her suitcase, but when I offer her an egg, she takes it and rests for a moment.

"Delicious," she responds.

"Yes...," I sigh deeply before getting to work on my own suitcase.

Early in the morning, the diesel engines wake me up. I jump out of bed and rush to the window. The sun casts its first rays over the emerald lake and the mountain range is reflected on its surface. Breathtaking. This may be the last time I see the sun rise over Sarangan. A feeling of sadness comes over me. If only we could stay.

I turn my attention to the blackened remains of the burned-down houses, hear the rumble of the approaching trucks. A stark contrast to the serenity of nature. Mount Lawu, the majestic sentinel, rises against the sky, its vegetation lush and vibrant. Telaga Pasir glistens like a sapphire jewel nestled in the heart of the earth.

A rustle behind me. I turn around. Aunty Hilda is awake.

"The trucks are coming," I say. "Look at how gorgeous the lake is."

She comes over and stands next to me. "Like a fairy tale," she whispers.

The minutes glide by while the two of us stay there at the window in our pyjamas. Silent. Immersed in our own thoughts. We see the Dutch Army dump trucks drive in, flying their red-white-blue flags, scaring up dust clouds. They come to a halt on the lawn. Dutch soldiers jump out. Before long, there's a loud banging at our door.

"Depart in one hour," shouts a male voice from the hallway.

I lift Aunty Hilda's suitcase into the first dump truck and help her climb onto the back. She takes a place on one of the benches mounted in the open flatbed. My own luggage is definitely heavier than fifty-five pounds, but I pretend it weighs nothing and hurl my things into the back of the truck. I manage to smuggle a typewriter and two backpacks full of tobacco. Nobody weighs anything, and no bags are inspected.

Otto and his family join us. My legs feel heavy. Sitting beside Otto on the bench in the open flatbed of the truck, together we stare over the lake. I think of the skinny little boy I was when we first arrived, trying to drag his suitcases up the hill. In the six years that followed, I've become a strong young man, thanks to the strict discipline of the German School, the labour service, and the many outdoor activities on the water and in the mountains. I had so many friends here. For the first time in my life, I didn't feel alone. I think of pastry chef Meiners and how he taught me his craft. I learned to take care of myself and Aunty Hilda. I felt free despite living in captivity. Neither the Japanese nor the Indonesians ever really harmed us.

Our fully loaded truck slowly starts to sway. And we're off. Away from Sarangan. Away from the lake and the mountains. A stabbing pain pierces through my heart and my throat is tight. The worried look on Aunty Hilda's face makes me think of all the hard work she put into Hotel Beau Site. With limited resources available, she has taken excellent care of everyone for years. Will she receive her bonus? She needed to take the hotel through these turbulent times in order to get paid. I look at Otto and see that he's fighting back tears. I lay my hand on his knee. He lays his on top.

My beloved lake, Telega Pasir, disappears from sight. Farewell, Sarangan.

Chapter 32

THE POLICE STATION

By afternoon, we arrive in Madiun, where we are housed in police barracks for the night. The place is sterile and unwelcoming: white, bare walls, fluorescent ceiling lights. A single washroom at the end of a long hallway. We set our luggage on the floor and sit on it.

Moments later, Mr. Waldstein comes to us with a worried look on his face. In a somber voice, he says, "Within half an hour of your departure, the Dutch Marines pillaged all the apartments in Sarangan."

"How do you know?" asked Aunty Hilda.

"I forgot one bag," he said, "so they let me go back and get it. Our houses were already aflame."

We stare at him in bewilderment.

"There goes my bonus," says Aunty Hilda, pain showing on her face.

"So, I bet the Dutch Marine Brigade is eating away my food supply," I mumble in frustration.

For the umpteenth time, we've lost everything.

After an uncomfortable night trying to sleep on my suitcase, unable to ignore the bulges—my typewriter and my two backpacks with tobacco—digging into my back, we prepare ourselves for further transport to the next police station in Semarang. I sit with Aunty Hilda on the staircase of the open lobby.

"Listen," she tells me. "Tomorrow, we will be transported to Batavia. They may split us up en route to the Chassé camp, or when we get there, and then we might not see each other for a long time. After all, you're almost eighteen years old and an adult. It's time we talk. I want to tell you the whole story."

I look quizzically at Aunty Hilda and feel a strange, tingling sensation going through my body.

"The whole story? What do you mean?" I stammer.

"A lot happened in the first year of your life," she says decisively. She takes both my hands in hers—it's serious business. "I'm going to tell you everything. The story of you. Will you listen?"

I nod.

Aunty Hilda straightens her back and begins to talk, "In the 1920s, after Papi and I bought the hotel, we always went on leave to Austria separately, usually five or six months away. The hotel was way too busy for us to both leave at the same time, so one of us always stayed behind to run it.

"It was near the end of 1929 when Papi went on leave. He was visiting his family in Austria and using his time there to recruit employees to help implement renovations and innovations at the hotel. We had a hard time finding experienced and reliable staff here. Qualified employees usually already had good jobs in the Dutch East Indies.

"At his sister Lintschi's in Vienna, Papi met her friend Maria Seiferth. She and Aunt Lintschi were colleagues—they both worked as seamstresses and cutters in the clothing industry. Maria had a son, Ferdinand, and two daughters, Mary and Elsa. Mary worked at the same company as her mother and Aunt Lintschi. She was sick and had contracted TB due to the damp, drafty housing in Vienna."

She's talking about my mother.

"Maria Seiferth asked Papi if he could use good employees at his hotel in Lembang. 'My Mary is a diligent seamstress and cutter, and although she has TB, she's a hard worker. The healthy climate of Lembang might cure her. My son, Ferdinand, who's a waiter, might also come in handy,' she told him.

"Papi and I discussed it over telegraph. According to Aunt Lintschi, the Seiferths were reliable people. Mary could work as the head of the linen room. That had always been my responsibility, but the hotel was expanding fast, and I had way too much on my plate. We decided that Mary join Papi on the boat upon his return. We also offered contracts to Uncle Ferdinand, as a waiter, Aunt Lintschi, as a seamstress, and her husband, Uncle Pepi, as our plumber. They were to arrive later, on a separate boat."

Aunty Hilda pauses and takes a deep breath. The muscles in my back tighten, and I straighten my spine. Now, of course, I'm expecting some long-hidden secret, but I get a sense that there is no way to prepare for what's to come.

"I trained Mary in her new job. She was indeed quick with a needle, and willing to work hard, and she did her job well. Not long after her arrival, our cousin Hans Schmid happened to visit. He'd also immigrated from Vienna to the Dutch East Indies and worked as a manager in a medium-sized hotel in Surabaja. Hans instantly fell in love with Mary. He didn't waste any time and immediately asked her to marry him. Mary said yes. We were so excited for them."

Now I'm confused. "But wait a minute…How could Mami have married Mr. Schmid? She was married to Papi, right? Her last name was Treipl, just like yours and mine."

"Let me correct you there, after all this time," Aunty Hilda answers. "I was married to your Papi. Not your mother!"

My brain is spinning, and I'm puzzled. Never had it occurred to me that Aunty Hilda and my father were married. As a little boy, I remember running back and forth between the private rooms—the rooms that Papi and Aunty Hilda shared, and the rooms Mami and I shared—which I was always free to enter. How could I actually have thought that Papi and Aunty Hilda were related? As brother and sister? Looking back, it didn't make sense. No. I'd just never thought about it. They never told me anything, and I never asked.

Aunty Hilda continues, "Your mother married Hans Schmid, and it was a gorgeous day. We celebrated the wedding in Bandung, with coffee and cake at the pastry shop Maison Bogerijen, on Braga Street. It was a shame, though, that Mary left with Hans to Surabaya, which meant I lost my well-trained employee—someone I trusted—so soon after coming to work for us.

"But a few months later, we received terrible news. Hans Schmid had sent Mary out the door while she was pregnant. He filed for divorce and said he would send her back to Lembang. One day, she arrived on our doorstep, heavily pregnant, and without pretence, announced to me, 'I'm carrying your husband's child.'

"What?" I exclaim.

"Yes, that's right. Your mother was expecting a child conceived by my husband."

"Unbelievable!"

"While Mary was standing there in front of me with her big belly, it hit me that the entire marriage with Hans Schmid had been nothing more than a sham, a strategy. On her part, at least. That is to say, I think Hans really loved her, but she knew that she was pregnant by a married man who was also her boss. She needed a husband to resolve her situation."

"Yes, but…How did you know she was telling the truth? I mean…How did you know for sure that the child was Papi's?" I ask.

"I only had to look at him. I could read it in his face. And I started counting the months. Mary had not been married to Hans long enough to be nearly ready to give birth."

I try to imagine my mother with a big round belly. I've never seen a photo of her from that era, and now I understand why.

"Your father always longed for children," Aunty Hilda continues. "And your mother had nothing to lose. That was to her benefit. But the truth struck me like a sledgehammer. I had had two miscarriages. I could no longer have children, and my husband had conceived a child with our youngest employee. You were conceived during the boat trip from Rotterdam to Batavia, Vicky. Your mother was eighteen and your father forty-two when you were born."

The world around me spins: I'm an illegitimate child. If I were to stand up straight, I would lose my balance. The ideal image that I had of my mother's virtue has fractured. Was this done on purpose? Could she be that calculated? Or had it all happened by accident? Had my father loved my mother at all? And if my father wanted children so badly, why had he spent so little time with me? A feeling of longing for my parents, gone forever, crashes over me like a wave.

"Are you okay?" Aunty Hilda asks, worried.

"Not sure…I'm a little dizzy. I'm realizing that I'm a b-bastard," I stammer, "and knowing that my parents are no longer here, I can never ask them any questions, never find out the truth."

"Shall I stop? Is it too much for you?" Aunty Hilda asks.

"No, no. I want to hear everything," I say firmly.

Aunty Hilda regards me with a searching look. "Okay, where was I? Oh yes…We had a huge fight on the doorstep of the hotel, the three of us. I scolded your mother for being a schemer, and I was furious with your father for cheating on me. And all of a sudden—I remember it like it was yesterday—your mother turned to

Papi and said, 'Never forget that this is your child. I want you to adopt him, and me, so that we all bear the name Treipl.' What a slap in the face."

Aunty Hilda seems to be reliving the whole story—a wave of frustration is washing over her. Her face has turned red and her nostrils vibrate.

"At first, I refused to take your mother in, but in the end, we allowed her to stay at the hotel," she continues in a calmer tone. "And then, on January 19, 1931, in the Borromeus Hospital in Bandung, you were born. You were named Victor Franz Schmid. Hans Schmid wanted nothing to do with you because you were not his child, but you got his last name because your mother was still officially married to him. The divorce papers had not been finalized yet. Papi was present at the delivery. You will see that in the birth certificate I carry with me here."

Aunty Hilda lays her hand on the small leather bag she has carried on her chest throughout the war.

"Your father was delighted with you—the child I couldn't give him. You were a healthy baby and long desired, but it was a big problem for him that you didn't bear his surname. Of course, I was jealous and extremely hurt. I didn't want to give up your father without a fight, and also, half of Grand Hotel Lembang was mine, but I found the whole situation completely unacceptable. 'Either she goes or I will,' I snarled at him, though truthfully, I didn't wish to leave him. So it happened that you and your mother left for Vienna, a few months after you were born."

"Have I lived in Vienna?"

Aunty Hilda nods.

"I'll show you a picture of you sitting on your grandmother's lap in Vienna," says Aunty Hilda. "Taken when I went to visit you there. You were the cutest little boy, wearing a dark blue velvet jacket with white buttons and a white collar, and a matching little blue hat."

My grandmother in Vienna…Mami's mother. What a strange idea.

"I've never seen any baby photos of myself. Are there any?" I ask.

"No, not from when you were just born. This photo in Vienna is, as far as I know, the oldest photo of you."

"And you came to Vienna as well? Why?" I ask, amazed.

"I wanted to see if you were healthy. But wait a minute. I need to go back in time a little. So, your mother had left for Vienna, and in Lembang, your father and I were trying to overcome the shock of his infidelity and repair our marriage. We loved each other very much, and we both wanted children. Rationally, I understood that he had had an affair, but emotionally, the situation was hard for me to digest.

"I asked my family in Salzburg for advice. 'It's ridiculous what Franz thinks he can get away with,' they said. 'An illegitimate son, whom he wants to adopt, as well as the mother of the child, at your expense. Just terrible.'

"But I knew the Indonesians looked at it from a very different angle. The second wife, bini muda, is a common thing in Indonesian families. She needs to know her place, treat the first wife with respect, and she has rights and duties within the family circle. That got me thinking.

"More than a year later, it was my turn to go on leave for Europe. Although we didn't talk about it often, I knew in my heart that your father missed you tremendously and longed to see you grow up. I have to admit, I was curious about you too, so I decided to travel to Vienna to visit your mother and grandmother."

"Is my grandmother still alive?"

"I don't know. There's been no contact since your mother's passing," says Aunty Hilda. "Your grandmother was a friendly, simple woman. I could see she loved her little grandson. I introduced myself as the owner of the hotel in Lembang, where Mary had worked. Your grandmother proudly stated that her daughter was married to a wealthy businessman in the Dutch East Indies. I suspected that she was referring to Hans Schmid, but I decided not to disabuse her of that story.

"Although you looked healthy, the condition the house was in definitely did not. It was damp. I knew, of course, that your mother had contracted TB there, but the living conditions were far more miserable than I could have imagined. I understood that you, Papi's only son, were at significant risk of also getting TB. That tipped the balance for me. I decided to return to Lembang and work on a solution.

"We wanted you to have our last name, Treipl, but your mother would only cooperate in the adoption if she got that last name as well. And while the thought of that made me bristle and haunted my dreams, I knew I had to get over it to get you back to Lembang. So, in 1933, the adoption was confirmed. You will read in the adoption deed that Papi adopted both of you with my knowledge, but without my approval. The condition I set was that your mother could not claim any inheritance. She had to be satisfied with what she got. You were almost three years old when you returned to Grand Hotel Lembang."

Aunty Hilda takes the small leather pouch from around her neck and unbuttons it. She rummages around, then hands me the adoption deed and the photo from Vienna, precious to me as a jewel, though this is the first I'm aware of either. A shiver runs down my back, and tears prickle my eyes as disillusionment, sadness, and anger all wash over me. Out of frustration, I jump up and hit my fists against the naked, white cement wall. Tears are running down my cheeks.

"Why the hell have you guys never told me anything?" I exclaim.

Never did I know that I grew up in an unusual family. That I was "different" in so many ways. The images flash through my mind: Aunty Hilda and Aunt Lintschi in our house on Crater

Avenue, gossiping about my mother. The rooms in the hotel, how the one belonging to my mother and me was across the hall from Aunty Hilda and Papi's. Still, I'd assumed that Papi was married to my mum since he always came to her aid when I had misbehaved, and how else could she afford the most expensive clothes in the latest fashion trends? Now I recognize, painfully, that my dad was supporting my mum as his bini muda, his second wife. Now I understand why I remained an only child. How often had I asked my mother to make me a sister? I think back to the modest earthen hill of my mother's grave and the puzzle is complete.

"I'm sorry, Vicky," says Aunty Hilda. "I don't know exactly why I waited so long. In some ways, I was afraid. You were small when it all happened, and I had to guide you through the war. We had the same last name, so you could easily pass for my son. Ignorance is bliss. It was safer that way."

"Okay, sure, it was convenient and safe for all of you. But before the war, Mami and Papi, why didn't they ever tell me anything? And now it's too late! I can never ask them," My throat tightens with frustration.

Aunty Hilda has gone quiet, and in a flash of awareness I become self-conscious of how selfish my reaction is. Here I am, whining about myself, pining for the man she loved and the woman who stole his affection, disregarding her heroic generosity. She brought me and my mother back to Lembang from Austria, even though she could no longer have children of her own. She tolerated my mother living under her own roof. She lost her husband and her hotel and took care of me as if I were her own child. Straight through the war, even. Time and again, she put aside her pride and sorrow, and chose a future with me.

I sit down next to her and put my arm around her.

"Thank you for taking great care of me all those years. If only you had told me sooner, I would have understood things a lot better," I say.

"I wanted you to be old enough to understand. But you're right, I've waited too long. I never imagined, when I first married your Papi, that this would happen to me. To me, the whole situation was an absolute nightmare. I was jealous and felt ashamed. I wanted a normal family, a loyal husband, a child of my own. But you were such a cheerful little boy that I quickly forgot those negative feelings. You brought sunshine into our home, for all of us. But I must admit that I wasn't sad when your mother passed away. Maybe I was punished for that, because only a week later, we lost Papi. Your father was the love of my life," says Aunty Hilda.

I'm starting to sniffle. Aunty Hilda starts to sniffle also, and we wrap our arms around each other. We're just sitting there, on the staircase of the bare white open lobby of the police barracks, in each other's arms, laughing and crying.

"I've known you much longer than I knew my mother, and much better, too. You are my Mutti. My mother. From now on, I want to call you that."

Chapter 33

THE ABYSS

The Dutch Marines flew us from Madiun to Batavia in an ancient Dakota, a military transport aircraft developed early on in the war. An army of photographers and journalists had gathered to come to see us; they were snapping away with their cameras around their necks as we disembarked. "Remnants of Sarangan's moffen nest—filthy Germans—captured in Chassé camp," was the headline in the newspaper *Java Bode* the next day. It was humiliating—I wish they would have left us alone. We never hurt anyone. Moreover, we are no moffen. We're Austrian, not German.

Now, it seems, it's our turn to be imprisoned behind barbed wire. But it's January 1949, for crying out loud. The war has been over for four years. Aunt Lintschi and Uncle Pepi went back to Austria in 1947, and Bruno was released from the camp in the British Indies in 1945. He lives in Salzburg and has been a free man for four years. But here we are, in Batavia, captives.

The Chassé camp, located on the outskirts of Batavia, is a compound of stone barracks with tiled roofs, a camp yard around the buildings, its boundaries laced with barbed wire and guarded by Dutch police. Within each barrack, walls of thin plywood rise seven feet from the ground, creating a semblance of separation within the communal space. Above, all is open. We the interned all sleep under the same high ceiling, though I'm in the men's section, and Mutti has her bed with the women.

Hygiene is poor in the camp, and privacy is hard to come by. And although everyone whispers here, we overhear each other's conversations whether we want to or not— sound carries, reaching far beyond our intended audience. In an attempt to carve out personal space, we hang fabrics and clothes, a makeshift barrier against the intrusion of gazes and prying ears. I don't feel like connecting with anyone around me, not even Otto.

When the Japanese ruled, this very building served as a brothel. Within these walls, the European women who were interned here were forced to act as "comfort girls" to the Japanese soldiers. A chilling token to their presence, the names of the prostitutes are intricately carved into the wood. A reminder of the agony they endured.

Amid the discomfort, I'm lying on my camp bed, and my thoughts go to the poor women who were abused here. The burden of my body is palpable—my limbs are aching, my legs heavy, my head is pounding, and the weight upon my chest immense. A black cloud is hanging over my world.

My bed is full of bedbugs. They show up at night and I awake with new bites all over, in their signature zigzag trail, so that my skin looks like a pale galaxy on a clear, dark night. The lice stink when you kill them, a scent so nauseating it almost makes me throw up. Some people think they smell like dirty laundry.

These red bumps itch like crazy. There's no way I can keep my hands off them. Only when I've opened a wound with my scratching does the itching stop. I wish I could be free of the wounds festering on my ankles, my legs, my arms, my neck, and my back. I'm tired. Dead tired. I curl up and close my eyes.

But I can't sleep. My mind is too active. So many thoughts are spinning around in my head. The story Mutti told me about my origins has struck the deepest part of my soul.

I'm a bastard. My parents are dead. There are no pictures of when I was born or when I was a baby. I'm an orphan, and all I have is my memories. We've lost all our possessions. We lost Grand Hotel Lembang. I feel miserable. Uncertain. Angry. I'm a maverick. I always was, and still am, tossed this way and that between people still at war with each other. In the country that I love, the country whose language I speak, I've become one of the unwanted white rulers. All because of the colour of my skin. And yet, other white men have encircled me with barbed wire and forced me to rot here.

What is the purpose of my existence? Something churns deep inside of me; I can't express this feeling in words. I'd like to cry. I want to disappear, but I can't go anywhere. It's sweltering hot, and everything is dusty and dirty. I'm soaked through with sweat. I turn on my side and get bitten again. Disgusting bugs! I jump up angrily and give a vicious kick to the rickety camp bed. The whole thing collapses, and now my shin is bleeding.

Ouch! Damn it!

I grab my leg with both hands and squeeze it hard, watch the blood ooze out. The sheet crumpled beside my bed moves, and the piercing, furtive eyes of a little boy look out at me. I shoot him an nasty look, and the boy takes off. The curtain falls shut.

The pain disappears. I have blood on my hands. When will all this crap finally come to an end? We are treated as prisoners of war. The PID, the Dutch Political Intelligence Department, keeps interrogating us. We are forty-two mothers and children and a few fathers. We've been screened to the bone and are all as poor as church mice. What the hell could these people want from us?

I curl up on my collapsed camp bed and close my eyes again. This world is unfair.

Chapter 34

THE PREVIOUS GENERATION

Mutti and I are sitting on the front steps of the shaded porch, in front of the camp's main building. There's no strict separation between men and women, and we are allowed to be outside the barracks, so we meet whenever we want. We have nothing to do, which is actually mind-numbing. There is no labour service, but we must report to the PID every day.

"Mutti, can you tell me about Papi's childhood?" I ask.

Having been through one of the most painful experiences in my life, I now have many questions. Questions about things that—strangely enough—never bothered me before.

She bursts into talk as if she'd been waiting years for my question.

"Sure. Papi was born in Vienna, on April 1, 1889, as the son of an innkeeper," Mutti says. "They had little money. His father had great faith in humanity and lost a lot of money as a result. He used to record his customers' drinks with a piece of chalk on a board, and half-drunk people wiped the board whenever they saw an opportunity. That's why there was no money for Papi or his two sisters for secondary education. Papi had little respect for his dad's lifestyle. After primary school, your Aunts Lintschi and Minnerl had to find jobs. Working in the clothing industry, their long days brought a paltry income. Papi had a completely different future in mind for himself."

"Yes, Papi went to the hotel management school, but how did he manage to do that?"

"Well, he worked as a waiter for years, even though he didn't like the job, and saved all his earnings in order to realize his dream. From a young age, he aimed to study at the hotel management school in Vienna. He made great connections and always left a good impression. He interned in renowned hotels in Lausanne and London to gain international experience—that's where he learned to speak English and French. He succeeded with flying colours. His aptitude for languages came in handy here in the Dutch East Indies. He also learned to speak Sundanese fluently and was able to communicate with our guests in their own language."

"I sometimes hated him for working hard," I say. "He was always crazy busy, and it felt like he used that as an excuse for not spending much time with me. I barely remember spending time with him. He was always there, of course, but in a way, he was remarkably absent. Why did he want to have children anyway?"

"Papi loved you. More than you will ever know. He did everything in his power to safeguard your future and to pay for proper education," Mutti says. "Maybe that was his way of showing love. It's a shame he was only in your life for such a short period of time."

"Yes, that is a shame, yes. Looking back, it would have been better if we, as a family, had spent more time together. Look at us now. What has all that hard work and saving actually brought him—or us?"

"Well, you can't change the nature of the beast. Success, money, and status were important to Papi. He enjoyed it. He was small in stature, and he wasn't financially well off in his younger years. Because of it, he had a life-sized inferiority complex. That's why he always dressed impeccably. He was also terrified of germs. Just like me, by the way. Everything always had to look good and be ultra-clean and bacteria-free. If he were alive today, he'd have given you the hotel. He'd have taught you the tricks of the trade."

"I don't know if I would have wanted that."

"Oh…No?"

"No."

"Why not?"

"I don't know if I would like to run a hotel."

"Why do you dislike that idea?"

"Always people around that you have to satisfy, demanding customers and staff members putting pressure on you. I remember there used to be strikes at our hotel because the employees wanted a raise."

"Well, there are pros and cons to every profession."

"Yes, but for an introverted person like me, it wouldn't be easy to survive in the extroverted world of a hotel. My favourite memory of the hotel is sitting in those tall trees where no one could see me, watching things below."

"So, what is it you want for your life?" Mutti asks.

"I don't know yet," I respond.

"Well, I think we should fight for the restitution of our possessions no matter what," Mutti says firmly.

"I understand that's what you want, but…We're getting off topic…You haven't answered my question yet. Why did Papi want children so badly? And how come the two of you weren't able to have children?"

"Both of us really wanted a family, but your father and I were first cousins. Our fathers were brothers."

"Opapa and Papi's father, the innkeeper, were brothers?"

Mutti nods.

"Was it normal to marry your first cousin?"

"There were no laws against it. I know other people who did the same. People didn't travel very far to find a spouse. And the closer you were to home, the more likely it was you'd marry within your family. But I do think that was the reason I kept having miscarriages; we were too close of relatives. When I was being treated for my second miscarriage, I had to undergo surgery, but where we were, there was no hospital around and no running water. A local doctor treated me. Most likely poor hygiene caused me to get an infection and become forever infertile."

Mutti's face wilts. "After that, I became depressed. I lived at that estate without work, without any distraction, while most of the women around me had one child after the other. The job offer at the motel in Lembang was a gift from heaven. In many ways."

"Wait a minute…This is going too fast for me. Estate? Motel? Didn't Papi have a job at Hotel Homann before you bought Grand Hotel Lembang?"

Mutti offers a subtle smile.

"Hotel Homann was only his first job in the Dutch East Indies. A lot happened before we finally got to Lembang."

"Okay, let's go back in time then…So, you and Papi were cousins. Had you known him since childhood?"

"No. We met for the first time as university students. I was born in Pola, now called Pula, a long way from Vienna."

"Where is Pula?"

"Far south of Vienna, on the Adriatic Sea. It was the only port city of the great Empire of Austria. My father—your Opapa—was a rear admiral with the Austrian Navy and commander of various ships. My mother died at a young age, and because Opapa worked at sea and couldn't take care of us, my brother, Rudi, and I were placed in foster homes."

"What illness did your mother have?"

"She died of cancer."

"What was it like, living in a foster home?"

"I'd rather not talk about that. My happiness only started when I met your father."

"How did you meet him?"

"At a family reunion in Vienna. He was twenty and studying at the Hotel Management School. I was a year older, studying piano at the Vienna Conservatory. He came walking into that reunion dressed in a really nice suit...," Mutti's eyes are starting to glow. "He was handsome, of slim build, and he was a true gentleman. It was love at first sight. Your father was overflowing with ideas and plans, and we couldn't stop talking. To me, he was like a ray of sunshine in the darkness."

I had never thought of my dad that way. "He was overflowing with ideas, you say. He was adventurous, you mean?"

"Yes, he had big dreams. Actually, we both had big dreams. Austria wasn't big enough for our aspirations."

"How did you get the idea to go to the Dutch East Indies?" I ask.

"A newspaper ad. Papi had just graduated and was looking for a job. They were headhunting for hotel managers in the Dutch East Indies and Buenos Aires, Argentina. We liked both options, but we were particularly charmed by the Dutch worldwide empire. The Dutch are a hardworking and prosperous people, and our cultures and languages are not that far apart, so we chose the Dutch East Indies. Papi wrote a letter of application to Hotel Homann in Bandung, which was already one of the best-known hotels in Java at the time. They were looking for a manager, and he was hired right away."

"Did you know what life would be like, out here?"

"We didn't have a clue, but we were young and ready for a challenge." Mutti grins. "It was near the end of 1910, and your father was twenty-one years old. We got engaged in Vienna, and shortly afterward, he left by boat to faraway, mysterious Java."

"All by himself?"

"Yes. The plan was that I would follow if everything went well. I arrived a year later when Opapa had to go to China with the Austrian Navy. He delivered me to Java and witnessed our wedding. We got married in Bandung in 1912. After that, Opapa continued on to China."

"That's where the decapitation story comes in," I joke.

Mutti laughs. "He could tell that story a thousand times. I'm so grateful that he spent the last years of his life with us. Opapa loved Lembang, and you have, at least, known one grandfather."

"Yes, he sure felt like my granddad. He behaved like my granddad. But, when you think about it, he actually wasn't…How long did Papi work at Hotel Homann?"

"Three years. Then he got another offer from an important return guest, Mr. Fletcher, an Englishman. He was the superintendent of tea at Francis Peek, a large company with many plantations. He noticed your father's drive and ambition and told him, 'Franz, in ten years, you'll still be manager here, earning only slightly more than you do today. Come work for me instead. I'll offer you a job as a planter, and I promise that you'll become a manager in under two years, earning three times what you do today.' Planters were highly regarded in Dutch East Indies society, and Fletcher's offer was music to our ears. The deal was settled quickly, and so we left on the omnibus train to Semarang, over three hundred miles away, in Central Java, where we ended up at a breathtaking tea plantation on Mount Ungaran."

"That sounds like the start of a great adventure," I respond.

"It was, for sure, but actually, living on a tea plantation in 1913 was less than idyllic," Mutti replies. "It was a lush paradise, but it lacked basic comforts. There was no running water, and the medical facilities and hygiene were inadequate. We didn't live in a brick house either. Our house stood on stilts and was made entirely of bamboo. Papi worked long days. He rode on horseback through the vast tea fields to check the planting and picking. At night, we kept the horse in a stable underneath the house, covered top to bottom in chicken wire to keep the black panthers out.

"I was by myself a lot. There were few distractions, and no cultural activities whatsoever. All in all, it was a massive culture shock for a young Viennese woman with a conservatory degree."

"Were there no other women you could hang out with?" I ask.

"There were many native families—no European women. But as you know, white Europeans aren't supposed to be close friends with natives."

"I know you think that way, but I don't share your opinion. I find it terribly contradictory. Papi never let me play with the native boys and girls 'because I could become one of them,' he always said. But what exactly does that mean to a kid growing up in the Dutch East Indies? I am one of them. Why should I consider myself superior to the people of the country I belong to? The country I was born in? I have many good friends who are Indo. And don't you remember the special bond I had with several of our native Indonesian staff members? Babu Siti was like family to me. I don't see what's wrong with being friends with them. I think it's time for a change."

"It's not good for your reputation," Mutti replies calmly.

"Reputation? That's bullshit."

"If you say so. As long as you don't come home with an Indo girl."

I look at her, baffled. "We don't even have a home to come home to," I reply sarcastically and get up. I'm not too fond of the turn this conversation is taking. I respect Mutti, but when it comes to this, I don't agree with her at all.

"Why is that so annoying to you?" Mutti asks. "It's just the way our society is."

"Mutti, white men brought that hierarchy here. This country is in the process of becoming independent. We white people can't play boss forever. By the way…Soma was Papi's best friend. How does that work?"

"Raden Somawidjaja is of nobility."

"Ah, now we're getting to the point." The scorn sharpens my voice, and now an awkward silence hovers between us.

"Do you want to hear the end of the story?" Mutti asks, irritated now.

"Yes, of course…Please."

"Well, we were living on that plantation, and World War One broke out. The Netherlands remained neutral, so the war passed us by in a certain sense. But there were political consequences. Your father didn't get the promotion he was promised, even though Mr. Fletcher liked him very much. The English had priority over us. Papi did not get fired, but he had no other choice than to stay in the same position for another four years. During that period, I had two miscarriages…," Mutti turns her face away. "The first time I got terrible abdominal pains. When the blood came—it was a lot of blood—I knew immediately it was over. The second pregnancy progressed much further. It seemed to be going so well, until the doctor told us during the examination that there was no heartbeat. I had to undergo surgery. The baby had to be scraped out of my womb."

I sit down next to her and take her hand in both of mine. "I'm so incredibly sorry you had to go through all that. That must have been a hideous experience for you," I whisper.

"Yes, it was. I was inconsolable," she says. "Depressed even, I think. Papi became restless. He wanted to take me away from that plantation. One day he saw a vacancy in the newspaper for a manager at a motel in Lembang. The hotel looked basic and poorly appointed, and the salary was middling, but the excellent location was a bonus. Because Lembang is high up in the mountains, the temperature was always pleasant. We knew the fresh mountain air would be good for our health and could make for a restorative destination for our guests. That's why we were interested. Papi applied and was hired."

"Was that our hotel?"

Mutti nods. "Yes, its precursor. Your father went to work, and I slowly started to recover, partly because I loved it in Lembang so much. In 1922, we were able to buy the motel. We wanted to turn it into a modern mountain resort. The business did well, and soon we were always fully occupied, and we expanded considerably over the years. We called in architect Albert Aalberts, who designed the new dining room and the lounge in the main building, and we had the tennis courts and the swimming pool built.

Because Papi had been a planter, he was able to become a member of the Society of Planters of the Preanger region, in Bandung. That was a big boost for our network."

"At least there was something good about having lived at that plantation…"

"Yes, indeed. Through the Society of Planters, guests came from all over the world. But imagining what's left of the hotel now…It makes me sad."

"I'm guessing the Japanese have completely run it into the ground. They were going to produce food there for the Japanese military that soldier told us. And when the Waldsteins came to Sarangan they said it had become a sauerkraut factory. Who could have come up with that idea?" I say.

Mutti looks intently at me. "It's never too late."

"For what?" I ask.

"I want it back."

Chapter 35

LAWSUIT

After enduring a month of screening by the Dutch Political Intelligence Department, Mutti and I are found "harmless," and we receive a pass that allows us to go in and out of the Chassé camp.

The next day, Mutti pays a visit to the Orphan Chamber to receive the remainder of the sale of the hotel. Unfortunately, after what we've used up during nine years of war, only half of the money remains, further halved by the guilder's devaluation postwar. She walks out with 25,000 guilders left in her bank account. To help out, I exchange the three months' salary that pastry chef Meiners had paid me in rupiahs for Dutch guilders at the market in Batavia. Additionally, I sell my supply of Virginia tobacco and the typewriter. We commence our search for a rental apartment, but unfortunately, there's a dire shortage of living space in Batavia, so we have no other option but to stay in the camp for now.

Immediately, Mutti initiates the battle against the Dutch state to regain Grand Hotel Lembang. She conducts interviews with three different lawyers: an Indonesian, a Dutchman, and an Italian. The latter is the son of our old neighbours, the Ursones. Each of the men agrees to work for her with the understanding that they will only be paid if they successfully complete the job.

All three lawyers write numerous letters and make various pleas without any result. According to the Dutch state, Grand Hotel Lembang has been lawfully sold to Mr. Schalks.

Ursone argues that when the rumour spread that Grand Hotel Lembang was for sale, both his family and Annie Meister, the owner of Pension Van Hengel, had wanted to make an offer for the amount of five hundred thousand guilders—and yet neither Annie nor his family was afforded the opportunity to put in their bid to the Orphan Chamber. Why were they not given the chance to make an offer? With what right could Mr. Schalks buy the hotel behind closed doors for just one hundred thousand guilders?

But the judge doesn't respond to Ursone's claim, his reasoning being that judicial decisions made during the war can no longer be challenged. The chapter is closed.

Grand Hotel Lembang has been sold, against the Orphan Chamber's promise, for a meagre amount. The seized jewels and gold bars are also missing. It's as if they never existed. We've heard that when the Dutch sent loads of gold bars from the Dutch East Indies to Australia, some of those planes crashed and sank to the bottom of the ocean.

"This isn't going anywhere. We'll probably never get our hotel back," I yell at Mutti in frustration. "The Orphan Chamber has been lying to us from the get-go."

We're sitting in the shade of the porch at the camp's main building again.

Mutti straightens her back. "Vicky, my entire life savings is tied up in that hotel. It's all I have left. Will you promise me something?"

"What, then?"

"Promise me that you won't give up the fight? There must be a way to reclaim our possessions. One day you'll meet a nice woman, and you'll have a family, and it'll be our family hotel again. I'll help you run it, and when I'm old and grey, I'll have a house to live in."

Mutti's voice sounds almost desperate.

The hard reality is this: Mutti is sixty-one, the age when she should be coming to the end of her working years, and yet her retirement provision has disappeared like snow under a late-spring sun. And while I understand her wishes, these court sessions are getting on my last nerve. The injustice rankles me as it does her. Yet the whole process frustrates me. I'm not sure that I want to continue pursuing this. I foresee years of struggle with a significant chance of failure. Why would I sacrifice my life for that?

"We're flogging a dead horse," I say.

"No, there must be a way," Mutti persists.

"But, Mutti, the judge already said that the Dutch state has legally closed off all decision-making that took place during the war. They won't change their stance. There will be no compensation. They aren't even going to say sorry." It's all so unfair.

"What bothers me the most is that Mr. Drijfhout's so-called 'administrative records' have gone missing. He said he was going to 'register' and 'manage' our possessions, right? Well, it was pure theft. And I knew it. Is there no justice remaining in this world?"

I sigh deeply and shrug my shoulders. "I'm not sure. It doesn't look good, though. I need to rethink our situation."

I hate to disappoint Mutti. I will not soon forget the torment on her face when she realized that she alone was still willing to fight to get the Grand Hotel Lembang back. But the feeling comes over me that my life has just been a succession of things happening to me. That I'm not in control of anything. And as grateful as I am for all that Mutti has done for me, I have to stand up for myself. I don't see myself fighting for this hotel for the rest of my life. Does it even make sense to prioritize possessions at all? We could lose everything in the blink of an eye all over again.

Chapter 36

MY FUTURE

We're not alone in our quest for justice. Numerous men at the Chassé camp—Germans, Hungarians, and Austrians who served the Dutch East Indies government before the war and, therefore, had become Dutch citizens—are entangled in endless bureaucratic procedures to regain their Dutch citizenship. This is essential for them to access their rightful pensions. Those men don't have a pass like we do to come and go from the camp, and we try to help them by delivering their letters when we're outside the camp.

Mr. Waldstein receives news that he isn't going to be reinstated as a Dutch citizen, simply because he briefly worked for the Indonesian government. How was he supposed to feed his family during the war? But the Dutch have a problem with it. All those years that he was the head of the Topographical Service at the Dutch Ministry of Water Management suddenly don't matter. They're not going to give him his government pension rights back, and he's asked to repatriate to Europe. Otto's father is still fighting for rehabilitation as well, and their family doesn't have passes either. It makes me think hard.

One day you'll meet a nice woman, and it'll be our family hotel again. When I'm old and grey, I'll have a house to live in. Mutti's wish has triggered a whole process in my head. What is our future going to look like? What do I want my future to look like? The hotel was her dream. Not mine. But what do I really want? What is my passion? I have no idea…

My former employer, Mr. Meiners, has risen to the position of head of the Kitchen and Beverage Department at the luxurious Hotel des Indes in Batavia. He has extended an invitation for an interview.

As I make my way towards the camp's entrance, I pass by the stone house of the camp boss. Two guards with guns slung across their shoulders are standing at the gate. I raise my pass, they nod in acknowledgment, and I step through, leaving behind the confines of the camp. Transitioning from behind barbed wire to the prospect of having an interview in the city; what a bizarre contrast this is.

Hotel des Indes is located on the Molenvliet canal, next to the impressive Dutch Savings Bank. Mr. Meiners receives me at his office, shows me around, and offers me a position as his assistant. I feel honoured; the job is appealing, as is the salary, but something stops me. I request some time to think about it.

The shortage of living spaces remains a challenge in Batavia, and we're yet to secure a rental place. Batavia's climate is unforgiving—hot and humid, conditions that don't bode well for Mutti, who struggles under the oppressive heat. Then there's the injustice of this place, the lack of money, the insufficient food, the bedbugs—these hardships all take their toll. Often, I find Mutti in the twilight of the bedroom, reclining on her camp bed, a damp handkerchief pressed to her forehead. Listless. That's not like her. While she's granted me the opportunity to determine my own path, her heart yearns to return to Bandung or Lembang, and she is anxiously awaiting my decision. The more time passes, the more weight rests on my shoulders.

The answer to my questions comes from an unexpected source. Mrs. Wisgrill, one of Mutti's best friends, invites us over for dinner. Having left Sarangan before us, she now works as an English teacher at the Carpentier Alting Foundation, a Dutch high school in the city.

Dinner at Mrs. Wisgrill's feels like a brief respite from the monotony of camp life. Her spacious home, that she shares with her three daughters, offers momentary relief from the barbed wire and barracks. The luxury of a seemingly free world still feels surreal to us. Although we have passes to get in and out of the camp and, in principle, we can go wherever we want, we do not yet feel free.

Mrs. Wisgrill cooks us a delicious dinner, a welcome respite from our meals at the camp's soup kitchen, and tells us enthusiastically about her job. About how the school started running again in 1946 and that a 'recovery period' was introduced to help the children, who had gone without education during the war years, catch up in their lessons. One tactic, for example, was to join two years together. By 1948, the school was fully operational again. The Dutch highschool system now offers various pathways to graduation, and different grades, each with its distinct trajectory and time span.

Mrs. Wisgrill's enthusiasm is infectious. As she speaks, my mind goes back to the great time I had at the German School in Sarangan. I loved going to school and had so many friends. I finally belonged. I became fit and strong and learned a lot. The disappointment of not being able to finish my studies still stings.

And in a sudden moment of clarity, a decision crystallizes in me. I know what I'm meant to do. I'm sure. Very sure. I wasn't born to run Grand Hotel Lembang, and I don't want to accept Mr. Meiner's job offer at Hotel des Indes either. I want to finish high school, graduate, and go from there.

Later that evening, back at the camp, I discuss it with Mutti.

"Mutti, do you think Mrs. Wisgrill can get me into the Carpentier Alting Foundation?"

"You want to go back to school?" Mutti's surprise is evident.

"Yes, I think it would shape my future better if I finish high school," I say.

A moment of silence follows.

"Vicky, it won't be an easy path. All courses are taught in Dutch."

"Well, I speak Dutch, don't I? It doesn't matter if it's hard. I want to graduate from high school," I respond. "It's not my dream to keep fighting for our hotel, Mutti. I've thought hard about it. I'd have to sacrifice a large part of my life to it, and we haven't had any success so far. I don't want to live in the past. I want to live my own life."

There, the words are out. Mutti stares at me, and a wave of heat flushes my cheeks. I shift restlessly, fidgeting with my shirt.

"I'm sorry to hear that," she murmurs. "It was a good life."

"I know."

"It was a wonderful place to live," she says.

"I know."

Mutti pauses for a minute.

"Vicky, I support the idea that you finish high school, but what do you envision beyond graduation?"

"I find that a difficult question. I don't know yet."

"Don't write the hotel off too quickly," Mutti insists.

I sigh deeply, my eyes fixed on the ground. I'm getting fed up with the hotel discussions. I wish she would stop talking about it.

"What are you going to do with Mr. Meiners's offer?"

"I will express my gratitude and tell him that I choose to finish high school."

"You sound determined," she says.

"I am."

Mutti stands up, pacing as if in deep thought.
"All right then. I will talk to Mrs. Wisgrill."
I dance with excitement. "Thank you, thank you, thank you!"

So, instead of me going to work for Mr. Meiners and bringing home a salary, Mutti is going to spend her last pennies on my education.

Chapter 37

THE CARPENTIER ALTING FOUNDATION

It is April 1949, four months after entering the Chassé camp. I'm eighteen years old and have been admitted to the third of five years of the secondary school at the Carpentier Alting Foundation.

I'm sitting in the library on a dark brown, wooden chair behind a wooden desk. Various desks are spread around the room, and shelves filled with books divide the space to create more privacy. Nothing is hanging on the white walls. It's very quiet here. A few other students around me are hard at work. I don't know them; no one from my class. I have to do assignments for algebra, geometry, and trigonometry. But oh, how I hate them. Not only have I never had these subjects before, I have to do it all in Dutch. My Dutch is much worse than I thought it would be. I speak it but forgot much of the grammar while attending the German School. I sigh deeply and open my trigonometry book. Triangles, sine, cosine, tangent. When will this ever be relevant to my life? I really don't see the point.

I slam the book shut and the student at the table next to mine shoots me an irritated look. I pull a face to make light of my outburst, but the other student doesn't see the humour in it. If only Otto were here—we always managed to find a reason to laugh together. But he's still at the Chassé camp and has no pass to get out; his father is still fighting for rehabilitation. Otto's getting bored stiff in the camp, as there is nothing to do, although he now has a girlfriend. Between my school commitments and his girlfriend, we see less of each other. Nevertheless, I bring books from the library back to the camp for him to read.

I open another book. Algebra. I used to think I was good at math. Addition, subtraction, multiplication, division—no problem for me. But algebra is different; it's calculating with letters: $a\times(b+c)=a\times b+a\times c$. Okay, I think I understand this one. I pick up my homework assignment: "Eliminate the parentheses of $(a+b)2\times(a+b)2$." I think. I'm quite sure the result of $(a+b)2$ is $a2+2ab+b2$. But then? I get to $a4+4a2b2+b4$, but the answer listed in the back of my textbook is different.

I don't know any of this shit. Answer B, maybe? I'll have to ask the teacher in class tomorrow, and I'm not too fond of doing that. Asking questions means standing out, and my cheeks tend to burn whenever I call attention to myself here. I'm the oldest student in the class by far, and I don't want to look stupid. Hopefully, I'm not the only one who doesn't get it...

The Carpentier Alting school is a white-chalked stone building, all classrooms attached to a porch, a high roof with red roof tiles. Towering palm trees grow alongside the lawn. I bought an old bicycle for next to nothing and ride from the camp to school in my best clothes. The hardest part is leaving Mutti behind by herself. She always sees me off and stands there until I'm out of sight around the corner.

Before I arrive at school, I make a habit of pausing to squeeze and kill the bedbugs under my belt. I'm ashamed of them and don't want the other children to see them. Most of the children at school are Dutch. They don't know where I live because I haven't told them. When the subject of war comes up, I safely keep my mouth shut. I've learned how to keep quiet.

Every day after school, I go to the library because it's impossible to concentrate on homework in the camp. And even though I work hard, I'm getting one bad grade after the other, even in German class. My only good grades are in statistics, visual arts, and physical education. I excel in volleyball. But the bad grades frustrate me immensely. I don't feel as much at ease at this school as at the German School. Here, I'm an outsider yet again.

By the end of the school year, my grades are still too poor to advance to the fourth grade. I feel guilty—Mutti knows I'm taking this seriously, but that doesn't change the outcome. She pays for school, and I want to graduate. But with my performance, that seems unlikely.

Fortunately, Mrs. Wisgrill makes a case for me during the teacher report-card meetings. She suggests that I take extra Dutch lessons during the summer holidays and choose specific majors, with an emphasis on economic subjects and modern languages. "Mark my word, he'll be in good shape halfway through next school year," she tells Mutti. Thanks to Mrs. Wisgrill, despite my bad grades, I'm admitted conditionally to fourth grade. I overflow with elation upon hearing the news.

Meanwhile, we're so over life at the Chassé camp. The climate here is stinking hot and sticky. We're technically allowed to move to the city, but there are still no rental spaces available in Batavia. Mutti wants to leave Batavia, but it would mean having to find a new school for me. She initiates a conversation with Mr. Zwaan, the principal of the Christian high school in Bandung. The school is well-regarded, and if he allows me in, we will also receive a residency permit for Bandung. The school is Protestant. Mutti is a Catholic, and I more or less gave up faith when I turned sixteen. The principal nevertheless accepts me as a student. Conditionally, in fourth grade, just like the Carpentier Alting school; I'll still have to prove myself to stay in grade four.

Finally, Mutti and I secure a rental home in a nice neighbourhood in Bandung, conveniently close to the school. The prospect of leaving the camp fills us both with excitement and anticipation for the new life awaiting us, but before I move forward, I'll have to find Otto. Leaving him behind while I'm embarking on a new chapter feels bittersweet.

As I stroll through the camp, a mingling of fragrant blooming flowers and swirling dust fills the air, accompanied by the joyful laughter and play of children. I find Otto engrossed in a book on his bed. "Otto, I came to say goodbye," I say softly, trying not to startle him. He jumps up, and we step outside, looking for a quiet corner at the camp. The late afternoon sun is hanging low. We stand together awkwardly, wordlessly, the air heavy with sadness and anticipation. I break the silence. "Otto, I'll be attending the high school in Bandung after the summer, and we finally found a rental home as well. It's a chance for a better future, and I'm excited about it. I have to go. But leaving you here…It's not easy."

Otto manages a small smile, "I understand, Vicky. I'm envious, but I would have done the same thing if given the opportunity. I desperately want to finish high school, too." Otto sighs deeply, "I'll get there one day. But my dad will have to resolve his dispute with the government. It's taking forever."

"I know," I nod, "but yes, you'll get there. This camp is just a temporary hurdle. You'll overcome it. And we'll stay in touch, write letters."

"Absolutely," Otto exclaims. "And we will see each other again once I have a pass."

"I'll be waiting for that day."

I choke back my emotions as I grasp Otto's shoulder. We exchange a heartfelt hug, holding onto the familiarity and warmth we found in each other. Then I start to walk away, waving. Otto watches me go. A fine layer of loneliness settles in my heart. How I'll miss my dear friend.

Throughout the summer in Bandung, I receive extra lessons, and my Dutch progresses in leaps and bounds. Mutti rents a piano and, for the first time in years, starts playing regularly. While I once favoured my Mami's piano playing, I now enjoy listening to Mutti play. She begins teaching and starts earning an income. Slowly but surely, both she and I start to renew our zest for life.

One of Mutti's clients is a friendly man, a Hungarian. His name is Sándor Gudjár. He visits every week and plays the piano very well. They often play four-handed pieces and they always seem to be in the middle of an endless, lively discussion. I'm delighted for Mutti that she has found a new friend.

School starts in September. I still have to work hard, but now I can follow the classes quite well, and my performance is improving. At Christmas, I eagerly receive my first report card: all my grades are good, and I'm officially admitted to grade four. I'm allowed to stay.

On December 27, 1949, over the Christmas holidays, the Netherlands, under enormous pressure from the United States, finally recognizes Indonesian Independence. The transfer of sovereignty is signed in Amsterdam, and Sukarno becomes the president of the republic.

A new era begins. The Chassé camp has been closed, and many of my friends, including Otto, begin attending high school in

Djakarta, the new name for Batavia. I still see Otto, but only during the holidays, because his father has a new job in Djakarta. The Waldsteins never left for Europe, and Mr. Waldstein gets a job with the Indonesian government again. They move back to Lembang, near the Bosscha Observatory, and their oldest daughter, Helga, joins my class.

In May 1951, I'm in the middle of my final exams. I'm now twenty years old. The school year was a blur, and I live from exam to exam, but then, I pass gloriously. Mutti is so proud and gives me an extraordinary gift: a chance to get my driver's licence, a symbol of newfound freedom and independence.

The summer holidays are approaching, a welcome end to the academic rigours. I spend my time swimming with my classmates at Tjihampelas, the pool in northern Bandung. With each splash, game, and dive the weight of responsibilities and studies lifts, replaced by the simple joy of being alive. For the first time in a long time, life feels carefree again.

Chapter 38

THE PAMANUKAN AND TJIASEM-LANDS

Three weeks after graduation, I bump into an old school friend who tells me enthusiastically about his work in the cultures—the tea, rubber, and coffee plantations—of the Pamanukan and Tjiasem Lands. He also says that there's a vacancy for an assistant at the head office in Subang, and he gives me the name of the director to get in touch with.

I'm excited about his story, so I discuss the issue at home with Mutti. Subang is located north of Lembang, on the north side of Mount Tangkuban Perahu. Being accepted would mean that I leave the house, coming home only on weekends. It would mean a significant change for Mutti. For both of us. But I must start earning my keep somehow, so she agrees. With her help, I write a letter of application, and I'm invited for an interview.

Sitting at a table at the head office in Subang with the English chief officer, who doesn't speak a word of Dutch, I do my utmost to make myself understood in my high school English.

"Victor, a pleasure to meet you, chap. Please, tell me something about yourself."

"Yes, sir. Well, I just finished high school at the Christian Lyceum in Bandung. My mother and I live in Bandung, but I grew up in Lembang. I speak several languages, including German, Dutch, and Malay, and I learned English at school."

"I see. Why do you want this job?"

"I find that a tricky question to answer, sir, because this will be my very first office job. I worked at a bakery, though, and I have a great recommendation from Mr. Meiners, my old boss. I love to learn, and I'm good at math. I'll do anything that needs to be done."

"Are you aware of what we do in this company?"

"Ha, I have an answer to that. Fortunately, I went to the library in Bandung to collect information. It was there that I discovered that P&T-Lands, with more than seventy thousand hectares of land between the Pamanukan and Tjiasem rivers, is among the largest companies of its kind in the world and the largest in Java. An Anglo-Dutch company, it's part of The Anglo-Dutch Plantations of Java, Ltd., whose management is based in London. They sell tea, rubber, kina, cocoa, coffee, kapok, sisal, pepper, and rice worldwide."

"Impressive. What do you do in your spare time?"

"I love sports, sir. I was a fan of volleyball at school. I'm good at athletics, long-distance running, and I like to swim."

"That all sounds good. We like active people. We English folks like ball games, such as hockey, tennis, cricket, and golf. We play sports every day after work. Does that appeal to you, Victor?"

"Yes, sir."

"You play volleyball, you said?"

"Yes, sir."

"We don't have that here yet. Maybe you can help us out setting something up. You're hired, Victor Treipl."

"Thank you, sir. I will not disappoint you."

"Brilliant. Here's your contract. It is a full-time job. Your salary is two hundred and fifty rupiahs or two hundred and fifty Dutch East Indies guilders a month. On top of that, twenty-five guilders in British pounds are put aside for you on a monthly basis in a savings fund at the Barclays Bank in London. You'll get a room at the P&T motel, nearby. Please walk along with me, and I will introduce you to the transportation service. They drive back and forth between Bandung and the head office. We expect you to arrive here next Monday, at 7 a.m."

I can't believe my luck. Real life has finally started. I have a feeling that the deciding factor was my liking sports. I get a job as an import assistant in the indenting department, the company's central purchasing department. Everything their twenty-plus estates need—from machine parts to diesel engines, to whiskey and bicycles for employees—is imported by this department from England, the Netherlands, and Germany.

My very first day starts with great dismay, though. The Friday before I started, a Dutch employee in the process of delivering the weekly wages to his gardening team was shot and robbed of all the money. He didn't survive the shooting. They bury him on my first day of work.

In six months, I'm fully trained. To me, memorizing data is practically a sport. When the English chief engineer calls over the top floor's railing, "What's the order number of that stainless steel order?" I recall off the top of my head and shout, "Order number 20124, sir." For some reason, it takes my boss, Rob van der Veen, much longer to come up with the answer and he has to search through the files.

But I soon find out that my eager behaviour is not appreciated. The administrator, who is the head of domestic and foreign departments, takes me aside and requests that I communicate such things to Rob van der Veen only, who will then pass the information on to the chief engineer.

"You'll have to respect a certain hierarchy here," he warns.

"Yes, sir. I understand," I answer, feeling subdued. It is my first experience with internal politics.

The company is wealthy, and its culture of luxury touches every aspect of its employees' lives. It feels like living in a bubble. I have an excellent starter job and earn a decent salary, from which I can pay Mutti a monthly allowance. I live in the P&T motel, where a babu takes care of me—cleaning, doing laundry, cooking for me. At the end of every workday, I play hockey, tennis, cricket, or golf with coworkers. I often go to the pool. And the chief officer is true to his word: just like he said in my interview, they ask me to set up a volleyball club. In the evenings after we've had our exercise, everyone goes to the social club for highballs and other alcoholic beverages. The men dress up and wear their short hair combed smooth; the unofficial uniform is a white jacket, a white shirt, and a black bow tie. The English bosses play snooker, and the alcohol flows freely. The chief engineer in particular likes his alcohol. Yet he shows up in the office on time every morning. In what state, well, that doesn't really matter.

The workweek ends on Saturdays at twelve-thirty p.m., after which I take the transportation truck to Bandung, along with several other colleagues. We all gather at the designated spot for the truck, and when it arrives and lumbers to a stop, we step into the back and take a seat on the benches. It's a two-hour drive before I'll be home with Mutti, with several stops along the way. For the first half-hour, there's a lot of chatting. But after that, everyone's fighting sleep, and doing their best not to fall off the bench when they lose that fight. On Mondays at six a.m., they pick me up, and by seven a.m., I'm at the office again.

Mutti always looks forward to seeing me. However, I also

dedicate a substantial amount of time to reconnecting with my old friends in Lembang, a short half-hour drive away by car and hired driver. Mutti indulged in a second-hand piano purchase, and her connection with Mr. Gudjár has deepened. Sándor Gudjár is a charismatic man of shorter stature and a stocky build, with a large head of hair and a curly moustache. He has twinkling blue eyes, likes to talk, and smiles a lot and often. She's from Vienna, and he's from Budapest; they have a lot in common. Their shared piano playing has brought them closer and spurred them to venture out together more often—both avid walkers and hikers, they find common ground in their outdoor pursuits. On Saturday nights, they eat out at various restaurants along Bandung's Braga Street, which offers a delightful range of choices, a combination of Indonesian and European food. Occasionally, they even treat themselves to a movie outing or take in performances by local musical drama groups. The bond between Mutti and Mr. Gudjár has brought a new radiance to her life, and witnessing her happiness warms my heart.

Meanwhile, my friends—Helga and Jutta, and several others—are turning Grand Hotel Lembang's pool into their go-to hangout place. The Schalks brothers, the owner's sons, seem to be the driving force behind my friends' frequent visits. Ben and Cor, with their blue eyes, blond hair, and charming demeanour, are a popular duo, my age. Yet, it feels awkward for me to join them. After all, they live in our hotel. Maybe their bedroom is even my old bedroom. In a way, I'm intruding. But what can I do about it? I want to hang out with my friends, right?

While I haven't discussed my excursions to the hotel with Mutti, I did once venture down that road, trying, very carefully, to gauge her opinion on the topic, but that conversation didn't go well. I asked her what she thought of Mr. Schalks, the new owner.

"He's an asshole," Mutti remarked candidly.

"An asshole?" I couldn't believe she said that. "That's quite the allegation. Why?"

"He knew the hotel was ours and that there was something fishy about the deal with the Orphan Chamber."

I don't entirely agree with her. Mr. Schalks was allowed to buy the hotel for what he knew was a very reasonable price. And why wouldn't he? If I had been in his shoes, I probably would have done the same. I understand Mutti's aversion, but it doesn't make him an asshole.

So, I've decided to go to the hotel and just not talk about it at home. I do try, though, when I'm there, not to draw attention to myself, to blend in with the larger group. To be invisible—without having to climb the ironwood trees as I used to, whose upper branches would not now hold my weight. But one day, as I sit on the pool's edge, my feet cooling in the clear water, and Helga splashing around on a tube nearby, a tap on my shoulder startles me. I turn around and see Mr. Schalks.

He must have seen the shock on my face. "Don't worry, I didn't mean to scare you," he says. "I just wanted to say that I know who you are and that you're friends with my sons. I can imagine that your mother might not be pleased with the state of affairs after 1940, but I'd like you to know that you're welcome here. There will always be a bed available for you in one of my sons' bedrooms, and for you, meals and drinks are on the house. No need to thank me for it every time. I just want you to feel at ease here."

I stare at the ground. Mr. Schalks kindly pats me on the shoulder. Then I get up. Grateful but slightly shaken, I reach out my hand to him and stammer, "Thank you so much for the offer, Mr. Schalks. I really appreciate it."

He shakes my hand, nods, and walks away.

Helga, having overheard the conversation, hoists herself out of the pool, and says, "Wow, that was a kind gesture. He's a remarkable man. Will you tell your mother?"

"Yes, I agree that he's a kind man," I answer, though a critical voice nags at my conscience. I will never, ever be able to tell Mutti this. Think about it: instead of fighting for ownership of the hotel, I hang out at the pool and every now and then even stay overnight with the Shalks brothers. It's treason, says the little voice in my head. But three lawyers have failed to bring us justice. I don't believe anymore that the Dutch state will compensate us.

"Helga, I can't tell my mother about this. It would break her heart. I'm asking you: please don't say anything to my Mutti. Will you promise me that?"

Helga stands up from the pool's edge and lays her hand on my shoulder, "I understand, Victor. It's a complicated situation. Of course, I promise you that."

I exhale deeply.

To shift the focus, I playfully nudge Helga into the pool, and with a mischievous grin, I follow suit, splashing into the water. We share a laugh as we resurface. The refreshing pool serves as a reprieve from life's complexities. I find myself drawn to Helga, who used to feel like a sister, but now I appreciate her on a deeper level than mere friendship. However, she hasn't shown any romantic interest in me. It seems that her attention is instead captivated by outgoing Cor Schalks.

The vibrant energy of our group of friends radiates nearby, and the camaraderie continues. I lay my hands on a floating tube, effortlessly pulling myself onto it and a familiar game begins: the friendly competition to assert ownership over the prized tube.

Chapter 39

MR. VON ZBORAY

I'm in trouble. I messed up. That's why I'm here, in the chief engineer's office, with him and the assistant manager of my department.

"How the hell did you manage to drive the car off the road, Treipl? No, let me rephrase that: why were you even driving the company car in the first place?" the assistant manager asks.

At P&T-Lands, staff members aren't allowed to drive a car themselves. Each vehicle has an Indonesian driver. I wanted to go to the pool and do some laps after work, but the pool is a forty-five-minute walk outside of Subang, so I called the transportation service to drive me there. I must confess the whole story. How do I explain, honestly, in a way that won't make things even worse for myself? I shift uncomfortably in my chair.

"I'm sorry, sir," I start. "I was at the pool, and on the way back, I persuaded the driver to allow me to drive the last leg home. I do have my driver's licence. But I made a bad judgment call. I went over thirty miles an hour on the dirt road. It was too fast, and I slipped off the road and ended up in a cluster of bamboo…"

My mind flashes on the actual events. As I was steering the car, the driver was backseat-driving like a nervous monkey on caffeine, clearly deviating from his job's script by allowing me to take the wheel. Feeling a surge of confidence, I decided to show off my expertise, imagining I was a race-car driver. I hit the gas, jiggling the steering wheel, underestimating the car's capabilities. But oh, the car had its own plans—it tilted onto two wheels, real-life acrobatics in progress, and I unintentionally parked the whole thing on its side amid those bamboo stakes. Can you believe it? Miraculously, nobody got hurt, and despite my initial shock, I couldn't help but find the situation quite comical. A vague grin appears on my face.

"What's so funny, Treipl? This is serious business. You violated the rules and caused damage to the company car. This is going to cost you your job."

I'm stunned. I knew such a strict consequence was possible, theoretically, but didn't imagine they'd apply it to me.

"Oh, no, please! It won't happen again. I'll pay back the damage if only I can keep my job," I beg.

"Absolutely not. Rules are rules. We can't make any exceptions for you. You will be handed your letter of resignation in an hour. You can wait outside until it's typed up."

"No! This can't be true. My mum and I depend on my salary."

"You should have thought of that earlier," the assistant manager replies coolly.

He gets up, opens the door, and gestures for me to exit. I leave the office, my head spinning. It never ever occurred to me that I could lose my job so easy. P&T is a major, essential employer in West Java; a dismissal will surely ruin my professional reputation. So much for my future…How will I face Mutti? What will she say when I show up at her door without a job?

I take a seat in the hallway.

Mr. Von Zboray walks by and sees me looking crestfallen. He's the superintendent of rubber, a naturalized Hungarian, and he knows me well.

"What's going on, Victor?" he asks.

I explain the story with a red face.

"I must admit, that wasn't a good move. But I don't like discrimination. Listen up. Recently, the superintendent of tea, an Englishman, totalled a company car. But he got a new car. He wasn't fired. I'm going to file a complaint against your termination."

I look at him in astonishment as he walks away. There's a glimmer in my chest—of hope, of relief—and I perk up a little.

Half an hour later, Mr. Von Zboray and P&T's CEO stride past me without so much as a glance my way and enter the assistant manager's office. Their voices volley but I can't make out what they're saying. After another half hour, Mr. Von Zboray comes out and gestures at me to follow him. I get up in a hurry, and the two of us walk to his office. He closes the door behind me.

"Take a seat, Victor," he says.

"Thank you," I say shyly.

"Listen. You've threaded the needle. I can make you a proposal. You have the choice to either tender your resignation or take a job as a planter on a P&T rubber plantation in Central Java. After six months, you can choose to either remain a planter or return to your old job at the indentation department."

I don't need to overthink this. "I gladly accept the job as a planter. Thank you so much."

"Good choice. That's what I like to hear. Your termination letter will be destroyed, and you'll receive instructions from me on how to travel to the plantation. They'll expect you there next Monday."

I am beyond grateful. I say goodbye to Mr. Von Zboray and my colleagues at the office, pack my bags, and call the transportation service for a driver to take me to Mutti in Bandung.

Chapter 40

AT MUTTI'S

Mutti stands in the doorway, watching the driver unload my suitcases. I read her thoughts, *He's been fired*, but she says nothing and receives me warmly, as always. I bring her up to speed about the car in the ditch, the conversation with my boss, and Mr. Von Zboray's offer. I try not to leave out any details.

She keeps silent. It's a discomforting silence.

"Vicky," she finally says. "I was hoping that one day you'd come up with a plan to reclaim our hotel and belongings. That you would fight for a future I can be part of. But now, you're going off to live even farther away from me. Semarang is not around the corner. You won't be coming home at all for the next six months."

"Listen, if I hadn't accepted this job, we wouldn't have any income," I say. "I'm extremely glad they didn't kick me out. Mr. Von Zboray saved me. P&T is the largest employer in the entire region.

And as far as our hotel is concerned, haven't we already discussed that topic extensively?"

"What do you mean? I agreed that you could finish high school. I sacrificed my last cents on it. I also told you then that you shouldn't give up on our hotel too quickly. But apparently, you forgot about that altogether?"

"Mutti, it's no longer 'our' hotel. We've hired three lawyers, and we lost the lawsuit. We've exhausted our options."

"You haven't tried anything at all," she shouts. She suddenly stands up, rips off her apron, squints out the window at the hospital in the distance as she stomps to the kitchen, where she throws her apron over the kitchen chair. I follow her there.

"Listen, the Orphan Chamber's paperwork has gone missing, and the legislation has changed so that, as far as the government is concerned, they don't owe us anything," I object.

"You could fight them on that."

"That'll be a titanic battle. With, as I see it, a high probability of failure. Do you want me to sacrifice my life for this cause?"

"You're just not willing to fight," she says. "To stand up for yourself."

"What? How can you say that?" My anger rises like bile. "Are you trying to provoke me? Well, how about this: it doesn't sit very well with me that you kept things from me for so long. Important things. Things that affect who I am and how I feel, my identity. Now that I finally know who I am, I'm busy trying to make a life for myself. I have a good job, my first real job, and I make a living for both of us. Why can't that be enough for you? You're upset because I'm not interested in running the hotel. Great. I get it. But guess what? That was your dream, not mine."

"Alright then, Vicky. Well, what am I still doing here? You're all I have left. If you abandon me, what am I supposed to do? I may as well leave."

"And go where? To Europe? Why? You can't be serious. You're the only family I have."

"I know that. But you're gone all week, and now you're about to leave for Semarang, for six months. Thank God I have Sándor. He's the only reason I'm still here."

Her words hurt—they hit in the pit of my stomach. "I don't want you to leave. You're my mother. I'm sorry you're by yourself so much," I say. "I'll look for another job, closer to home. Or I'll call you every day. I promise I'll pay more attention to you."

"Don't feel obligated now to be stuck here with your old mum." As she walks out the kitchen, she casually adds, "That plantation you'll be working at is right next to the tea plantation where Papi and I used to live."

A light shiver passes through my body. That's where they lived in that bamboo house on stilts, in the middle of nowhere, with no running water and panthers roaming around at night. Would it still be as rustic out there as it was back then? I stay behind on the living room couch, my head roiling with doubts.

Chapter 41

KALI MAS

As per Mr. Von Zboray's instructions, I take the train to Semarang on Monday. Mutti's goodbye feels somewhat reserved. Different than usual. During the train ride, our argument keeps running through my mind. I shouldn't have gotten so angry.

In Semarang, I'm picked up at the station by Mr. Siogo, the assistant of the P&T estate Kali Mas, which means Gold River. Upon arrival at Kali Mas, Mr. Kramer, the administrator, welcomes me and shows me my room in his big beautiful house. Then he takes me to the office and introduces me to my colleagues, Bolt and Siogo.

Mr. Kramer briefly explains my duties and asks, "Victor, do you have a driver's licence?"

I'm completely baffled. Surely they won't have me driving? "Yes, sir."

"Good. Then, as of now, you'll be responsible for driving the Jeep. Siogo's been the one driving it so far, but he doesn't have a licence, so that's an accident waiting to happen," says Mr. Kramer.

Priceless! I wish I could share this story with Mutti. She would've found the humour in it. I imagine her shaking with laughter; her laughter is so contagious when she lets it out.

Every morning at six a.m., I drive with Bolt or Siogo to the rubber forests to inspect the work of the Indonesians tapping the latex from the trees. The latex is harvested by slicing a quarter-inch groove into a rubber tree's bark with a hooked knife and peeling back the bark.

My task involves scouting areas of the forest for new rubber plantings. I've noticed that the other assistants are more than willing to delegate this job to me, and I soon discover the reason why. The rubber trees must be meticulously planted in straight lines, maintaining a four-meter distance from one another. Determining the most efficient direction for these rows requires trudging through the ten-foot-tall elephant grass. This grass has razor-shape edges, leaving me with bleeding legs at the end of the each day. However, the work doesn't bother me. It brings back memories of joyous times spent playing in shorts in the same grass around Ursone's farm. Moreover, the cuts tend to heal swiftly, making it a manageable experience overall.

There are few distractions from the work. In the evenings, I retreat to my room to enjoy reading the newspaper or immersing myself in a captivating book. My taste in books is quite diverse, ranging from English espionage novels to philosophical works like Herman Hesse's *Siddhartha,* or any other compelling book that happens to cross my path. Or I visit my colleagues, who live with their wives and families in the houses around the administrator's house. For supper, I go to the Siogos', and I pay them for my meals. Siogo's wife is a lovely lady and a great cook. Bolt, though, knocks back a bottle of gin every night.

Three months go by. I'm reading in my room, as I do so often now, when Mr. Kramer calls from the hallway.

"Victor, your mother is on the phone."

"Thank you, sir, I'm coming.'"

I throw my book down, walk down the hall, and pick up the receiver.

"Vicky?"

"Yes, Mutti, it's me."

"Vicky, something terrible happened." Her voice sounds raspy and broken.

"What is it?"

"Sándor has had a serious motorcycle accident."

For a moment, I'm speechless. I try to make sense of her words. I can picture Sándor with his contagious smile and curled moustache.

"Oh, no. How did that happen?" I ask.

"He was hit by a car. At a crossroads. It wasn't his fault."

"Is he okay?"

"He died of his injuries last night."

I have to sit down. My head and shoulders hang, and I'm dizzy with the unfairness of this tragic loss. Mutti was so happy with her new friend, and she so deserved to find love.

Mutti, in her distress, starts talking very fast. "It happened yesterday morning. I got a call from a nurse at the hospital. She told me that Sándor had had an accident. She didn't want to explain much, but she said things didn't look good and that he'd been taken to hospital by ambulance. She said Sándor was conscious and had given her my phone number."

The line crackles.

"Vicky, are you still there?"

"Yes, I'm here. I'm trying to process the news."

"I ran straight to the hospital," she continues in a shaky voice—the Bandung Hospital; you can see it in the distance from her living room window. "His left leg was shattered, he had a broken wrist, but worse, he was spitting blood. His lungs were perforated.

When he saw me, he was still smiling, but then he lost consciousness." Mutti begins to sob intensely on the other side of the line. Oh, my heart breaks for her!

"I'm so incredibly sorry," I stammer. "I wish I was with you. What's going to happen now? Does he have any family around?"

"Only his brother. I called him right away. The funeral will take place tomorrow. He'll be buried in the European cemetery."

My mind goes back in time to Mami's earthen hill. To Papi's coffin on the shoulders of six Indonesian men. Now Mutti must go through it all again.

"God, I wish I was there with you," I say. "This is all so awful."

"Thank you, darling. Yes, I also wish you were here. You're so far away…"

There's a silence. The line crackles again.

"I love you so much, Mutti, and I will be there with you in my thoughts. I wish you lots of strength tomorrow," I say.

"I love you too, my dear son. It was wonderful to hear your voice."

We hang up.

I slump into the hallway chair, my fingers tangled in my hair. Why? Finally, she found a partner again and wasn't alone in her world. In Sándor Gudjár's presence she seemed transformed— more playful, laughter dancing in the air as they bantered. And the music, oh the music. They'd entwine their melodies at the piano in the cozy living room.

Classical pieces for the four-hand piano would come to life under their skilled fingers in the afternoons, when the room bathed in a soft, golden glow and the slightly cooler air carried the scent of the evening breeze through the open window.

Mutti's smile, radiant and free, while playing with Mr. Gudjár, warmed my heart. I recall the delicate sounds of the piano keys, the soft, rhythmic tapping of the piano pedals, and the occasional squeak of the piano bench as they shifted their weight. Her playing, more refined and melodic, combined beautifully with Mr. Gudjár's robust and lively style, despite his lack of a conservatory education.

Why must she endure so much suffering? I wish I could dash home, be there to support her. Why this cruel physical distance keeping us apart?

Chapter 42

BACK TO BANDUNG

Six months pass. My contract with Kali Mas is about to expire when I find myself standing in front of Mr. Von Zboray, tasked with making a choice. Rather than stay in Semarang, I choose to go back to the job at the Subang office, where I'll be closer to Mutti. He tells me that I'll be trained to replace my old boss, Rob van der Veen, who is leaving for the Netherlands for half a year.

It is the last week of March 1953. I take the train to Bandung and walk from the station to Mutti's house on Frans Hals Lane, near the hospital and the Christian Lyceum. I'm looking forward to seeing her again. I haven't told her that I'm coming home today—I wanted to surprise her. I gently turn the doorknob and open the door.

"Mutti! I'm home!" I shout cheerfully, lowering my luggage to the floor.

I listen. No response. Maybe she's in the kitchen? I walk from the hallway to the living room.

The piano is gone.

It feels as if life is flowing out of me.

I accelerate my pace to the kitchen, shouting, "Mutti! I'm home!" The kitchen is empty. There is nothing, absolutely nothing, on the counter. I open the refrigerator. Empty. I'm terrified now. I run to her bedroom. Empty. I open the wardrobes. Empty!

Slowly I lower myself onto the bed.

She's gone. She left without saying goodbye. My throat tightens, and I panic. It can't be true. I force myself to think clearly. Where would she be? Visiting a friend? Surely, she wouldn't have taken the boat to Europe?

I walk back to the living room, to the small desk in the corner of the room. There is an envelope. FOR VICKY, it reads.

The bottom drops out of my stomach.

I pick up the envelope, take it over to the couch, and plop down. I'm too scared, at first, to open it. I turn it over in my hands and stare at Mutti's handwriting for some time. FOR VICKY. The tears start running down my cheeks. I walk into the kitchen, take a sharp knife from the drawer, and carefully cut open the envelope.

Bandung, Friday, March 6, 1953

Dearest Vicky,

As you read this letter, I'll be aboard the boat en route to Europe. Back to Austria, the land of my roots. Today I'll close the door on this house and leave my life in the Dutch East Indies behind me for good.

The past few months have been exceptionally harsh. Sándor's death was the final blow, and his funeral…The grief was utterly overwhelming. I also visited Papi, and when I stood there at his grave, it felt as though the past forty years flashed before my eyes. I felt that my time had come.

After the funeral, I spent hours at the piano, alone, contemplating our argument. I'm not mad anymore. Only deeply disappointed and incredibly sad to have burned all my energy, and for nothing.

I was a wealthy woman once, the owner of Grand Hotel Lembang, the most luxurious and largest hotel in the entire area. It was here, in 1912, that I got married, and now, more than forty years later, I'll return to my homeland, with a few cents in my pocket and my loved ones left behind, resting in the Dutch East Indies' soil. Our dreams shattered.

With a trunk and a few bags, I'll board the train bound for Tandjong Priok—the port of Djakarta. I have terminated the lease as of April, sold my piano, straightened out my finances, and said farewell to a few cherished places. I went to the Pasar Baru and had a delicious gado-gado meal. A smile on my face as I observed the market vendors, advertising their products as usual. I strolled past the windows of the shops on Braga Street. Past the Bombayer, where I used to buy silk. Past Maison Bogerijen, with its inviting patio and exquisite treats. Past Borromeus Hospital, where you came into this world.

I hiked up the Tangkuban Perahu to the old fortress, past the gigantic trees overgrown with lianas. I remember how immensely we enjoyed our walks there, the coolness and the jungle's symphony, the babbling mountain streams, and the chatter of macaques. You were only little then, and you were so skinny. You frequently had to pause to catch your breath. In my solitude, I once more pointed out the flowers and plants, teaching you their names.

I also walked by the hotel. That was too much…Almost unbearable. It has been renovated and looks like a genuine hotel again. However, I couldn't bring myself to enter. I just couldn't.

I did glance across the property—from the charming cottages with their white walls and red-tiled roofs beneath the trees to the family bungalows, the expansive front lawn, and the meandering stone garden paths. I took in the tall tjamara trees producing welcome shade, the elegant white marble goddess statues gracing the front yard, the pond surrounded by a stone wall and blooming lilies floating on the water, the salmon-coloured hibiscus shrubs and the tall white tube-rose flowers in full bloom in the garden beds—their scent, oh, how indulgent. I traced the pebble driveway leading up to the main entrance and lobby and the grand main building, where our family life unfolded. Those were the happiest years of my life, Vicky, and those times can never be reclaimed.

Finally, I bought carnations for the very last time and visited our three graves, as we so often did together. Papi, Opapa, and your mother will forever remain here.

I've written to my brother, Rudi, and will rent a room in his house. I intend to visit Mrs. Wisgrill, who now lives in The Hague, and then continue to Salzburg. I'm excited to return home after so long.

I couldn't bear to say farewell to you, my dear son. I don't want to say goodbye to you. I'm closing this chapter of my life in the Dutch East Indies, but yours continues, although I hope, one day, you'll come to Austria.

Take good care, my dear son. I'll write to you once I've arrived. Please, write back!

Alles Liebe—With all my love,
Your Mutti

I can't move. Tears cloud my eyes. Austria? What am I supposed to do there? She's gone. I can't believe it. She's turning a page, visiting every place dear to her, and forever closing the book of her life in the Dutch East Indies. And she's done it all without me. The many times I called her, she never said a word about it. All the time she was mulling it over, she chose to avoid discussing anything with me.

My chest hurts. Slowly I begin to realize that Mutti will never ever come back. That I'm left behind here by myself.

Chapter 43

AUDITOR

I'm all alone. Restless. Purposeless. The hole Mutti leaves behind is enormous. Who should I tell my stories to? Who should I go to for advice? Nobody knows me as she did. She was my counsellor, my teacher, my protector. I miss her tremendously. When will I hear from her? I can do nothing but wait for a letter with a return address.

All kinds of thoughts are spinning through my mind. She hadn't even waited for my return. She left without saying goodbye. She must have felt terrible after Mr. Gudjár passed away. She didn't speak about his death often, but I didn't ask her enough about it either—I see that now. I shouldn't have left her alone for so long. She'd been by herself for more than two months before she left for Europe. If I had fought for the hotel, she might have stayed. But I didn't. Have I been too nonchalant about everything? Too selfish?

I have no family whatsoever and no partner. I don't know what it is with women. I've had girlfriends and unanswered crushes on girls, like my childhood friend Helga, but none were serious and they didn't last long. I haven't met my soulmate yet. What do I have to do to find her? What does she look like? "Don't come home with an Indo girl," Mutti had said.

At a loss as to what else to do, I immerse myself in my work in Subang. Fortunately, at least, that is successful. Rob van der Veen's job is a piece of cake. I can also manage my old responsibilities simultaneously and even have time to read the newspaper to stay updated on business and world news.

Mr. Cemac, the company's chief financial officer, has noticed my efforts and offers me a new job as an assistant accountant in the accountancy department. Along with the other accountants, I now get to visit the estates and their associated factories: rubber, tea, sisal, and kina. There are twenty-two locations. We keep an eye on all the bookkeeping and inventory, the workforce, and the cash and barter payments. Each estate takes a week at a time.

My Australian boss encourages me to master accounting theory and offers to fund my studies and provide the necessary time. After researching the available options, I decide to enroll for the course to become an English chartered accountant. I work for an English company, so I may as well align with their system, I figure.

I immediately get a promotion and become an auditor. Finally, no longer a bloody assistant. My new position allows me to visit the estates on my own, where I must examine the estate managers' accounts, an administration that is strictly closed to outsiders. I scrutinize money flow, check supplies and cash, inspect the machinery, and look at what the manager is spending money on. It's a responsible job for a young lad like me. My boss urges me not to abuse my power and to report only to him. I am deployed to conduct fraud investigations, such as sifting through a major rice theft, while being careful not to respond to any bribes from the estate manager. It feels great that my boss is trusting me.

My salary goes up considerably. I now earn a thousand rupiahs a month, and the contribution to my savings fund is increased, which means I can send Mutti more money now. My account at Barclays Bank in London is growing, and Mutti receives a transfer every month. I assume she's grateful for it. I still haven't heard from her.

In the months that follow, I do nothing but work and study. On any given night, you can find me sitting behind a stack of books; the reading is harder than I thought, and I'm starting to regret choosing the English accountancy system. I should have chosen the Dutch chartered accountant course. I had already learned the Dutch system in secondary school. I find the English way of accounting very difficult. My English also turns out to be poor. Many technical terms are foreign to me. But it's too late; I'm already in the middle of the training, so I struggle on.

Due to my academic commitments, I find myself staying an increasing number of weekends in Subang. The town is built around the P&T headquarters and the social club. The European employees live nearby in elegant, expansive stone houses. The Indonesian settlement starts farther out in the rural area, beyond the European enclave. Accessible via winding dirt roads, the Indonesian settlement consists of bamboo houses covered with palm leaf roofs. The residents work their fields with buffaloes and sell their wares in food stalls, tokos (shops), and at markets. I don't live in the motel anymore. I move from one spacious house to another, each time for several months, all belonging to managers on leave in Europe. They are luxury lodgings. Every home has servants, gardeners, and babus employed. My own trusted babu, who cooks, washes, and does the housekeeping for me, moves with me from one place to the next. When it comes to sports, in addition to tennis courts and a golf course, there are volleyball courts and an associated club, to which I've contribut-ed. There's a movie screening every Saturday evening.

I am friendly with some of my colleagues, but when I spend time with them, we keep the conversations light and superficial. We must dance around so many sensitive topics. Everyone has a camp history of some kind. And since the main language is Dutch or English, I don't speak German with anyone. I hold my own, but I feel lonely. Very lonely. I miss Mutti. I miss the depth of our conversations. Our connection.

Then I go for my first exam at the British Council in Bandung. I fail.

Chapter 44

MUTTI'S LETTER

Salzburg, June 2, 1953

My dear son,

I am writing you this letter at the desk in my new room at my brother's, your Uncle Rudi's, house. He and Aunt Mizi aren't wealthy. They can barely survive on his meagre retirement. My monthly rent is a welcome addition for them.

After arriving in the Netherlands, I stayed with Mrs. Wisgrill in The Hague for two months, where I was received very hospitably and slowly got used to life in Europe. The continent is still licking its wounds. The war has only just ended, and so much has been destroyed. The Netherlands is in reconstruction, but Austria remains occupied by the Allies.

I am grateful that I can live with my brother. Rudi and Mizi have a daughter, Ria, as well as their son Bruno, whom you know. Ria is married to Erwin, who is a doctor, a general practitioner. Bruno was married in 1951 to Luise.

Bruno and Luise have been leasing a hotel on Lake Wolfgang, a beautiful lake near the town of Sankt Gilgen. I went to see them there. Lake Wolfgang is an excellent location in the summer. There are plenty of tourists, but during the winter months, it goes completely silent. Unfortunately, the income from the summer season isn't enough to get them through the rest of the year. That's why they had their eye on Hotel Rupertihof in Salzburg-Stadt, but they needed money to be able to lease it. So, I made a deal with them: I offered them what's left of my money, and in return, I get a sandwich lunch and a dinner every day for the rest of my life. I'm content with it. It is a fifteen-minute walk from Rudi's house to the hotel.

The impact forty years in the Dutch East Indies has had on my life is only now beginning to dawn on me. I miss the oasis of Grand Hotel Lembang. The wonderful climate. The scents and colours of Java. The markets and trips to the sea. I was a rich woman, in many ways. Now I am poor, and I lost my dear husband too soon. For our big dreams, we paid dearly.

Luckily, I still have you. Tell me. How are you doing? How is your work going? Where do you live now? Have you found a girlfriend yet?

I thank you a thousand times for your monthly financial support!

I hope you're doing well, and I look forward to hearing from you.

Alles Liebe,
Mutti

26 Gärtnerstraße
Salzburg-Stadt
Austria

Chapter 45

KARLA

After failing my first exam, it starts to dawn on me that doing nothing but working and studying isn't bringing me joy. So, I've decided to be a little kinder to myself. I study at a slower pace now, and I leave Subang on the weekends.

I am drawn to Lembang, where I find my greatest joy, and I've accepted Mr. Schalks's offer to stay overnight at the hotel. This has strengthened my friendship with the Schalks brothers—Ben and Cor. Cor, the older of the two, is known for his easygoing nature and great sense of humour. On the other hand, Ben, a bit more reserved like myself, has a thoughtful and introspective personality and is a skilled mechanic. Both own motorcycles, and they take turns in having me with them as a passenger. Occasionally, they let me ride. Motorcycles are a common thing on Java; Uncle Ferdi had one when I was a little boy, and even though Mr. Gudjár was recently killed in an accident, the riding draws me in. In fact, I love the riding so much that I buy a motorcycle as well, a shiny Jawa Twin.

I swing my leg over it and grip the handlebars with my thin leather gloves. With a twist of the throttle, I bring my motorcycle to life, its power roaring beneath me. I glance at Ben and Cor doing the same thing, their smiles matching mine, and we exchange nods of excitement. The journey begins, and we make our way towards the rainforest trails, the tires kicking up a fine spray of earth. The wind rushes past me, tugging at my curly hair, rustling the leaves overhead. The sunlight filters through the jungle canopy, creating a pattern of shadows. The sounds of the rainforest envelopes us, the resonant calls of the macaques, and occasionally the rush of water. The fragrance of tropical flowers intensifies as we drive deeper into the jungle. We take turns at taking the lead. My heart soars with each turn of the trail, the scents, sounds, and sights reminiscent of my hikes with Mutti.

After an exhilarating ride that usually lasts for most of the day, we return to the hotel hungry and thirsty. I settle into an extra bed available in Ben's bedroom, which used to be mine. Mami's old bedroom is now Cor's and Mr. and Mrs. Schalks have taken over Papi and Mutti's bedroom. Surprisingly, all our old furniture is still there, although the pictures on the walls have changed. Spending the night in this familiar place feels oddly comforting. The Schalks family goes out of their way to make me feel at home.

I am loving my weekends again.

My Dutch colleague John is another source of inspiration for me. He's an outstanding photographer, who not only captures great images but also develops them himself. John showcases his stunning enlargements at the social club, where he sells them. Inspired by his work, I decide to purchase a Contax 35 mm camera and a light metre, embarking on a journey of photographing everything that catches my interest.

John generously invites me into his darkroom and teaches me how to handle the chemicals. Develop, stop, fix, rinse, and dry.

He shares all the secrets of producing high-quality enlargements and small prints on white paper with me, and I find it extremely intriguing.

One day, unexpectedly, John gets into an argument at work and quits his job, which is an unprecedented act out here. In haste, John, along with his wife and child, departs for Holland. But before leaving, he offers to sell me his camera and darkroom equipment. An offer I eagerly accept. Additionally, John also gives me his last print order, consisting of about a hundred photos, so I immediately recoup part of my equipment purchase. What a truly generous and exceptional person he is.

Now, I commute to work in Subang and to the various estates I need to audit. I can go wherever I want, which gives me an incredible feeling of freedom. I like taking pictures of the landscape— rice fields, native villages, indigenous men carrying produce on their shoulders, farmers herding geese on the road, native women washing laundry in the river, and fishermen on wooden boats with small gaff sails and long wooden beams on either side for stability.

I enlarge the most captivating images and offer them for sale in the social club, following John's example. My favourite shots feature the Indonesian people in their natural surroundings. My bathroom serves as a darkroom, and I arrange for photo delivery through P&T's post office, with payment collected through the accounting department.

Bottom of FormThanks to my photographs, I'm starting to make a name for myself. Several of my English colleagues have an airmail subscription to the British newspaper The Times, and one day, a colleague points out a column to me called "People and Nature." The editors are asking for photos of exotic landscapes, and that idea really sparks my enthusiasm. That very night at home, I sift through my collection of photos, struggling to get the best ones. I separate all the photos with the theme "people and nature" from the other pictures, eventually narrowing it down to three: one of the women washing laundry in the river, another of the fishermen on the lake in their wooden sailboat, and a third one of an indigenous man balancing freshly harvested rice plants on either side of a bamboo bar on his shoulders. I submit my three photos to London, and a few weeks later they are published in the English newspaper. The Times compensates me with a generous sum of English pounds, motivating me to send in more of my work.

As a result of this success, my colleagues invite me to their parties and celebrations and pay me to capture pictures of their events. Through these opportunities, I meet a lot of new people, and I finally begin to shed my introverted shell.

On one of my motorcycle trips, while driving through Bandung, I pass the house of an old classmate, Karla van Os. We attended the Christian Lyceum together. I remember her as a friendly, athletic girl, someone I've always had a fondness for. The impulse strikes me to take a chance, so I make a U-turn and knock on the door.

After a few moments, the door swings open. It's Karla's mother. "Good afternoon, Mrs. Van Os," I greet her with a warm smile, "My name is Victor Treipl. I'm an old classmate of your daughter's. Is Karla at home by any chance?"

Mrs. Van Os nods and gestures for me to come in. "Yes, she is," she replies. As I step inside, hurried footsteps descend the stairs, and there she is—Karla standing in the hallway.

"Hey, Victor," she exclaims, a bright smile on her face. "Long time no see. How nice of you to come by."

We spend the rest of the afternoon strolling through the neighbourhood, reminiscing about our school days, and catching up on years that have passed. As we talk, I can't help but notice how attractive she is, and I wonder why I've never truly noticed it before. Karla impresses me not only with her looks but also with her intelligence. She's currently studying at the Technical University in Bandung, pursuing a career as a medical analyst.

As the day nears its end, I gather up the courage to make a hesitant proposition. "Karla," I say, my voice filled with anticipation, "how about we go to the cinema in Bandung this Saturday night?" She looks at me, her eyes lighting up, and with a smile, she replies, "Sure! Yes!"

A feeling of lightness and happiness washes over me as we make plans for our Saturday night outing, and I can't help but look forward to what the future might hold.

Bottom of FormThat night I lie awake and think of Karla's stunning wavy hair, her friendly face, and the way her green-blue eyes briefly held mine. Ah, Karla van Os! Butterflies are in my stomach.

There's an American movie playing with Audrey Hepburn and Gregory Peck, Roman Holiday. I buy our two tickets. An Indonesian on his betjak, a two-seater bicycle taxi, takes us to the cinema.

We sink into the dark red plush chairs. Audrey Hepburn plays Princess Ann, a young princess who travels through Europe with her entourage. That is how she ends up at the embassy in Rome. She's had enough of all the formalities and decides to rebel against protocol. She manages to escape through the window, intent on one night of freedom.

I carefully look over at Karla. The images on the large screen dance across her face and neck. She's wearing a white blouse with sleeves just over the shoulder. Her wavy hair is elegantly done up. She turns her head towards me, her smile beaming. Nervously, I take her hand in mine and squeeze it gently. While Princess Ann is seduced by journalist Joe Bradley, riding a scooter through Rome and dancing to her heart's content, I fantasize that Karla is sitting with me on the back of the motorcycle.

Afterwards, mesmerized by each other and in the thrall of the romance of the American movie, Karla and I float back to her home on the betjak. I kiss her hand at the front door, then take off on my motorcycle to my bedroom at Grand Hotel Lembang.

Now, more than six months later, we call each other every night. On weekends, we're inseparable. Usually, I drive from Subang to Bandung. We go to parties, the cinema, and the pool at Grand Hotel Lembang. I join the local motorcycle club, eight boys with BMWs and Harleys and me on my little Jawa. Everyone has their own motorcycle angel, and Karla is mine. We make long trips through the lush Preanger area around Bandung, to the botanical gardens of Buitenzorg, the mountains of Puntjak, and Telaga Warna, the coloured lake.

Karla's parents are strict and deeply Catholic. They are from Nijmegen in the Netherlands. Spending the night with Karla is absolutely out of the question. Karla herself is also terribly prudish. I can talk to her about anything except sex.

"Before you get married, that topic is taboo," she tells me.

But that rule apparently never applied to her older brother, who had to marry the Indo girl he got pregnant. But of course, I accept this like a gentleman and learn to get used to Karla's family customs.

On the Saturday of Karla's birthday, I make reservations for a table for two at a chic restaurant in Bandung. But on top of the pass of the Tangkuban Perahu, I get engine trouble. Whatever I try, I can't get the damn bike to start. There's no other option than to start walking. I decide to turn around and walk back to Subang, to the local mechanic's shop, where I usually get my bike checked. I'm pushing it in front of me, sweating badly, my head restless with thoughts of Karla. She's waiting for me, with no way of knowing where I am. I must get to her somehow.

Eventually, I walk by a P&T building at the bottom of the mountain. I park my Jawa and run in. They allow me to use their phone.

"Karla, it's me. Congratulations on your birthday!"

"Where are you? I've been terribly worried," she says.

"My engine broke down. On top of the pass, of course. I had to walk all the way back to Subang. I'm so sorry."

"Oh, no! What a pity! Well, park your motorcycle and come by taxi," she suggests.

"But it's getting way too late."

"I was so looking forward to it." There's disappointment and some irritation in her voice.

"Me too, Karla. Look, listen, I'm really sorry, but I think we should postpone until next weekend," I answer.

"Well…Alright then," she says.

I hang up the phone. I have a knot in my stomach. Our evening is ruined, I can't do a thing about it, and it's all my fault. I push my bike to the workshop. Just my luck, they're closed. Of course—it's the weekend. I'll have to wait until Monday.

The next day I call Karla again, and she tells me that she went for dinner with someone else. "With whom?" With Friso Wittenberg. He has a crush on her. Oh, I could kick myself. I should have taken that taxi. But at the same time, how could she do this to me? At the slightest setback, she turns to someone else. Friso, of all people. Is this fickle behaviour a one-off, or a warning of what's to come?

Chapter 46

PASSPORT

In the summer of 1954, I have an audit assignment at an estate south of Sukabumi, in West Java. The journey from Subang takes four hours, and one of the P&T company drivers drives me out there in a magnificent grey Wolseley, the British luxury car for the upper class, which is very low to the ground.

On the bad dirt road to the estate, the car's crankcase, the lower part of the engine that contains the lubricating oil, hits a rock. Within moments, we've lost all our oil and the car's engine comes to a sputtered halt at the side of the road. There's no other option than to wait for help, for someone to drive by.

After an hour, a cloud of dust finally appears in the distance. The driver positions himself halfway in the road, waving, and the car stops. It's a small truck on its way to the same plantation we were headed to. I jump in and get a ride while my driver stays behind with the Wolseley. I assure him that I will arrange for reinforcements.

As I start my audit, after having shared the story of my morning car troubles, I'm given unsettling news that the woods along that main road are life-threatening because of the gangs of robbers. "There's always something to steal from the Europeans, and because they don't give up easily, usually people die," they tell me. That idea makes me feel quite restless, especially with my driver's safety in question. Although an employee of the company is already dispatched to assist, I can't help but worry.

By eleven a.m., there's still no sign of my driver and his Wolseley at the Sukabumi estate. Anxiety now gnaws at me, but I am powerless to do anything but wait. It isn't until lunchtime when my driver's face finally pops up. Unharmed and smiling, he had managed to have the Wolseley towed.

By the end of the day, the car is back in working order, and with a sense of relief, we set off on our journey back to Subang, leaving behind the ominous woods and their grim reputation.

For another business trip, I must audit an estate on the south coast of Java. Another company driver takes me through the village of Garut, where there are regular uprisings by Muslims. All is quiet when we pass through. But an hour later, upon arrival at the company, we see a crowd of people standing around the administrator's, Mr. Werner's, car. He and his elegant East Indian wife are standing there too, in the middle of the commotion, pale as ghosts. He's gesturing frantically with his arms, and all eyes are on the car.

My driver brings our car to a halt next to Mr. Werner's. Bewildered, I look at the side of the car. There are at least twenty bullet holes in it! The occupants are unharmed, miraculously. We passed the same spot just a little later than them, and nothing happened to us.

The incidents do make me think: the bullet with my name on it is somewhere waiting for me. It just hasn't been fired yet. Indonesia is independent now, and the presence of Europeans is less and less desirable. Many Dutch and Indo people have started packing their bags and arranging transport to the Netherlands.

A few days later, Mr. Cemac, P&T's chief financial officer, calls me to his office.

"Victor," he says, "you are treated and paid as a European here, but you can't actually prove that you are European because you don't have a passport."

I look at him dubiously and wonder where this conversation is going.

"Without a European passport, you're not entitled to go on leave abroad or to deposit savings in the savings fund in England," he continues. "That savings fund costs the company dearly in foreign currency and is only intended for Europeans."

I find my work as an auditor interesting. I get to travel from one estate to the next. I have a lot of freedom. I make a good living and take a few days off every now and then to tour the country on my bike with Karla and my friends. I haven't felt the need to go on leave abroad so far. But that savings fund issue, that does bother me.

"What are you trying to tell me, Mr. Cemac?" I ask, somewhat concerned.

"If you don't have a European passport, you will eventually be classified as an Indonesian citizen, and you will not be able to keep the same working conditions at the P&T. Do you want that?"

I don't have to ponder this for too long. I'm not particularly fond of relying on my white privilege, but the reality is, based on my appearance, I'd never be seen as Indo or Indonesian. Even if I chose to acquire Indonesian citizenship, they would never fully embrace me as one of their own. On the other hand, without a European passport, I anticipate Europeans would treat me unfairly.

So I say, "Although I was born and raised here and speak the country's language, I am neither Indonesian nor Indo, Mr. Cemac. I'm a white European born in the Dutch East Indies. I have fair skin, and unfortunately, even if I wanted to, I would never be considered one of them."

"You're right about that. I have a proposal for you. I'll be going on leave to Europe soon and plan to visit Vienna. If you give me your papers, I can arrange an Austrian passport for you."

His words need to sink in for a moment before I comprehend the magnitude of his offer.

"But…Why would you do that, especially for me?" I stammer, amazed.

"I like you. You're a good employee of this organization. You have potential, and I'm eager to support your growth."

My cheeks glow with the heat of my self-conscious gratitude.

"Thank you so much, Mr. Cemac. I gladly accept your offer."

Chapter 47

CHANGES

Karla's embrace from the back of my motorcycle feels somewhat distant. She's unusually quiet. I decide to park the bike so that we can walk and converse without the wind in our ears.

"Is something the matter?" I ask her.

She hardly dares to look at me, but the truth comes tumbling out. "Victor, my father's work contract is coming to an end and my parents have decided to repatriate to the Netherlands." She pauses and lowers her eyes.

My feet are nailed to the ground. I can't move. I wasn't expecting this answer at all. "But…That doesn't mean that you are leaving for the Netherlands, does it?"

"I've been thinking about it for a long time, Victor. And the answer is yes, I will go with them."

"But why? Why don't you just stay here with me? You're twenty-one. You can make your own decisions, right? Your brother is married to an Indo girl. I'm sure he will stay in Bandung."

Karla keeps looking down while turning circles in the soil with one foot. She says nothing.

Suddenly I get it. Of course, she can't stay because we aren't married. I smile and take her hand in mine. "Karla, will you marry me?" I ask.

She has tears in her eyes and that warms me to her, despite the unpleasant surprise she's sprung on me. But her reaction is not as romantic as I would've hoped for, had I given more thought to this moment.

"I expected you to do this, Victor. I wondered the same, myself, and discussed it with my parents. They're strongly against a marriage between us because you're not a believer. They think I should marry a Catholic boy in the Netherlands."

This baffles me. All this time I've been spending with the Van Os family, never once have I heard a discontented word from Karla's parents.

"But doesn't our relationship matter to you at all? Don't you even want to fight for us? If I understand correctly, the matter has already been completely settled?"

Karla stares down to the ground again. "I'm sorry," is all she says.

"I'm sorry? I'm sorry? Is that all you have to say? So, for you it's just easy come, easy go?"

I look at her in disbelief. Karla has opened a hole in me. A big bloody wound right into my heart. I thought we had something good going. I imagined spending the rest of my life with this girl. Marry her, have children, and build a life here together. But instead, Karla's just shattered me. Humiliated and offended, my fists ball in my pockets. I'm not good enough. I just can't believe this. I walk back to my Jawa and give the kickstand a huge kick.

Karla watches from a distance, and says, "Maybe you better take me home."

"Yes, you hurry up," I say curtly.

She walks over and climbs on behind me. Without a word, I hit the throttle and drive straight to her parents' house. As she gets off, I mutter, "I'll call you tomorrow," and tear down the street. I don't know exactly what conversations Karla has had with her parents, but the outcome is clear: my sweetheart did not choose me. The clouds wilt into wisps before scudding away in the wind.

On the phone the next day, Karla doesn't change her decision, and a few weeks later she leaves with her parents on the boat for the Netherlands. Karla is gone. It is the autumn of 1954. I am all alone once again.

Chapter 48

TABEE, INDONESIA

It is Tuesday, November 8, 1955. The flagship of the Royal Rotterdam Lloyd, the *MS Willem Ruys* is a little over 650 feet long and 80 feet wide and accommodates up to nine hundred passengers. I'm standing on the tween deck looking up. Two impressive exhaust stacks protrude from the top deck, flags waving softly from the main mast. Up top is the bridge, the ship's control centre. The first-class cabins are one deck above me. P&T has reserved a second-class cabin for me on the tween deck. They paid for the whole trip. The ship is so large, there are tennis courts, volleyball and shuffleboard courts, a swimming pool, passenger decks with sun loungers, a smoking salon, a library, a lounge and bar, a dining room…There'll be music and entertainment, delicious Indo-European food, and land excursions planned: three weeks of sailing on this luxury cruise ship. I should consider myself lucky and feel elated, but instead, I'm in a state of ambiguity. I am physically on the ship, but my heart is not here. What is it I expect to find in Europe?

I take a deep breath, pulling the air through my nostrils deep into my lungs: a mixture of sweltering heat, sweat, spicy cigarettes, the brine and dirt of seawater, but above all, fish. The port of Djakarta, a hub of chaotic activity, is busy with cargo ships, tugs, and colourful wooden fishing boats on the water. The Indonesian carriers are running back and forth across the wharf with goods on their shoulders. They load and unload the ships. The deep groan of the ship's horn echoes over the deck. The sound announces our departure, and the cruise ship slowly starts moving. My native Java, so familiar to me, slowly slides away. A wave of panic moves from my crown to my feet. What the hell have I gotten myself into? Will I ever see my homeland again? My fellow passengers wave to their loved ones on the quay, who are waving too, throwing colourful streamers at the ship. No one waves me goodbye.

I think about Karla. Her green-blue eyes, her dark blond wavy hair. A few months after her departure, I received a letter with her new address in Nijmegen on the envelope's back. She told me her life in the Netherlands wasn't very exciting and she hadn't met a decent Catholic boy yet. We began to correspond.

It's been so long since I've seen her, smelled the scent of her rose perfume. My heart goes both ways. To the Netherlands, to the woman who will not let go of me, even though she left me so easily, and to Indonesia. I love this country. I was born and raised here. Is leaving the right choice?

I'm thinking of Mutti. Of the big fight we had. Of her letter and unexpected departure. I want to settle our argument. I need to see her. She'll always be my mother, my dearest relative, and no one can replace her.

Then my thoughts wander to the bullet holes in Mr. Werner's car. The risk of such an attack happening to me one day is significant. I lay my right hand on my chest, feel the Austrian passport in my shirt pocket. Mr. Cemac kept his word.

The port of Djakarta is slowly disappearing. The phrase *Tabee, Indonesia* runs through my mind. Farewell Indonesia. A wave of heat erupts from my chest to my head. I panic. I must get out of here, away from the deck. I want to be alone. I start squeezing through the crowd, exit the tween deck and run down the corridor towards my cabin at the end. V.F. TREIPL AND A. WENAS, it says on the nameplate.

Once inside, I shut the door firmly behind me and drop onto the bed. I take a deep breath and close my eyes. Luckily my room-mate isn't here. Tears are burning behind my eyelids. I'm a twenty-five-year-old man of Austrian descent born in Java. I've never been off the island. Here, on the eastern horizon of the world, is where I grew up. It's what I know. West Java is my home. Lembang is where my roots are. I'm upset, nervous, and melancholic, but I can't possibly stay.

A few months ago, I began to prepare for the big crossing. I had steamer trunks made, and everything I own I packed in them. They are now piled up in the hold, down below. Three weeks on the boat, from Djakarta to Singapore, Ceylon, Suez, Naples, and Southampton to final destination Rotterdam. And then?

I have no idea what Europe looks like or what to expect. Do they have rainforests there? What is the weather like? I may have fair skin, but I'm a boy from the tropics. I love the heat and the sweet smells of Indonesia.

The Indonesian government has given me a re-entry permit, which is quite exceptional. Many Dutch people don't receive permission to come back once they've decided to leave the country.

And yet, I have decided to leave for good. I didn't tell anyone at work. They think I'm on vacation and are expecting me back at the office in six months. I ruminate on this decision, internally recount all my reasons: I want to go to Europe because I am entitled to long-term leave. I want to go to Europe because Indonesia is starting to become dangerous for white men like me. I want to celebrate Christmas at Mutti's in Austria, and I want to settle our fight. I want to go to Europe to visit Karla. I will only return to Java with a permanent life partner.

Having calmed down a little, I wash my face in the small sink. I straighten my clothes, leave the cabin and begin exploring the *Willem Ruys*.

Chapter 49

UPROOTED

We have arrived on the Red Sea. I'm on deck, where it's warm. The sea is narrow, with land on both sides. In the distance, a caravan of camels. The clatter of cutlery and hum of conversation in the lounge and dining room rises on the salty air from below. I recognize the music of a traditional Indonesian krontjong orchestra. Over the twang of the ukulele and banjo, over the rhythms of the cello and guitar, an ethereal female voice seems to float. Music straight from the heart; it draws me in.

As I walk down the wide stairs, my feet sink into the thick carpet. My hand slides down the shiny, smooth handrail. Elegantly dressed women relaxing in lounge chairs sip their cocktails and engage in animated conversations. Men are drinking and laughing loudly at the bar. It's almost dinner time on the *Willem Ruys*. The tables, stylishly set with white damask cloths, are starting to fill up in the dining room. Spicy smells of food invade the room. Rijsttafel tonight—an elaborate Indonesian meal adapted by the

Dutch, consisting of rice accompanied by many side dishes in small portions.

I take a seat at the table I always share with the same familiar guests. My roommate and colleague, Amin Wenas, who is on his way to his new job in England, is a nice guy from Menado, a town on the island of Celebes, and he applied for the same job in London as I did. He already passed his accountant's exam (I haven't yet) and got the job. A Dutch couple, Ton and Ria, and their two children are our other table companions. Most of their stories are about the Netherlands. They've worked as contractors for P&T for five years and they, unlike me, are on their way home. On the way to everything familiar to them.

After dinner there is dancing, but I don't feel like it. I stroll back to my cabin. It's the same ritual every day, here on the boat. I participate, but I'm not present. My insecurity about the future puts me in a fog for the whole journey.

When we get to Suez, we discover that our cruise has organized excursions to the Pyramid of Cheops, the Cairo Museum, and the Mohammed Ali Mosque. Everyone joins in.

Afterwards, all I remember of the outing are the narrow, low corridors in the pyramid. So low that you had to duck everywhere, and so narrow that oncoming lines of tourists would have to wait for each other to pass.

From Naples, the *Willem Ruys* sets course for the Bay of Biscay, where the weather is changing, and the sea is getting rougher. One by one, passengers disappear to their cabins. The *Willem Ruys* advances through the violent, pounding ocean swells. I haven't earned my sea legs, apparently, and stumble to my cabin, where Wenas is sitting on his bed eating grapes.

"Nice and sweet, these grapes. Would you like some too?" he offers generously.

With my hand over my mouth and unable to answer, I run back into the hall. I gag and vomit my breakfast into the toilet. For a week, I can't get a bite down my throat and stay in bed, sick as a dog, until we sail into milder waters, to the Southampton harbour. Wenas disembarks, and we continue our journey to Holland.

The Rotterdam sky is lead grey. A cloud cover hangs over the land like a low ceiling, and an icy wind blows. I don't see any mountains, just flat land, the quay, and buildings, which must be part of the city of Rotterdam. I've prepared for this trip and am wearing warm clothes, but the cold cuts through my bones. It's a stark contrast to the tropical climate of Java. I am out of place and uncomfortable. It's early December, winter in the Netherlands. I shiver.

The *Willem Ruys* is moored with large mooring lines, and everyone tries to get off the ship as quickly as possible. My Sarangan friend Guido Dubois is picking me up. He's invited me to spend the first few weeks at his parental home. I know the family well. Guido's mother is a friend of Mutti's. As I walk down the gangway, Guido stands out from the crowd immediately. He hasn't changed a bit and grins broadly. We grab each other amicably by the shoulder.

"Here, you need this," says Guido, handing me a long winter coat. "You're shivering like a tropical flower!"

Grateful for the coat, I wrap it around me. There are lines painted on the quay, squares with numbers in them. I watch amazed as Dutch social workers direct the Indo-European passengers to the squares, where blankets and clothing are distributed to them.

"They're transported by bus to their new homes in various cities of Holland, depending on their employment prospects," Guido explains. There's an exodus of Indo-Europeans, whom the Indonesians consider white.

I pull the winter coat closer around me. After my luggage has been unloaded, we start the drive to Guido's house in his father's cream coloured Simca Aronde. A long tunnel carries us underneath the river Maas. Never before have I driven through a tunnel, let alone underneath a river. I cower, claustrophobic, and collapse a bit on my seat, then breathe a sigh of relief as we finally rise back to ground level.

Guido chuckles. "I felt the same way when I drove through this tunnel the very first time."

The road is wide and paved. Guido calls it the "highway." I look out the window as the Dutch landscape passes by, flat as a pancake. No volcanos or tropical rainforests; instead, the view consists of factory smokestacks, church towers and brick houses, and rectangular plots of land divided by canals. Oh, and plenty of cows, huddled together to shelter themselves from the cold wind. Everything is grey and drab, except for the grass on the meadows. Meanwhile, the rain's pelting the car's windshield horizontally. The windshield wipers swish away at full speed. Have I mentioned I'm freezing?

We arrive in The Hague at Guido's parents' house in the Quail Lane. Rows of multi-storey brick houses with balconies and red roofs line either side of the street. The outdoor furnishings are sober and small. Lace curtains inside the windows. Guido turns the key in the front door of number 32. In the Dutch East Indies, houses weren't locked. The lace curtains across the street move.

"Welcome, Victor." Mrs. Dubois meets me in the long, narrow hallway and hugs me. "Did you have a good trip?"

"I don't know, I still feel very out of place," I answer dazedly.

Guido and I haul my trunks and bags up the steep wooden stairs, our breath visible in the chilly air.

"It's freezing cold in here," I sigh.

"Nice and fresh, you mean!" Guido laughs. "According to good Dutch practice, no matter how cold it is outside, there's always a window open for fresh air."

Guido leads me to his old bedroom. Guido is now married to my old schoolmate, Jutta Waldstein, and they live in a small home in de Flower neighbourhood, only a fifteen-minute walk down the road. His brothers and sister also have their own places.

We stack my luggage at the foot of the bed. Out the window is a small, grey-tiled terrace, enclosed on three sides by a wooden fence. The flower beds are dry and deserted. There's a shed at the back of the garden. It strikes me that Dutch life mainly takes place indoors.

The living room is cozy and warm, although the petroleum stove emits a sulfurous smell. Mrs. Dubois has prepared supper, and we reminisce about the Dutch East Indies. There are no servants here. The Duboises cleanup and do the dishes themselves. It's not like they're poor either. Guido's father, a Belgian by birth, has been reinstated as a Dutch citizen after long legal proceedings, and he was allowed to keep his government pension. The whole family lived on that until the children left home.

"Holland has no babu and no djongos," says Mrs. Dubois. People don't have servants in Holland. "They have strange customs, Victor. If you visit the Dutch and are offered a biscuit with your tea, don't take more than one. Be careful with your fingers because they might close the container lid on you. And if you haven't left the house by five-thirty p.m., which is dinner time, they'll try to stare you out of the house instead of offering you a plate."

I'm very grateful for the Dubois's hospitality, but without them admitting it outright, it hasn't been easy for them to adjust to a Dutch lifestyle. I closed the bedroom window, but still, I'm shivering under the woolen blanket. My teeth are chattering. I'll have to get myself together. The Dutch East Indies are no more. If only I could get warm, somehow, first.

Chapter 50

NIJMEGEN

I rent a car, buy a map of the Netherlands, and embark on the solo drive to Nijmegen to visit Karla. As I approach the outskirts of the city around lunchtime, my nerves jangle me. A strange feeling takes up residence in my gut. What will she look like? What will her parents think? What will I find there? My wife? My destiny?

The Van Os family lives at the Bloemenburgerhof, a street right in the centre of Nijmegen. Most houses in the Netherlands are built in rows, which strikes me as orderly but rather soulless at the same time. I park in front of the door and ring the bell.

It seems to take forever, but I finally hear steps in the hallway. Karla opens the door. She smiles, and I melt. I take her hand. She gives me a quick kiss on the mouth and pulls me in. Amazed and slightly overwhelmed, I step into the narrow corridor. Is she less prudish than she used to be? What happened?

I take a quick look around. High white walls and glaring ceiling lights. A small coat rack with coats, caps, and hats to my right.

I close the door behind me. Karla offers to take my coat, and I can't take my eyes off her. Her wavy hair, her full lips, her slim waist.

Taking my gloves, she asks, bluntly, "Will you marry me?"

I don't know what to answer. That voice I know so well rears up in my head defiantly, suddenly clear on what it doesn't want, screeching, *No! No! Don't do it!* Why such a rush all of a sudden?

On the outside, I stay cool. Button by button, I open my coat. I consider my answer for a moment. "I'd like to get to know you again first."

"Why? I'm still the same person," she says, with a nonchalance appropriate for discussing lunch plans or which hat to wear.

"Everything is different, Karla. You're different. You've been in Holland for quite some time now, and you've adapted. I still have to get used to everything here."

"I understand that, but I can assure you, I'm still the same person I've always been."

"Let's go for a walk together," I suggest. I don't feel like having to face Karla's parents right away anyway—those people who so unabashedly renounced me in the Dutch East Indies.

"Okay." She shrugs, and gives me my gloves back, lifting her woolen coat from the coat rack. I help her into the coat.

She smiles. "You always were a gentleman. We can walk along the Waal River down here."

"That's fine," I reply.

First, we explore the old town. Karla regales me with anecdotes pulled from Nijmegen's rich history, which goes back two thousand years to when the Romans settled here. I'm impressed. The war destroyed a large part of the city centre, but judging by the construction sites, it looks like a lot of work is being done to restore it. We walk over a bridge over the Waal to the Ossenwaardpad, a narrow trail along the riverbank. I take Karla's hand, try to reach for a sense of normalcy, of connection. But nothing feels normal. On the contrary, this is all so weird after such a long time, and in a strange country.

I decide to confront her about the hurt she caused. "So, tell me, why did you leave Bandung?"

"You know why. My parents had to go back to the Netherlands."

"Yes, I know, but you could have chosen otherwise," I respond. "Why do you suddenly want to marry me now, and back then, you didn't?"

"I've been thinking about it," she says.

"What's changed?" I ask.

"I realized that you'd go out on a limb for me."

I'm not convinced yet. Her approach seems self-centred, leaving me with the impression that I'm just a puppet being manipulated to fulfill her desires. "Your parents wanted you to marry a Catholic boy. I guess you haven't found Mr. Right yet?"

Karla's attitude tightens. She wrenches her hand from mine, clearly uncomfortable with my bringing this up.

"Let me rephrase it," I continue. "Why am I good enough for you now but not then?"

"I don't care what my parents think anymore," Karla says, suddenly resolute. "I want to get out of here."

I stop and stare at her.

"Your mother is also a Catholic. We can go to church now and then, right?" she says. "That would solve the problem. I want to go back to Java with you."

I am baffled. I should be flattered by the fact that she wants to come with me, back to my native soil. Returning to Java with a spouse would be a dream come true. But her response doesn't feel right.

Thirty thoughts a second are flying into my mind; then, the answer comes to me, and it's unequivocal. Now I can see that for her, it's not about me at all, about who I am, about love. All she cares about is getting out of this hamlet. She has always tried to manipulate me. Have I ever steered this relationship myself? When have I ever made a clear choice about Karla?

"I don't want to marry you." The words are coming out of my mouth as if they weren't mine.

She stares at me. "Well, in that case, I don't want to see you again," she says calmly.

I look her in the eye. I'm trying to fathom her. She's calculating. There's no emotion. She doesn't shed a tear. Her heart is cold as stone. I've never seen her green-blue eyes be so intensely cool as they are now.

"Goodbye, Karla. Fare you well," I say and start walking back towards the bridge.

She stops and doesn't follow me. She doesn't even attempt to run after me. And as sure as I am about this decision, something in me is dying. This relationship is really over now.

My stride is hesitant at first but gets firmer with every step I take as the distance between us gets bigger.

I arrive at the car, get in, and leave. I feel good about it. Very good, actually. Finally, I'm listening to my intuition. Finally, I've made a clear choice that I can get behind. Karla is not the woman of my dreams.

Chapter 51

ARRIVAL IN SALZBURG

The breakup with Karla happened abruptly. Her apathetic behaviour quite honestly stunned me. Her cold, icy words, "Well, in that case, I don't want to see you again," were almost unbelievable. Yet, as I listen to my heart carefully, I've known deep down from the early stages of our relationship that Karla was selfish. Her choices often gravitated to what was most convenient for her. One vivid instance was that night when my motorcycle broke down; instead of offering support, she effortlessly went out with Friso. The tipping point came when she relocated to Holland with her parents. She had the option to stay. To choose us over convenience, but that wasn't the path she took. Even though the prospect of a shared future in Java is now lost, and I'm wrestling with the consequences, surprisingly, the wounds from this breakup with Karla aren't as deep as I expected. I honestly feel comfortable with it all.

Besides the Dubois family's enormous hospitality and that of other old Dutch East Indies friends I visit, Holland is a sobering experience. The Dutch are actively grappling with their own wartime past, working to rebuild their lives and their country. Most Dutch people who never left the country know very little about the Dutch East Indies and believe that the suffering over there could never have been as bad as it was here. Their response to any mention of the fighting and camps in Indonesia is usually something along the lines of "Nothing was worse than the bitter-cold winter famine, when we all ate flower bulbs," or "The sun was shining in the Dutch East Indies, wasn't it? I bet you could pick fruit from the trees over there!"

Nobody shows any interest in my story. Moreover, I'm not Dutch. Even though they would have difficulty knowing it just by looking at me, I'm Austrian. I'm the enemy. I need to be careful about sharing my opinions about the war. So, I've decided to shut up. I'm good at that. I learned to be silent from a very young age.

In mid-December, Guido drives me to the train station in Utrecht, and together, we load up my trunks and all my luggage. After we share our heartfelt goodbyes, I embark on my travels from Utrecht in the Netherlands, through Arnhem and Munich, Germany, and across the Austrian border into Salzburg. I can't wait to reunite with Mutti again, and discover what Austria looks like and what the country has to offer me. Maybe my future lies in the mountains.

When I get off the train at Salzburg station, my luggage unloaded beside me, it hits me just how freezing cold it is on the platform. In no time, thankfully, an Austrian customs officer shows up to process me.

"Where are you from?" the officer asks stiffly without introducing himself.

I hold out my hand. He shakes it with some reluctance.

"Nice to meet you. My name is Victor Treipl. I came from Holland."

"What is the purpose of your visit?"

"I've come to visit my mother."

"How long will you stay?"

"I don't know yet. Maybe I'll find a job here."

That seems to set his alarm bells off.

"That suitcase. Open it up!"

With a red face and submissive demeanour, I open the lock and unclasp my trunk. The officer starts to feverishly rummage through my belongings as if he suspects I've got gold or weapons in there.

"Sir! Sir! I'm Austrian. I have an Austrian passport." I hold the passport open to his face. He looks up for a moment, grunts, and then just continues rifling through my things.

"What is this?" he asks, pulling out my hand-carved wooden garuda statue, a legendary Hindu bird-like demi-god that has the body of a human, the face of a man, wings, and an eagle's beak.

"It's a wooden sculpture from Indonesia, sir. I lived there for a long time." I do not tell him I was born there; I doubt he would be pleased to know that.

Roughly and without restraint, he continues his search, finds a stack of my black and white prints, and looks at them one by one. It feels like he's studying my underwear.

"May I ask what you're looking for, sir?"

He doesn't answer, tosses my photos back in the suitcase, and makes a complete shambles of my carefully packed belongings. And now he's starting to unzip my bags. I'm about to reach a boiling point.

"What gives you the right to make such a mess?" I exclaim.

"You said you were from the Netherlands, but all your stuff indicates that you come from somewhere else," the officer roars.

Just as I'm about to launch into a tirade against the customs officer, Mutti's cousin Bruno, Grand Hotel Lembang's resident entertainer, appears around the corner. He looks so much older. He reads the situation immediately, points to me, and says to the officer in a polite tone, "Sir, this man belongs here. This is all he has."

But the officer, charged up with a sense of his own power, doesn't know how to quit. Bruno shoots me a meaningful look and strides off purposefully into the customs office. Moments later, he comes out with the customs police inspector, whom he introduces as his friend.

"Peter, it's alright," the inspector tells his subordinate. "You can let him go now."

The man stops his prying and looks at the inspector in astonishment. I breathe a sigh of relief.

"But, boss! This man is from the tropics and says he's going to look for work here," the officer argues. "We can't just let any foreigners come in and take all our jobs. Work is already so scarce for Austrians."

"I am Austrian, sir," I answer, showing my passport to the inspector. He nods reassuringly.

"Come on, Peter. It's okay," he says again, directing his employee to the office.

To me, he says, "You can close your bags now. You're free to go."

The men disappear into the office.

"Phew," I sigh. "That was an enchanting introduction."

"Shake it off," Bruno grins broadly as he extends his hand to me. "Good to see you, Victor. How are you? You've grown since the last time I saw you." He gives me an amiable slap on the back of the head. He may look different, but otherwise, he's just how I remember him.

He doesn't wait for my answer and barrels on, "Come on, I'll offer you a room in our hotel. Let's throw your stuff on that luggage rack. My car is parked at the entrance here."

Bruno drives us to Hotel Rupertihof, a cozy-looking hotel with a gabled roof, white plaster walls, small dormer windows, wooden balconies, and dark carved wooden trim on the façade. The wide front door is adorned with Christmas lights and an evergreen wreath.

"We're waiting for the first snow to fall. It won't be long," he says.

"Oh!" I exclaim. "I've never seen snow in my life. It seems so magical to me."

Inside, he introduces me to his wife, Luise, who appears warm and energetic. She shows me to my room, and I begin unpacking, mentally preparing to be reunited for the first time in two and a half years with Mutti, who'll join me at Bruno's hotel for dinner.

Chapter 52

MUTTI

I'm sitting alone by the window, at an elegantly set table in Bruno and Luise's inviting restaurant. As Bruno and Luise diligently attend to their culinary and serving duties, I gaze out at the world beyond. Under the amber light of the streetlamps, Mutti's petite figure draws nearer. Her brisk stride is unmistakable.

I remember our conversation in that bare, white hallway of the police barracks as if it were yesterday. *Listen. It's time we talk. I want to tell you the whole story.* Afterward, I was frustrated and disillusioned. Upset that she'd kept the family secret from me for so long. Disappointed with who I'd become, and unsure as to what I should do with my life. My thoughts flash to our blazing argument concerning the hotel. Her words still echo in my ears. *Alright then, Vicky. Well, what am I still doing here? You're all I have left. If you abandon me, what am I supposed to do? I may as well leave.* It hadn't been an empty threat. She did leave. Without saying goodbye, even, and I couldn't believe my eyes when I saw that she had disappeared. She, too, was frustrated and disillusioned. Frustrated because I didn't want to fight for the hotel, for a future in which she could play an active role, and disappointed with what had become of her life after forty years in the Dutch East Indies.

But we must reconcile. After all, she's still my mother. There's just the two of us. We must talk things over. That's why I'm here in Austria.

She comes up the stairs wearing a long, dark blue wool coat and a colourful silk scarf around her neck, an elegant little hat slanted to one side, and leather gloves on her tiny hands.

My brave little Mutti. She fits perfectly into the Austrian street scene, from what I've seen for the first time today. I walk up to her, arms outstretched. She opens her arms to me, and I'm relieved to see a playful look dance across her features.

"I'm so glad you're here," she says.

"I've missed you, Mutti. I didn't know what to do with myself after you left."

As we draw closer, the silky texture of her scarf gently caresses my cheek, carrying with it the subtle fragrance of her familiar perfume—a soothing blend of lavender and vanilla. In that delicate moment, memories rush through my mind like an old film reel: the painful loss of my parents, the echoes of our hotel and livelihood slipping away. With those recollections, her unwavering care for me emerges—the courageous woman responsible for protecting an eight-year-old boy. Together, we weathered the storm of war and faced hardships that tested the limits of our endurance.

Thinking of our arduous journey, it's remarkable how we navigated every obstacle together. In moments of despair, Mutti comforted me. She was my protector, sharing her food rations and warning of the threats that lurked in the outside world. She always, without fail, had my back.

Tears shimmer in our eyes as our grip tightens. This is more than just a hug; it is the deep bond between a mother and her son, a manifestation of the resilience built through our shared trials.

We take a seat at the table. The waiter pours us water, and I order a carafe of wine to celebrate our reunion. The restaurant soon fills with hotel guests. It's a cozy stube—a classically Austrian room. Wooden paneling along the walls, mood lighting, wooden chairs with a heart set into the back, tables set with white cloths, and a Christmas arrangement, a taper candle surrounded with greenery, berries, and pinecones on each table.

"How are you, Mutti?" I ask. "Is life in Austria what you expected it to be?"

"Yes, I like it here. I'm doing fine because of the monthly allowance you send me. I am eternally grateful to you. As a good family does, my relatives have taken me in, but life isn't easy. They work hard.

"When Bruno finally reached his family in Salzburg after the war, he found out that they'd lost everything. Uncle Rudi had been commander of Salzburg's fortress but decided to quit his job during the war because he didn't want to work for the Nazis. As a result, the government pension he receives is extremely poor. To earn a living, Bruno became a sales representative for the company Steyr, which produces agricultural machines, and travelled all over Austria to do so. He's a good talker, as you know, and has been able to successfully expand his business over the years. Luise is an excellent hostess and runs the hotel more or less on her own. I try to do my part with advice when she asks for it. And I maintain Rudi and Mizi's garden and that of the hotel. A person must have a task in life."

The waiter serves the starter from the menu of the day. Consommé Celestine. Delicious, clear herbal soup with sliced pancakes. My old favourite.

"Mmm, tastes good," I say, and I remember with a warm feeling all those times in my youth when the djongos, the male servants, served me that same soup.

Mutti grins from ear to ear. We toast and clink our wineglasses. It is good to see that she's at ease. She knows her way around here. I can sense this is her home.

"You wrote to me that you had a girlfriend and that you were going to visit her in Holland. How did that go?"

"Karla. Yes. I visited her in Nijmegen. But I found out in a hurry that she's not the right woman for me."

I tell her about our relationship, my failed proposal, and how Karla decided to return to Holland with her parents. I tell her about my work, promotions, and successful photography assignments. I hesitate but then decide to tell her I had bought a motorcycle and went on numerous trips all over West Java.

Mutti seems to be at ease. She smiles and tells me she never doubted that I would find my way. I tell her about the bullet holes in Mr. Werner's car, the Austrian passport, my mediocre results in the English Chartered Accountant course, and my decision to leave Indonesia. But I can't possibly say a word about Grand Hotel Lembang and Mr. Schalks, my Saturdays in the pool, and the nights spent in his sons' rooms.

The conversation inevitably comes to our quarrel.

"Mutti, I'm sorry that we argued like that about the hotel and that I left you all by yourself so many times," I say.

"That's kind of you to say. Thank you. Me too. I wouldn't say I enjoyed that fight. I shouldn't have let it go so far," she says, taking a sip of her wine. "And yes, I was often alone, but there wasn't much you could do about that. It was unfortunate that you had to move to another city for work, but sacrifices must sometimes be made for a good job. That's part of having a career."

The waiter brings us the main course. Wiener schnitzel with lemon and potatoes with butter and parsley. Delish! As I savour each bite, I can't help but think that Mutti did well to make a deal with Bruno that will let her eat here for the rest of her life.

"Do you still think I should go after our assets?" I ask.

She thinks, seems to choose her words carefully. "I thought about it for a long time and concluded that you were right. That you should go your own way instead of chasing shadows from the past. No matter how sour it is that we've lost everything."

"I'm glad to hear that," I say.

There's a silence, and we both focus on our food.

This is as good a moment as any to share my plan with her. "I have decided not to return to Java unless maybe with a European life partner."

"Oh?" There is hope in her voice. She wants me to stay in Salzburg.

"There are few marriageable women in the Dutch East Indies. The European women who didn't already have a partner were leaving for Europe in droves."

She sits up, on the edge of her chair, like she's always done when she's excited or tense.

"What's next for you, then?"

"Well, now that my relationship with Karla has ended, I think I should look for work in Europe."

"You mean in Austria? I have a lot of connections, and so do Bruno and Luise. We can help you find a suitable job," she says ardently.

I raise my hand. "Okay, okay! Thank you for your offer. But before we start talking about work, let's celebrate Christmas together first. I am on leave and still employed by P&T, so there's no rush for me to start job hunting."

She nods, holding back her enthusiasm. I refill our glasses and observe her closely. There's a gentleness in her expression, and a look of apprehension in her eyes. Our bond is deep. Very deep. An unspoken agreement that assures me we'll persistently find solutions and navigate the challenges fate throws our way. We've proven resilient, having weathered the storm of losing my parents, our cherished hotel, and the revelation of my true background. I envision future challenges: questions about putting down roots in Europe, the prospect of our continued togetherness, the nature of the job that will sustain us both, and the possibility of creating a family for Mutti to be a part of.

Yet, our shared history tells me that, together, we'll navigate the unknown, grieve our losses, and forge ahead into a future that we shape with the strength of our enduring connection.

"What do you want for Christmas?" I'm pleased that I can now afford buying her a nice present.

Mutti smiles. "My only wish has already been fulfilled."

Chapter 53

A WHITE CHRISTMAS

I've been in Salzburg for a week now. This morning when I wake up and draw the curtains aside, everything is white. From the balcony to as far as I can see, every surface is covered in a glistening layer of wintery wonderland. It looks like a fairy tale.

With my winter coat over my pyjamas, I step outside onto the balcony. The snowfall has come to a halt. The depth is astonishing. It is as if a whole foot of snow had descended overnight, wrapping the world in a serene stillness. The snow feels cold between my toes but melts immediately. I walk around in it and, looking back, behold my own footprints. Hilarious!

I brush some snow off the balcony railing, and it sails off, soft, light, and glittering. Only when I press the snow firmly in my hands does the stuff take on substance. A snowball! The very first snowball of my life. I throw it down to the street and accidentally hit a passerby on the shoulder. The man turns around, looks up, and sees my smiling, bashful face sticking out above the balcony railing.

"Frohe Weihnachten!" he chuckles and walks on. Merry Christmas!

"Frohe Weihnachten!" I shout after him, as cheerful as a child.

I go back in and get dressed as quickly as I possibly can. I run down the stairs and take a long morning walk through the postcard-perfect streets of Salzburg. Festive decorations and lights abound, and the aroma of hot chestnuts and freshly baked cookies fill the narrow downtown streets. So, I think to myself, *this will be my first white Christmas.*

Christmas preparations are in full swing at Hotel Rupertihof. The hotel is fully booked. In the heart of the cozy living room stands a magnificent Christmas tree, its needles emitting a delightful fir fragrance. The tree is decked out with an array of decorations, glass baubles in various shades of red and silver dangle from its branches. At the top, a radiant silver star glows.

I share my excitement about my first snowball and my morning walk with Mutti, Bruno, and Luise while we sit at their kitchen table for dinner, and their laughter fills the room.

"You should go on a ski holiday, Victor," Bruno says.

"A ski holiday?" I burst out laughing. "Until this morning, I had never seen snow in my life. Now you're asking me to race down a mountain on those long slats."

"Oh, you'll figure it out soon enough. You can borrow my gear and take a few lessons in Berchtesgaden. It's nearby. Suitable terrain for novice skiers. I'm sure you'll like it."

In the days leading up to Christmas, Mutti and I visit several Salzburg attractions. Most are within walking distance in the Altstadt, the old town. Unfortunately, the Second World War left its mark here. Many buildings are battered, and most are badly neglected, although I can easily imagine the old splendour.

We visit Hohensalzburg, a medieval castle on the Festungsberg, a mountain that towers eighty metres above the city centre. Salzburg is full of churches, and free concerts are given everywhere. I love the baroque Salzburg Cathedral and the Gothic Franciscan Church the most. We also visit the Getreidegasse, a narrow little street with numerous medieval houses, baroque facades, passage-ways, and shops. House number 9 is Mozart's birthplace. I love it all. What a new world this is to me.

Christmas in the snow is enchanting. This feels like the way Christmas should be. We attend the Weihnachtliches Adventsingen, Advent singing, outside in the snow on the Cathedral Square. On December 24, we celebrate Christmas Eve with the family. Bruno and Luise, Ria and Erwin, Uncle Rudi and Aunt Mizi, and Mutti and me.

Although I'm meeting some family members for the very first time, it feels special to be together and speak German all evening. The hotel kitchen has prepared a delicious dinner, and there's a little present under the tree for everyone. On December 25, we go to mass together in the Salzburg Cathedral. It's an impressive experience, and I appreciate being part of this.

After Christmas, I take ski lessons in Berchtesgaden. Bruno has lent me his ski clothes, and I'm borrowing his wooden skis with a strange kind of binding on them. The toe of the leather shoe stays stuck to the ski while the heel is free to move up and down. The instructor makes us walk sideways on our skis all the way up the hill, then slide down again. Each run takes less than five min-utes. And then the whole show starts all over again. I eventually manage a few slaloms. By the end of the afternoon, I'm completely exhausted. But that night I fall asleep satisfied.

It's a Christmas of many firsts. My first time in Austria, my first encounter with snow, my first time meeting my Austrian family, and my first time on skis. I hope there'll be more of these delightful firsts in the coming year, like finding a fulfilling job and the possibility of meeting an interesting and charming girlfriend.

I've started looking for work. Until just before I arrived in Austria, the Americans had been stationed in Salzburg and the Russians in Vienna. A post-war rehabilitation like the one that's been going on in Holland hasn't yet been initiated in Austria. The economy remains depressed, there's little money to go around, and my Dutch and English qualifications and Dutch East Indies professional background do not match the Austrian demand. Mutti goes to great lengths to get me on track, contacting all kinds of family members, but there's no suitable job available. A family member in South Tyrol owns orchards and produces packaged and canned juices; I could manage their book-keeping, which appeals to me, but the caveat is that they wouldn't be able to pay me yet. *To that, I say thanks, but no thanks.*

Although my stay in Holland was a sobering experience, I'm now starting to see the situation with a fresh perspective. A fair number of Dutch people have lived in the Dutch East Indies for a few years, and many Indo-Europeans recently moved to Holland. I have my own network of old friends and ex-colleagues in the Netherlands. Years of trade with Indonesia have resulted in a lot of Indo-European influences in Holland. I can buy Indonesian food at the toko—a store selling Indonesian food products and takeout meals, and I can buy Indonesian spices and teas at the grocery store. And after all, I grew up with the Dutch way of thinking, I speak the language, and have a Dutch high school diploma.

I tell Mutti about my musings.

"So, you're going to seek your fortune in the country that has taken everything from us?" she replies.

"If you want to look at it that way, yes," I answer. "But you know, even though I'm of Austrian descent and speak German fluently, I don't know this country or the mentality of the people at all. Not to mention my diplomas are worthless here."

"But you don't have a Dutch passport. Would they even accept you?"

"I don't know. I'll have to find out."

Mutti looks disappointed.

"Listen, dear Mutti. It's not like you to think small. To think in terms of problems instead of solutions. You yourself travelled across the world to seek your fortune."

"Well, that hasn't quite served me well, has it?"

"Holland is only a train ride away. I promise our bond will not weaken, even if we don't see each other every day. We can call and write," I suggest.

Her face brightens a little.

"I'll do everything I can to take care of you. For the rest of your life. But I must follow my own path."

A radiant smile appears on her face. "Thank you, my son, for taking great care of me. I feel very grateful to have you in my life. And I know you are serious, when you say, 'I must follow my own path.' I've heard those words before. I understand the importance of granting you independence."

I send my letter of resignation to P&T. Although my boss would have liked to see me back at the office and had been counting on my return, he provides me with a impressive letter of recommendation.

I'm getting better at making critical decisions. I used to let everything take its course and let others decide for me. But I'm finding out that I need to follow my heart, dare to choose different paths and be independent. I am filled with a profound sense of empowerment.

I pack my bags, say goodbye to Mutti and my other family members, and take the train back to the Netherlands.

Chapter 54

THE NETHERLANDS

I arrive in the Netherlands in February. It just happens to be the second coldest month on record since January 1823, temperatures so severe that just a day after the cold sets in, the ice on the canals is solid enough to skate upon. On February 14, the gruelling "eleven cities tour," a renowned Dutch long-distance skating event, takes place. However, the extreme cold takes a heavy toll and kills several participants.

I obtain a residence permit and find a room with a landlady in De Bilt, near Utrecht, and land a job in accounting at the fruit processing company Veluco, owned by the Oostrom family.

Every week I have to visit the "immigrant reporting centre" at the police station in De Bilt to show my passport and provide them updates on my residence and employment status. Once a month, a social affairs officer comes to the office to check on "the foreigner." I open the door, speak to the man politely, and lead him to my boss, who then takes over from me while giving me a big wink. The officer has no idea that he just spoke with the so-called foreigner.

I master the work well, and I like my boss very much, but I miss the freedom I had in The Dutch East Indies, the audits at the estates, life in the tropical sun, the smells, the colours, the people….

I must do all the housework myself. That takes some getting used to. *Holland has no babu and no djongos.* I buy a subscription to meals from the Chinese restaurant down the street for the sake of convenience, so at least I don't have to cook for myself all the time. I work, come home, do some shopping, pick up my takeout dinner from the restaurant, do the dishes, read a book, and go to bed. Holland, with its relentless cold, feels monotonous and isolating. Establishing social connections proves challenging, as most people seem to remain cocooned within the warmth of their homes. On my walk home from work, all I encounter are drawn curtains and empty streets.

I conclude that maybe a class of some kind will inject a little variety into my routine. I sign up to study economics, but the first math exam is such a shocking failure that I quit after the first week.

I can't seem to find my footing, and depression grows on me like an ugly moss. The lead-grey Dutch skies aren't helping. Soon, I fall seriously ill, diagnosed by the doctor as suffering from "malnutrition due to a lack of vitamins." His remedy is straightforward: cancel my subscription to the Chinese restaurant and start cooking healthy meals for myself. Tired and weak, I drag myself through the winter, facing dysentery for the first time in my life. My friend Otto had it several times in the Dutch East Indies; I never did. I wonder how he's doing. He became an optometrist and left for Melbourne, Australia, a few years ago. I haven't heard from him since.

In Holland, they aren't sure what to do about dysentery. "A disease from the tropics," one nurse whispers to another. Have I been carrying those bacteria all along? Who knows, but it sure takes forever to get the right medication.

I may have set my mind on the Netherlands, but the reality is I find life here disappointing, and I'm experiencing considerable problems adjusting. It's only when the sun comes out, the trees burst into leaf, and the shy flowers start to bloom that I brighten up a bit.

One day I decide to visit an old acquaintance from Lembang, Herman Bongers. Herman is considerably older than me, an ex-sailor and English teacher, who had come to Indonesia with his family just after the war for a four-year contract. For one school year, he was my English teacher at the high school in Bandung, and now, the family lives not far from my current rental in De Bilt.

Herman is a tall and robust man, his reddish-grey hair and neatly trimmed beard lending character to his appearance. His spectacles add an air of wisdom to his friendly demeanour, making every conversation with him a comforting experience. Over time, our visits grow more frequent, and Herman evolves into a father figure, offering advice and valuable guidance.

I share my burdens, workplace woes, and educational challenges with him. Herman possesses the rare gift of truly listening, devoting his full attention to my concerns. One day, as we sit across from each other at the table, he says, "I would advise you to make a choice."

"A choice?" I ask. "What do you mean?"

"Well, you're no longer welcome in Indonesia, right? You can reminisce about it all you want, but the Dutch East Indies you grew up in are no more, and the Indonesians would rather see white men leave. You have an Austrian passport, but you don't belong there either. Holland still offers you the most opportunities and connections. Why not become a Dutch citizen? That might open more doors for you. It's just a matter of getting used to that idea and going through the process."

A matter of getting used to becoming Dutch. It echoes through my mind. *I'm not sure if I want to get used to that idea,* says another voice.

"Maybe you could teach German," Herman says, interrupting my thoughts. "You speak the language fluently and your Dutch is impeccable. Teacher training would likely be a breeze for you. You'd earn a good salary and could build a decent pension."

I look at him in surprise.

I brood over that conversation with Herman for a long time. I can't help but factor in what I imagine Mutti's opinion might be. "Holland is just a train ride away," I had told her. Working in Holland is one thing. Becoming a Dutch citizen is a whole different story, especially considering the post-war feelings....

However, after much deliberation, I decide to follow Herman's advice. I apply for Dutch citizenship. The naturalization process will take five years. Herman generously offers me an interest-free monthly loan. As a result, I can move on from my budding career as an accountant and register for the full-time teacher training program, with a first-degree secondary education qualification. When I'm not in class or studying, I earn money by tutoring and giving homework assistance.

And who would have thought: my energy starts flowing again. It feels like I'm getting a second chance. I've decided not to disappoint Herman.

Chapter 55

HETTY

One of my former managers from the Dutch East Indies, André Esveld, who returned to the Netherlands in 1957, invites me to dinner. He was a big boss at P&T when I started my first job there. He recently retired in Subang and now lives with his second wife, Georgina, in the village of Ede.

On an idyllic, sunny Saturday afternoon in the spring of 1958, I take my Volkswagen Beetle to their house. They live in a spacious bungalow on Buurtmeester Street, with a sprawling lawn and trees around it and a pleasing view of the greenery. What a lovely spot this is!

André shows me his home and garden while Georgina cooks an Indonesian meal. We laugh a bit about the past, especially about the after-work social activities where I met André.

"Those were the days," André sighs. "Life is a bit different nowadays."

"You live in a great spot here, though. You don't have a whole lot to complain about, I'd say?"

"No, it's not too bad, but P&T isn't exactly generous with its pensions. I'm only fifty-four, so I took a position at an optician's office in Arnhem."

While we're standing in the garden reminiscing, a lady on a bicycle suddenly appears in the driveway—an attractive, slender young lady in a summer dress with long legs and wavy dark blonde hair. She is taller than I am and flashes us a charming smile. She puts her bicycle on the stand, runs straight to André, and hugs him. My curiosity is piqued. Who is she?

André introduces me, "Victor, this is Hetty, my youngest daughter from my first marriage. Hetty, this is Victor, a former colleague from the Dutch East Indies."

Hetty has beautiful bright blue eyes. We shake hands shyly.

"Nice to meet you, Hetty," I say to her, and to her dad, I say jokingly, "Your first marriage? Youngest daughter? How many gorgeous daughters do you have? Why haven't you told me about this long ago?"

"Hetty and her sister Jeanni stayed here in Arnhem during the war," André answers seriously.

My intuition tells me I shouldn't pry any further. In Arnhem during the war? Was Hetty here with her mother, the first wife? Arnhem was one of the most heavily bombarded cities of the Netherlands during the war. What should have been a quick triumph for the Allies turned out to be one of their worst defeats— the now-famous "bridge too far." So, I change the subject.

"Hetty, if I may ask, is it a coincidence that you're here visiting your parents, or do you live nearby?"

"Yes, you two should get to know each other a bit," says André, patting me on the shoulder. "I'm going inside to see if I can help Georgina with anything."

He walks back to the house while Hetty and I sit down on the grass.

"I live here," Hetty says. "I was twenty-three when my father came back into my life, and I'm trying to make up for the time I missed."

"How old were you when your father disappeared from your life?"

"Five," she says.

"Hm…That's a long time ago, indeed a lot to catch up on. Luckily you can still do that. Are you in school, or do you have a job?"

"I'm a full-time phys-ed teacher and travel back and forth between two schools, the Amersfoort Lyceum and the National High school in Utrecht. How do you know my dad?"

Hetty's intense blue eyes, like two sapphires set ablaze, fixate on me with unwavering intensity. But her gaze holds too much daring beauty; I cast my eyes downward, overwhelmed by a sudden shyness.

"From P&T. I was just a kid, and he was one of my bosses."

Here in the grass in front of her parents' house, Hetty is a cascade of words, full of life and interest, and she's asking me one question after another. I tell her that I'm from Lembang, that as an eight-year-old boy I lost my parents, that the war broke out, and we lost our hotel. And I tell her about Aunty Hilda, who became my Mutti.

Hetty listens to my story, mesmerized, and is already getting ready to fire the next question at me when I raise my hand in protest. "Wait a minute. It's your turn," I laugh. "Who are you, and where are you from?"

I learn that Hetty is twenty-four years old and was born in Subang, West Java. Her mother wanted to divorce her father when Hetty was a little girl. She was five years old in 1939 when her mother brought her and her older sister Jeanni to the Netherlands. Hetty's mother then went straight back to the Dutch East Indies to join her new husband, abandoning her daughters. A few months later, the war broke out. Hetty's mother ended up in a Japanese camp, where she gave birth to her baby Miep. Miep's father worked as a forced labourer on the Burma Railway and died of exhaustion. Meanwhile, Hetty and Jeanni lived with a foster family in Arnhem and spent the last seven months of the war in a bunker. They survived the war without any contact with their father or mother.

"Wow, I'm not the only one with a gripping family story," I respond. "Why did your mother take you to a foster family in the Netherlands?"

"That question still haunts me," she replies. "Maybe she thought we were safer here, I don't know. But I do know from my dad that he had agreed to my mother delivering us to a foster family for a year. We called them Uncle Arnold and Aunt Jul—short for Julia. At the time, it was quite normal for Dutch children to be brought to the Netherlands to attend school, but I honestly feel that we were too young. And then the war interfered. To my mother, the war is a closed book. She can't talk about it."

"So, she did survive the war."

"Yes, she did. And after the war, she returned to Holland with Miep. We all lived together in Den Bosch, with my grandfather, my mum's father, and his wife, Marie. It was a house full of women of all ages and various heights, and we all had different surnames." Hetty laughs. "People tend to be pretty short in the south of Holland. Everybody called me 'the tall one of the Esvelds.' My height has always been my biggest frustration."

"There's nothing wrong with your long legs," I laugh.

Hetty lowers her eyes and blushes slightly.

There's shouting from the patio. "Dinner's ready!"

We look at each other.

"I believe we aren't nearly done talking just yet. I'd love to get to know you better." There's one more question I need an answer to. I dare to ask it. "Could I take you out sometime?"

"I'd really like that," Hetty replies bashfully.

We walk back to the house. Georgina has gone to great lengths with the Indonesian meal, and after dinner, she hands me a large piece of delicious coconut cake to take home. By way of goodbye, I kiss Hetty's hand. My eyes hold hers for a moment. Knowing that we will see each other again next weekend, I feel as weightless as a ray of light dancing through the Indonesian jungle.

Later that night, at home in De Bilt, I'm dreaming away on the couch. Henriëtte Johanna Esveld. The phys-ed teacher with her long legs. This woman is different. This woman radiates strength, is independent, and has a will of her own. She was born in Subang. Even though she was very young when her mother took her away from there, the Dutch East Indies are also part of her life. She understands me. Hetty Esveld—she's the woman I've been looking for all along.

Chapter 56

CONVERSATION IN LOUPIAC, FRANCE

January 19, 2020

It's Dad's eighty-eighth birthday. We're sitting on the couch together, and I hand him the final draft of my book. Our book. The document is ready for proofreaders, and Dad is the most important one.

"Here you go, Dad. I started it exactly two years ago, and this is the result," I say. "I'm proud to have gotten this far, and at the same time, it feels extremely challenging to hand the manuscript to others and to receive their feedback on it. I hope the story will feel close to your heart. That it will touch you when you read it."

Dad's sitting next to me with the stack of papers on his lap, and tears well up in his eyes. "It's unbelievable that you did it. That you really turned my story into a novel. You've done a great job."

I put an arm around his shoulder. "Thank you. But it would be best if you read it first," I laugh. "Hopefully, you still think this way afterward. Remember how it started?"

"How what started?"

"Our first Skype call. I asked you, 'Do you still miss Java?' And you told me that you spent years looking for your own identity and that you had silenced yourself, but it eventually made you physically ill."

"Yes," he says. "After medical science couldn't find a cause for my frequent dizziness and fainting, I visited a psychologist. In our very first meeting, he said, 'Go write down your past.' I was surprised he asked me that. In the beginning, nothing came. Maybe two sentences a week, that's it. I had learned to shut up and keep quiet about my origins for so long that I'd elevated it to a noble art," Dad chuckles. "But over time, the memories began to bubble up, then the sentences started flowing, and at one point, I could hardly stop writing. Though there was some trial and error, I started to open my mouth more often, express my opinion, and share my story with you and with dear friends. As you know, my writings were more matter of fact. They were just snippets of memories, and there was no chronological line in them. It is a gift to me that you've converted it all into this book. I could never have done that myself. And I could never have shared my deepest feelings with a stranger either."

"Thank you for your confidence and your faith in me, Dad. Because you were Austrian, your experiences are so different from those of the Dutch and Indo Dutch. That has always intrigued me immensely. You and your family have been treated rather unjustly by the Dutch. How does it feel for you to bring this story to the world?"

Dad thinks about it and says, "I always thought the story was worth telling, that it matters, but some of my old Sarangan friends stopped me. During the reunions that we organized over the years I raised the subject several times. But especially my friends who had become Dutch citizens were afraid of reprisals. I didn't feel that reprisals would ever happen, but some of my friends' parents had to fight for years to get their Dutch pensions back, and of course, I didn't want to endanger them in any way. So, I kept putting my idea about a book aside over and over again. Many of the residents of Sarangan have since died. Besides, we changed their names in the book. Although I hope people can identify with this story, it can't be taken personally."

Dad is silent for a moment and then adds, "It's okay. The time has come. My story should be told."

The truth is, unless you let go, unless you forgive yourself, unless you forgive the situation, unless you realize that the situation is over, you cannot move forward.

- Steve Maraboli, Unapologetically You

EPILOGUE

My parents, Victor and Hetty, married on July 13, 1963. It was a joyful day and the beginning of a long life together. A pastor from Den Bosch ecumenically married them in the Catholic Church of Ede. My grandmother—Oma Mutti—was Dad's witness.

Unfortunately, André Esveld died before he became a father-in-law to my dad. In the summer of 1958, he became seriously ill, diagnosed with bone cancer. He underwent treatment, but to no avail. His wife Georgina, a registered nurse, nursed him at home until his passing. André suffered terrible pain. My mum lost her father on June 3, 1959, just two years after she'd met him again. He was only fifty-six years old.

In 1963, Dad became a Dutch citizen.

I was born in October 1965 and my brother Bruno in October 1967.

My dad graduated from secondary teacher training, and he also obtained a degree as an interpreter-translator of German in 1965, two months after my birth. He had a part-time job in the evenings at the Thorbecke high school in Arnhem. My parents had an agreement that Dad would be a stay-at-home father and take care of me, while my mother was the breadwinner. However, when I was three months old, the Wageningen high school called him during the Christmas holidays, encouraging him to apply for a job. Their vice-principal, Mr. Boerwinkel, had been Dad's Dutch teacher at the Christian Lyceum in Bandung. Mr Boerwinkel was the one to interview him, and he hired Dad on the spot. Dad started a full-time job as a German teacher in January 1966. He retired in 1988.

My mum worked for forty years as a phys-ed teacher at the Amersfoort Lyceum and retired in 1995. As an empowered woman dedicated to her career, she was ahead of her time. Working full-time while raising young children, she was often criticized for not being home with Bruno and me by male colleagues and the school's deputy principal. But she stood her ground and was always supported in her career choices by Dad.

My parents led a socially active and adventurous life. In 1966, they bought a ruin in the French province Ardèche, which they converted over a period of ten years, during the school holidays, into a full-fledged holiday home. This is where their great love for France arose. In 1997, they emigrated to the tiny town of Loupiac, in the southwest of France, where they bought another ruin, which they turned into an oasis. Dad died there at ninety years of age, from the effects of Covid-19, on November 23, 2021. Mum didn't want to live without her Victor and died of a broken heart, a year later, on November 19, 2022. They were both born in January and died in November. Their marriage lasted fifty-eight years and their French friends called them les amoureux—the lovers.

Grand Hotel Lembang remained in the Schalks family's ownership until 1965, when it was eventually sold. In the summer of 1990, my family—my parents, my brother Bruno, and I—took a trip to Indonesia. We stayed at Grand Hotel Lembang, where the old glory of yesteryear was still present. In the hotel's gardens, I sat in a rattan chair for a photograph, almost mirroring a photo that was taken of my grandmother Mary—Dad's biological mother—in 1939. I seem to resemble her. Presently, the hotel still operates under the same name, although a Chinese owner has since taken over and significantly renovated the premises.

Since World War II, the Dutch government has never returned any of the Treipl family's belongings, nor paid any **compensation**.

Before the Japanese occupation, the Java Bank secretly diverted gold supplies from the Dutch East Indies by boat to New York and by plane to Australia. Some of those planes crashed into the ocean. The Treipl family's gold bars have not been recovered to this day.

My grandmother Hilda Treipl (Mutti) spent her senior years in Salzburg, in a small bungalow that was part of a nursing home. There was a lovely garden around it, and walking in nature remained her passion and her life. She never remarried. My parents supported her financially until she passed away. She died in 1981, at the age of ninety-three, and was buried in Salzburg, Austria.

Everything can be taken from a man but one thing:
the last of the human freedoms –
to choose one's attitude in any given set of circumstances,
to choose one's own way.

- Viktor E. Frankl, *Man's Search for Meaning*

ACKNOWLEDGEMENTS

This book has been a deeply emotional and collaborative journey between my dad, Victor († 23–11–2021), and me. Despite the distance, our conversations over Skype were filled with his memories. Some of Dad's memories were recessed and had to be brought back to life through repeated questioning and relentless research on my part. Other memories were so vivid they appeared before me. After two years of hard work, the dream of this book came true. I'm deeply grateful for my dad's openness—the will to face the sometimes painful past—and the freedom he gave me to shape this book's storyline. It has further deepened the special bond we already had.

I also thank my mum, Hetty († 19–11–2022), the main co-reader. She had heard the stories countless times and provided additions my dad had forgotten. I'm thankful for her input and her never-ending interest and encouragement.

My Dutch writing coach, Nanda Huneman, helped me set the storyline, gave me unvarnished feedback, showed me new perspectives whenever I was stuck, and challenged me to use fiction while writing this life story. Thank you!

A big thank you to my sister-in-law, Ella McQuinn, and Leo MacDonald. Because of you, this novel found its way into the hands of HarperCollins Holland. Many thanks to the HarperCollins Holland team for the excellent collaboration and for producing and promoting the attractive Dutch edition of this book.

Margo LaPierre, I can't thank you enough! You were the editor of my dreams. Margo performed a substantive and stylistic edit to my English translation. A poet herself, she has an incredible feel for the rhythms of language, and her detailed editorial letter and notes are of outstanding artistry and skill. She's also a huge encourager. Collaborating with her, I started writing again, deepened characters and relationships, and turned mere summary into imagery and scenes, resulting in an enriched and revised version of my novel. Working with Margo has been an absolute privilege and an experience of literary companionship.

Lastly, I want to express my immense gratitude to my husband, John McQuinn, for who he is. As I spent days, months, years writing in a language you don't speak, then translating those words into English, editing my manuscript and going through the process of publishing it, you have been my rock. Thank you for the hugs and the words of encouragement, cups of coffee, breakfasts, lunches, and the glass of red wine on my desk at the end of the day. They got me into a flow where I forgot about time and kept writing.

ABOUT THE AUTHOR

Birgit Treipl (1965) is a Dutch Canadian author. She was born and raised in the Netherlands and holds a BA in marketing communications. Her career began in advertising, and she later founded a successful marketing and communications recruitment agency before immigrating to Canada. An outdoor enthusiast, she first moved to British Columbia and now splits her time between Nelson, British Columbia, and Seabright, Nova Scotia. *Even Without Blood*, drawn from her family history, is her first novel.

www.birgittreipl.com
www.facebook.com/birgittreipl.author
www.linkedin.com/in/birgittreipl